Praise for

RUNNING FROM LIONS

"From the very first page I was completely sucked in. Vaca's characters are very well developed and his writing style makes the story leap off the pages and come alive. He creates a real connection between the readers and his main characters."

-Bitten By Books

"Smooth writing. Though the Young Adult market is crowded with dystopian stories, this has a different take on it."

-NovelRocket.com

"Vaca casts a spell with his rich universe, authentic characters, and tight plotting. A hypnotic, fresh take on the dystopian thriller. This writer is playing for keeps."

-Don Winston, best selling author of *The Union Club*

RUNNING FROM LIONS

Also By The Author:

Capernaum

The Surgers!

Probably, Most Likely

RUNNING FROM LIONS

———

Part 1 in
The Running Duology

by

Julian R. Vaca

Copyright © 2013 by Julian R. Vaca
All rights reserved. Published in the United States independently.

Visit me on the Web! www.JulianRVaca.com

Cover art by Matthew Covington | © 2013
Design by Katie Mae Vaca | © 2013

ISBN-10: 1491204575
ISBN-13: 978-1491204573

"...Deliver me, lest they tear me like a lion, rending me in pieces, where there is none to deliver."

-Book of Psalms, 7:1b-2

Chapter 1

I am the star you gazed on when you were six and stood on the tips of your toes and looked out your bedroom window at the twinkling sky. I shot across the firmament. Left a fading streak behind me. You marveled. Said a prayer, maybe. Or a wish. I could sense your eyes on me then...even now, as I will myself to stop.

I need this to stop.

Burn up.

Crash.

Chapter 2

I have memories of hands. Legs. A head. All the functioning body parts that you undoubtedly take for granted. But, to me, they are just memories. Even though I long to have myself back...to breathe and eat and sleep, like normal...I know it would do me no good up here in space...in my prison.

Yet, though my senses have abandoned me, I am confident I have not lost my ability to *feel*.

Why?

Because up here, among the other stars, I feel cold. Always the cold binds me and chokes me, forcing me to spin and soar in this prison.

So much cold.

Chapter 3

A landscape of distant, sparkling lights stretches before me, always, endless, forever. Expanses of black fill in the blanks between the stars, and there is an occasional stroke of pale blue and purple hues.

This beauty is my hell.

Although I might possess memories of a host – a working body that I may or may not have occupied at some point in the past – I do not possess memories of a why. Why I am here, that is. What damned me to this eternal cycle? To this beautiful hell?

If I had some grasp on time, I would bet this has been going on a millennia. Or two. Cursed galaxy, why not three? I could just as easily tell you how many other stars are up here with me, stuck in their respective routes, their respective prisons.

How I long for freedom. To burn up. Or crash.

To not exist anymore.

Cleary, that is the point. That is the key. That is why it is prison.

Chapter 4

I am fragments and particles.

Everyway, nothing and everything. I am lost, and yet straight on course. I am forever and –

Stop. You sound like you have accepted this fate. Like you have given up. I am none of those things. I am just a prisoner, trapped in this shell.

No. We are ending, yet eternal. Darkness, yet light.

Stop. I need to break free. Think! How did this happen? What did this?

No. There is no "thinking." There is only doing. And what we do, is shoot through space.

STOP. This is not natural. How long have I just accepted this? I *can* think...that has got to count for something.

No. There is no "thinking." There is only –

Shut up. Get out of me. I am thinking. That is what this is. And that means there is hope.

If I can think...

...I can will.

Chapter 5

There is a change in me.

It is subtle.

A spark.

A spark ignites the flame, which trickles, then goes ablaze. The wildfire is my consciousness. I am here. That much is true. Okay. Why am I here? I cannot remember much, if anything at all.

But, what I do remember is that being confined like this...trapped in space, touring the galaxies...is a lot like being confined to a single solitary place. Like a cell. Like a prison cell.

Good. Yes, keep going. My consciousness is back, and I am definitely in some sort of prison. Two things. What else? The memories...

...what was that about memories...?

Hands! Arms, legs, a body. A body capable of living. Yes. That is it! I am a life force. I am a being that can think, and I am trapped. There was something else –

You. I could sense *you* watching me. Marveling. That is it. You are the missing piece. My way out. My freedom.

Now I am

off

course.

Chapter 6 | Farah

It's not like you've never seen it before. Really, they're just stars. Desert sky's full of them. Watching down on us...hundreds of thousands of little strange gods.

I sit, cross-legged, in the wooden watchtower at the east end of my Village. My neck hurts and my back too, but every time I sag a little, I force myself to straighten up. Can't afford to get comfortable. My job's important, see.

Everyone my age has a job. It's how you survive out here, in the bowl. Dad's always reminiscing about a time – way before I was born, way before the great wars wiped out everything good – where you could pick any job you chose. Just like that.

I smile, cooped up in this little perch two-dozen feet above the ground, and dream about the prospect of picking my own job.

What would I choose? Probably something with animals. There aren't too many left now, but any time we come across a stray dog on our weekly scavenges near the dunes, I beg Dad to let me keep them. In fact, most of the animals in our Village are a direct result of my insistences.

Well, whatever hypothetical job I might've picked, it

definitely wouldn't have been night watcher. Seems the only time this place gets cold is at night, when all these stars are out. When I'm at my post. I sigh. Could be worse though. I could've been assigned to the stables, like my best friend, Lois. Any time I see her she's got a strand of hay in her long black hair, and she scowls when I take it out for her.

Maybe I wouldn't have picked a job with animals.

Near my feet sits a ratty, taped-up megaphone, and I scoot it away and stand up. The watchtower is made of scrap metal and slats of weathered wood, just like the tall fence that encloses our three-hundred-acre Village. The watchtower's only as wide as my wingspan, and it has just enough room for me to stretch. Which I do. My joints pop. I exhale in relief.

Below my post, in the Village mess hall, the tantalizing scent of honey bread and various spices of tea sift through the rafters and lay deliciously on the air passing and encircling the watchtower. One of the Village cooks is preparing a night meal for the patrol, which should be returning from their first shift any minute now.

I hear my stomach growl, and I blush despite myself. No. It wasn't my stomach. I look over my shoulder and see three pickup trucks approaching under starlight. The patrol. Right on time, I think, as I check my wristwatch. I hear the grinding sound as the east gate opens admitting the patrol entrance.

So. First shift's over. Which means in approximately four hours my shift will be over and I can return home, to my room, where my bed and a stack of salvaged CDs await. I'm almost done with "More Songs About Buildings and Food" by the Talking Heads. It's the only album I have by them. Could just as easily be the last copy of it in the world, too. That thought suddenly makes me appreciate having it.

Truck doors open and close, and the sound of banter fills the air faintly. Members of the patrol, a select group of men and the occasional woman, talk and joke as they head for the mess hall. I try to pick out Alex, my boyfriend, amongst them, but all I can make out are shadows.

–You know, Fare, Alex is always telling me. –With as much as you complain about night watch, you should consider training for patrol.

The only thing I get out of that is he thinks I complain. Do I? That much? Do I sound like an ungrateful brat?

I'm constantly looking for ways to impress him, to make sure he knows that while I may only be sixteen, I'm just as driven and motivated as he is at eighteen.

So I lie to him.

–Yeah, I'll say. –Patrol actually sounds like a good idea.

The problem is, it doesn't sound like a good idea. Can't let him know that. He thinks it's the greatest thing since...well, he thinks it's the greatest thing. Period.

I sigh again. Been doing a lot of that lately. It's not like I mean to, though, it's just that I'm getting close to that age where, by Village standards, I should be prepping for that transition from "job" into "role."

Is this my role? My destiny? To live out the extent of my life as grandmaster night watcher? How's *that* for a scary thought? Really, what's truly scary is that I can't think of anything else I'd rather do. What shoes I'd love to fill. If there was a role where someone's only task was to collect and log music, we wouldn't have a problem here.

Only that role doesn't exist, and what does, is night watcher. My job. And, at the rate I'm going, my eventual role.

I lean against the watchtower railing and survey the desert horizon. I stare at the millions and millions of stars, and they stare back. Yeah, it's not like you've never seen it, the view of the night sky, but at least it's beautiful, right?

A shooting star catches my eye. I make a wish, like in books, and hope it comes true. I want to want something. Anything. I wish for a want.

Wow, what a terrible wish.

That's when I hear a far off *crack!* and I spin my head. Eastward, from where the patrol came. The sky lights up with a radiant purple glow, a kind of spark, like lightning. Then, it fades.

What in the...?

Chapter 7

Yes, there is definitely a change in me.

I am certain now that I am off course. Whatever course I was on. Was I even on a course? Well, if I was, I am definitely off it now. My fellow stars whip past me faster than they usually do. That is how I know. That is how I am certain.

Something blue and green approaches. It is round. Bigger than the stars, bigger than me, and getting bigger the closer I get.

It is...a planet.

I am heading toward a planet.

This is my chance!

I will myself to head straight into the planet, but I am not sure I am even doing anything. I just keep thinking. Get there. Get there. GET THERE.

It must be working. The planet is huge now. Massive. I feel a heat, such as I have never known, wash over me. It is choking me. Suffocating. If I had lungs, which I am sure I did at one point, they would be full to the brim. Overflowing with this heat.

I am suddenly praying for the coldness I once felt. I never thought that would happen. The surface I am approaching widens, I get closer, and now I cannot see past it. The stars have left me. Space…it is gone.

All I see now is a stretch of brown, dark, no stars to bring light.

I am about to make contact.

I am about to crash.

Chapter 8 | Farah

I yank the megaphone off the watchtower floor and clamber down the rope ladder. My heart pounds in my chest. I've been assigned to the night watcher job for all of twelve months, and in that time, I've only had to sound an alarm once. That first instance was a mistake. A humiliating one. A costly one.

Here's my chance for redemption.

My sneakers hit the sandy ground with a *plop*, and a small cloud of arid dust rises around my ankles. I bolt away from the watchtower and fumble with the megaphone controls. C'mon! There's only like two buttons!

I huff. And then I puff. And then I gasp. I'm pathetic when it comes to exerting any physical energy. If that's not reason enough to avoid patrol roles like the plague, I don't know what is. I skid around a collection of rusty, sheet metal forts and merge onto the Village's main road. That's when I finally get the megaphone turned on.

"Twelfth alarm, twelfth alarm!" I bellow through the microphone. My frightened voice is amplified, and almost instantly lanterns begin to flick on inside forts and buildings.

"Unidentified signal!" I yell.

I have no idea to where I should be running. The protocol's fuzzy. All I think about is that purple flash in the sky and the lack of air in my lungs. Before I calculate my next move, I barrel through the side door of my fort.

Inside, Dad sits at his workbench, peering through his makeshift magnifying glass. Using two pliers, he examines some kind of gear. My dad's role in the Village isn't that desirable. He's been tasked with deconstructing various tools and trinkets, figuring out their inner workings, logging them, and then reassembling their parts. The products of his deconstructions leave our quarters stuffed with odd gizmos and metal things strewn about.

When Mom was alive, she often scolded him for the mess, saying it was uninviting. She said the clutter and disorder were the reasons they couldn't keep friends. Dad said it was because their "friends" couldn't appreciate the clutter and disorder.

"Dad!" I say, still using the megaphone without realizing it. "Did you hear? Twelfth alarm!"

"No, I didn't," he replies, rotating the gear under the glass. "Try using your megaphone."

"I – oh, right." I lower the instrument to my side and stride across the room. "Sorry."

"It's fine, hon'," he says, smiling to himself. He sets the gear down gently and then takes off his square-framed glasses. "You know my hearing's already as good as shot. So what's up?"

What's up is that I just sounded the twelfth alarm and you're so calm! But then, when does he ever act with any semblance of urgency?

"I saw something," I say, "in the sky."

"What kind of something?" Now I have his full attention. He turns in his stool and looks up at me. I watch his brown eyes go back and forth between my green ones. "A U.F.O.?"

"Dad, no, not this again."

"You said 'something in the sky,' didn't you?"

"Yes, but not *that* kind of something. It was, I dunno, like a flash, kinda like lightning."

"So..." He scratches his chin. "So a U.F.O. without the F?"

I roll my eyes. Before I can reply our door opens and Alex and a host of other patrol members step inside.

"Fare," Alex says, taking the megaphone out of my hand and setting it on a random crate. He then holds both my hands in his firm, blistered ones. "What happened? What did you see?"

"Please," Dad says flatly, "come in. Knocking's a thing of the past."

"It...I'm not sure what it was," I tell Alex.

His desert goggles are up and resting on his short black hair. As always, my eyes fall from his gaze to the long twisted scar on his neck. He refuses to tell me how he got it, even though he didn't have it before we started dating.

"She was probably daydreaming again, Al," one of the patrol members says snidely.

I look past Alex and see his uncle, Lark, standing in the doorway with his arms crossed. His rifle hangs over his shoulder by a leather strap, and the moonlight from outside outlines his clean-shaven head.

"Now see, how's that possible, Lark?" Dad replies, grabbing his cane and standing up. "You can't very well *day*dream at *night*! Why, that's a paradox, isn't it?"

Lark's smug face melts away immediately.

"Oh dear," Dad continues, "someone fetch the poor man a dictionary."

"I know what paradox means, you crazy ol' – "

"I was going to look up daydream for you."

A couple members of the patrol start to snicker. Lark unfolds his arms and takes a step forward – flashing what is supposed to be a mean look, yet only makes him uglier – but Alex turns to face him before things escalate.

"Uncle," he says, "why don't you wait outside with the rest of the patrol? Leader will be out on the main road soon, looking for Farah."

Lark, grinding his teeth, waves his hand and leads the rest of the patrol outside. Alex turns back around, grabs a chair, sits down, and looks up at me intently.

"Now. What did you see?"

I tell him. He processes it, and slowly the concern in his eyes starts to fade.

"What?" I demand, hands on my hips. "You don't believe me?"

"Of course I believe you," he says, unconvincingly.

"It's just...you said it was lightning, so – "

"*Like*," I correct him. "It was *like* lightning. Besides, the sky patrol isn't expecting a storm for another few months, right?"

Alex stands. "They've been wrong before."

"And they're wrong again?" I'm getting irritated, and I show it. "You think it's lightning I saw."

"Leader will want to send a team out there to investigate the source," Dad says, hobbling away from his workbench and brightening one of the hanging oil lamps in the room. "Always better to be safe than sorry."

"You think it's them?" I ask, turning to face Dad. "You think it's the undergrounders?"

"But how?" Alex says. "What in their limited arsenal could produce the type of effect Farah's describing?"

Dad shakes his head. "Be careful, Alex. You shouldn't put anything past them...you know that. Can't take any chances if there's a potential threat to our Village."

"Spoken like a born Leader," a female voice says.

We all turn and watch the tall, slender form of our Village's Leader step inside. She wears her customary duster jacket and boots, and the subtle streaks of grey in her yellow hair glow in the lamplight. We see her armed entourage as they wait outside.

Alex stands and joins Dad and me as we dip our heads down respectfully.

"Now," she continues, beaming at us. "Is that true?

24

Is there a potential threat to our Village?"

I gulp. Something about standing in Leader's presence always makes my throat dry up. I'd like to think it's reverence, but I'm pretty sure she just scares me.

"Y-Yes," I stammer, stepping forward. "Signaled twelfth alarm."

"You were right to do that," Leader assures, clasping her hands behind her back. "Could be the undergrounders signaling one another. Could be weapons testing. Or, it could end up being nothing at all.

"Either way, we have to be sure."

I nod and start to feel the tension leaving my body. Good. She said I was right to sound the alarm.

"So, Farah," she says, "be ready to roll out in fifteen minutes."

At first I don't realize what she means. Then, when I feel Alex and Dad's eyes on me, it seems to click.

"Wait, you want me to accompany the patrol?"

Alex starts to laugh, like he thinks this is a joke, and Dad clears his throat – leaning hard on his cane to step forward. "Leader, if I may, I do not think it is safe for her – "

"The patrol will need you there, Farah," Leader says, cutting into Dad. He swallows the rest of his sentence and stares at his boots. "They'll need you to verify the location of the flash. You're the only one who witnessed it, and you're the only one who can adequately lead our men to the flash's source."

My heart starts hammering again like before, when I first saw the light. "It was probably just lightning..." The words escaping my lips seem small and meek.

"Still," Leader says, walking over to me and placing a hand on my soon-to-be-trembling shoulder, "can't take any chances if there's a potential threat to our Village." She squeezes the skin around my bone with a sense of finality and takes her leave.

I have nothing to say. No, that's not true. I have *plenty* to say. To scream. I want to shout objections and tell Leader I can't go out there. I've never been past the dunes, where they say bad things happen. And that's where I'd have to lead Alex and the patrol...that's where I saw the sliver of light touch down.

But I can't move the muscles in my mouth. I just stand there.

"I won't let her out of my sight," Alex tells Dad.

"Damn right you won't," he answers.

Chapter 9

Oxygen starts at my nose, shoots down my throat and into my stomach, and then forces me to shake uncontrollably. My vision is obscured, but I choose to worry about that later. Right now the foreign sensation of breathing is all I can bear. My nostrils flare, working to compensate for my mouth, which, strangely, I cannot open yet.

Steady. Steady breaths ease the sharp pains and my body eventually goes lax. Good, one thing at a time. Slowly my lungs adjust and, before too long, there is a rhythm to my inhaling and exhaling. I can do this. I start to welcome the crisp air instead of fighting it, and that expedites my recovery.

I start to pay attention to the details. Take in my surroundings blindly. At first I give a start. The ground is loose. Millions and billions of little pebbles rub and slip against my naked body as I try to turn over. What is this? The touch and weight is familiar, but I cannot place it. Not yet. Seeing it would definitely help...

I raise my hands up to my eyes and start to rub. Tiny, dancing clips of white and blue permeate my sight, but after a short time, it fades. Now I can see clearly, and before me – stretching well past the limits of my reacquired peripheral vision – is the night sky and her stars.

They are so far away now, and I am thankful. I am free.

That is when I hear several loud *cracks!* in quick succession and a powerful light envelops me.

Chapter 10 | Farah

In my cramped bedroom, I throw several belongings into my backpack. I feel like this is punishment. I feel as if I've been sentenced to a death march.

"Pack lightly," Alex had said before he left our fort. "There's a chance we won't reach whatever you saw before daybreak. May have to stop for rest at some point."

I didn't respond. He gave me a reassuring kiss on the cheek and left. I turned to Dad, but he avoided my eye line. He limped away and returned to his workbench.

"Come see me before you leave," he had muttered.

I told him I would and then headed into my room, where I am now, fumbling with my portable CD player. The cover on the bottom that holds the batteries is broken, and I constantly have to tape it shut. Like right now.

"Think patrol will let you take that?" a voice asks. I look up and see my best friend leaning against the doorway. She takes a bite out of an apple and then steps in, closing the door behind her, except –

"Hey!" her brother squeals, holding his hands out and sidestepping past her. Digs, Lois's ten-year-old beanpole of a brother, glares angrily. "You knew I was behind you."

"You guys are up?" I say, kneeling down and picking up the fallen batteries.

"Yes, but he's not supposed to be," Lois says, shoving Digs and adding, "mom's gonna flip when she sees you outta bed."

"The whole Village is up," he says in defense, flicking some curly hair out of his eyes, "so get off my back."

"That true?" I say, sitting on the edge of my twin-sized bed. "The whole Village?"

"Practically." Lois takes another bite.

"Great."

It's not like I should be surprised though. I did sound an alarm after all. Now, more than ever, I pray I'm not wrong about this. One mistake as a night watcher is acceptable, sure. Everyone makes mistakes, right? But two... I shudder at the thought.

"I'm sure whatever you saw isn't a threat," Lois says, offering consolation. What she doesn't realize is that I'm not scared of what we might find, per se, but what we might *not* find.

"Says the girl who doesn't have to go out there," Digs quips. He dodges a smack from Lois and smiles victoriously.

"I wish you guys could come," I say, standing up to finish packing with my back to them. "I'm sure I'll need a laugh on the long ride."

"You'll have Alex," Lois offers.

"Yeah," Digs says with a snort as he leans against my scrap metal wall, "because Alex is a laugh riot."

I can't help but smile. "If Alex had your wit we'd already be married." I hear Digs almost fall over by my dresser.

"W-We would!" he stutters.

"She means her and Alex, doofus," Lois says. You can practically hear her eyes roll in their sockets. My smile deepens. I throw the last article of clothing into my backpack, put on a hoodie, and turn to face them.

"Well," I say, grabbing my backpack, "how do I look?"

"Ready!" "Terrified!"

I can't tell who said what, but it doesn't matter. I know exactly how I look. I'm not trying to be self-deprecating, I've just learned to accept some things the way they are. And right now, yes, I'm terrified. Pitifully terrified. Nothing can change that.

"Look on the bright side," Lois says between two more bites as we leave my room. "You're finally getting Alex to take you on a date – albeit, a forced one."

Behind us Digs pretends to dry heave.

"Yeah, yeah."

I half wave as they leave the fort, and once they're outside I hear Digs curse out loud. Lois probably threw her apple core at him. I walk over to Dad's workbench and cautiously avoid creating a shadow. He's studying a different, tinier gear now.

"It's like anything else," he eventually says, his voice heavy and low. Still he rotates the gear, poring over the details and impressions. "You remove one variable – even what seems to be the least important piece – and the whole thing's shot. Useless."

With steadied, practiced hands, Dad places the little gear back inside a rectangular device – right amidst scores of other small gears. It meshes in between the teeth of two larger, thicker gears. Then, he jots something down in his journal, closes up the rectangular device with two screws, and sets it right side up.

It's a music box.

"Does it work?" I ask, picking it up off his workbench and examining the craftsmanship under lamplight.

"Try," he replies.

I open it and see my reflection in the strip of mirror glued to the inside of the lid. No music plays.

"It used to," he says, "but now it's missing a piece. Clearly a vital one."

I look up from my reflected eyes and meet his. A moment passes between us. I close the lid and set the music box back down under his magnifying glass. He looks so tired, and, even under the poor lighting, I see creases forming around his eyes.

But he's not just tired. No, I've seen that look before.

Knock. Knock.

It's Alex.

"Ready?" he asks, opening the door halfway and leaning in.

I nod once and he leaves, keeping the door ajar. Dad clears his throat and starts to move things around his workbench idly. I don't really know what to say. It's not goodbye, right? We're just going out, confirming that all I saw was lightning – the first stages of an electric storm – and turning right back around. Simple as that. I watch Dad jot a few more things down in his journal before I finally head for the door.

"If you get scared," he calls over his shoulder, and I freeze in the threshold, "don't forget."

"It's like walking a rickety bridge," I recite, half grinning. "Don't look up, don't look down."

"Just look straight ahead."

I don't loiter any longer. After closing the door, I only have to walk a few paces down the main road until I find Alex and the rest of the patrol waiting in front of the trucks. A few people, families here and there, stand outside their forts and watch eagerly. A fist-sized lump starts to form in my throat.

"How you feeling?" Alex asks, taking my hand.

How do I look? "Good. Doing good."

He opens the passenger door, helps me in, and then closes it shut. He jogs around the front of the truck and climbs into the driver's seat. Four patrol members with rifles climb into the truck bed. I stare at their weapons through the rearview mirror.

"It's just for protection, you know." Alex turns the key and the engine rumbles to life.

I feign a smile and look out the window. Alex's Uncle Lark climbs into the truck next to us and, after slamming his door shut, he catches me staring. He blows a kiss and I look away, my stomach twisting into all kinds of knots. I put my hand on Alex's leg as we start toward the east gate.

"Mind telling Uncle Shark he's a creep?"

We drive for a few short minutes before Alex eases off the gas and we come to a halt. The nine-foot tall gate begins to grind open. Exterior pulleys and gears spin, and the gatekeeper flashes a toothless smile from his perch as we exit the Village.

The bowl. A never-ending expanse of sand and sky. The black and blue firmament surrounds us, encases us. It's understated symmetry: The night, with limitless stars, the ground, with limitless sand.

I lean forward and look through the windshield. There are no clouds. Not a single hint of a hungry storm. Thank God for that. Our Village barely withstood the last one.

And yet...

The lack of clouds confirms that whatever I saw wasn't lightning, right? I don't possess the tangibles that would deem me fit for sky patrol, but I'm certain I've never seen lightning without clouds or vicious winds or some precipitation.

When I confirm the destination with Alex, he lists off a few questions. How would you describe the sound? How long did the light linger in the sky? What colors did it have?

I tell him, and I can't help but notice the doubt in his tone as he breathes, Mhmm, over and over. I take my hand off his leg and rest it in my lap, taking in the outside star- and moonlit darkness. After a while, what's been like two hours passes, and I see his body

34

finally start to relax. He's in cruise control now, but the way he checks his mirrors tells me he's still focused and alert. A model patrolman.

I take off my hoodie as he reaches forward and plays with the radio. This is more out of habit than anything else. For years, Villages have been checking radio frequencies and scouring the airwaves for signs of other survivors. Dad said that in the beginning, when he was young, it was an effective way of tracking down survivor outposts.

It also helped establish the Villages. By Leader's estimate, there are some two dozen other Villages in the bowl – all living by their own rules, laws, standards and creeds. There had been multiple attempts, before I was born, to have a united front. Link all the Villages into one. But Dad said it got messy. He said it seemed the only thing anyone could agree on was that the Coasts were forbidden...

So, it was decided that peace – even in separate, divided, scattered Villages – was still the obvious preference to chaos.

Alex turns off the radio after a minute of static. "Hungry? There's some trail mix in the glove compartment."

I should probably eat something. It's been several hours since dinner. But I'm so nervous I probably won't be able to stomach even the smallest of snacks.

"I'm fine." I lean forward and rummage through my backpack, looking for my CD player. "Been thinking a lot about my role lately."

"Yeah?"

"I'll be seventeen soon. Makes sense."

"So, what role are you leaning toward?"

"Wish I could say. Shouldn't this be easy?"

"Not necessarily," he says, turning on the cab light.

It helps. A second later I find my CD player buried at the bottom. I grab it, zip up my backpack, and sit back.

"Took me a couple days to choose patrol," he adds, clicking off the light.

I keep a laugh inside. Wish I had that problem, except that I don't have anything to choose between.

"Look," he continues, reaching over with his free hand and stopping me from untangling my headphones. He holds my fingers and squeezes them affectionately. "Whatever you decide on – whichever job you choose – I'm sure you'll be great at it."

His words are well intentioned, but they don't ease my frustration.

"Thanks," I force myself to say.

Alex doesn't talk much, but when he does, it's usually to encourage me. I should really appreciate that more, given that he's related to Lark.

"You're tense," he says, massaging my knuckles. "You don't have to be worried. Everything's going to be fine."

I know he's referring to right now, traveling through the bowl, but I pretend we're still talking about my role-to-job switch.

"You think I overacted, when I signaled the alarm."

I sigh inwardly, watching the side of his face for a reaction.

He says, without pause: "It's not that. I...it's just, I had a feeling that Leader would propose this. Having you come with the patrol."

"You *did?*"

"It's how she works, Fare," he says, a touch of bitterness in his tone. "Any opportunity she gets to operate without board or assembly consultation, she's going to take it. Including risking a non-patrolman's life."

"That what you guys call us?" I say in a teasing way. "*Non*-patrolmen?"

Alex's brawny figure loosens as he begins to chuckle. He's always so handsome when he livens up, acts like a teenager. I let go of his hand and start to play with his hair.

"Did I get a genuine laugh out of Alex Windsor?" I say, acting shocked. "Non-patrolmen must be good for something!"

"Yeah, yeah," he replies, sounding more embarrassed than anything. "Can we just change the subject?"

"Lois doesn't seem to think you take me on enough dates," I tell him frankly.

"Lois works in the stable, shoveling manure. The fumes in there mess with her head."

"Alex!" I swat his forearm gently.

"It's true. Why do you think her face is always contorted into a pouty expression?"

"Very funny." I lean over the center console and rest my head on his firm shoulder. He tilts his head against mine, exhaling after a beat of silence.

"I guess I just didn't want to believe you," he eventually says, "because I knew the result would be this. You, put in harm's way."

"But I'm *not* in harm's way." I run my hand up and down his right arm. "You said everything's going to be fine, and I believe you."

He tilts up and then kisses the top of my head softly. I move to kiss him back, which I know is not safe while he's driving, but I don't care. I need to feel him. But Alex's face has changed, so I perk up. He's not paying attention to me. He's staring straight ahead, eyes narrowed. I follow his gaze and see.

The dunes are up ahead.

But behind the sandy hilltops we see sparks in the air.

Gunshots.

The undergrounders have beaten us to the chase.

Chapter 11

The light is artificial and it is blinding.

I squirm and try to stand, but a voice calls out behind the glow. I stay on my hands and knees, feeling more vulnerable than I could have ever possibly imagined.

"Well, what do you think we got, boys!"

The voice is deep, resounding. Either the crater I am in – the one I formed when I crashed – is amplifying my hearing, or his delivery is just that intense.

I am betting the latter.

"My, my..." the man continues, "that *is* something special, isn't it?"

I squint. The light that covers me is so bright all I can make out are silhouettes. I count nine forms surrounding me atop the crater. Some pace around, getting a good look at me. Others remain stagnant. Regardless, I am immediately embarrassed of my naked form.

Another voice speaks. "My God...what is it?" He sounds scared. More than I am.

"Don't you know?" the first voice booms, a hint of fervor layered beneath his tone. "It's our answer. Our ticket. Our *future*."

I cannot even begin to speculate what he means, but what I do take note of is his use of "our." He is suggesting that I am theirs. That they own me. I am an object, and most objects have an owner, and in this man's eyes that is all I am. Their object.

But I will not be taken so easily. I will not be a prisoner again.

I push off my hands, sway a little on my knees, and then plant a firm foot on the ground.

"Whoa, whoa," a third voice exclaims. "It's getting up! What'da we do?"

"Bind it," the first voice orders. "Mr. Toff will know what to do."

The light that surrounds me flickers – bodies are moving back and forth in front of it and behind it. They are regrouping. They are getting ready to take me in.

I have to act.

I leap to both feet – still unable to see well because of the light – and scramble forward. Then, what sounds like streaks of air whip past my head and puncture the ground. This creates mini eruptions. I try to take cover, but my options are limited.

"What are you doing!"

"You'll kill it!"

"Trying to immobilize it! Pretty sure Mr. Toff would prefer this thing dead over it escaping!"

I scratch and claw at the crater walls, which are slightly taller than me. I need to get to the surface. I have to get out of this hole! But before I am halfway up, the light smacks off unexpectedly and there's a spray of shards against my back. Something has ricocheted off the artificial light source and killed it. Now the men curse and scramble around.

"Form ranks, form ranks!"

"We're under attack!"

Alex sticks his hand out the driver's side window and rotates his fist in a circular motion, signaling for everyone behind us to stop. A second later our truck skids and brakes. The tires kick up sand as a result and form little puffs of clouds. Alex and I unfasten our seatbelts and exit the cab simultaneously. He jogs toward the dunes and I dart after him.

"It's them, isn't it?" I ask as we crest the nearest dune. As we near the top, we slow, get down onto our bellies and scoot so we can peer over the peak.

Sure enough, three Jeeps are parked surrounding a large hole. We're about fifty or so yards off, by my quick estimation, so I refrain from saying anything else. One man wields a powerful searchlight mounted on the rack of a Jeep, and he points it at something inside the hole.

Lark and two other patrolman crawl up next to Alex. They all cuss under their breaths.

"I knew we should've left the Village sooner," Lark mutters. "Now we gotta get our hands dirty." Left sooner? Weren't you the one who thought I was daydreaming?

"You think we should attack?" Alex asks. I can tell by his tone he's not fond of this idea.

"Without a doubt," Lark replies. "Whatever they see in that crater is valuable. And that means only one thing."

"What?"

"They'll try to use it against our Village."

Alex exhales through his nose. "I dunno, that's just speculation, uncle. For all we know – "

"*Look!*" I say, almost shouting.

Someone's *inside* the crater! Trying to escape! A second later one of the undergrounders opens fire, shooting warning shots around the trapped person.

"That's it," Lark says, standing up and grabbing his rifle off the ground.

Before Alex can object, his uncle takes aim with one eye shut and fires. Surprisingly, his bullet doesn't stray. The immense searchlight shatters into bits of plastic and glass, and the undergrounders scream and run into defense mode.

"Get back in the truck!" Alex yells at me, and before I react the rest of our patrol is running up the dune with rifles and pistols poised.

They pass me in what feels like a frantic cluster, but I hear Lark and Alex taking control and bellowing orders. Soon, nothing but gunshots fill the air. I slide down the sand hill, hands over my ears. Eyes clamped shut. So much shooting.

Don't look up. Don't look down. Just look straight ahead.

I open my eyes and stare through the settling sand clouds at our trucks. Bullet shells and casings trickle down the dune, rolling past me, rolling against me, nudging from behind, daring me to look back.

"Don't look up," I say out loud, and my voice sounds strange and hollow because of how hard I press my palms against my ears. "Don't look down."

Someone screams out in pain over the deafening gunfire. Please don't be Alex, I think. That's when a sickening realization overcomes me. If anyone gets hurt or, God forbid, *dies*, it will have been all my fault. I spotted the falling light from the night sky. I issued the twelfth alarm. And I led the patrol here...

A minute drags by like an hour. Then two minutes. Finally, after the longest one-hundred-and-twenty seconds of my life, a bizarre silence falls over the desert. I drop my hands and pivot my head, gazing up toward the top of the dune. Two patrolmen tend to a fallen, wounded form that writhes in pain. The rest of the patrol disappears down the other side, and I hear the far off grumbling noises of the retreating Jeeps.

I force myself to stand and scramble up the dune.

I force myself to be calm.

I force myself to believe it's not Alex rolling and moaning on the sand.

Chapter 13

I drop back down to the bottom of the crater and cover my head. The repetition of agonizingly loud *cracks* and *booms* encircle me. The sound is the most violent thing I have heard in a while. I know only pain and death will come of it.

I tilt my head and peer up between my arms. Two bodies are lying at the top of my crater – limp, unmoving. A third body falls and rolls down, down, down and then bumps into me. I flinch, scoot back, but not before a pair of lifeless eyes steal my gaze. The man is bleeding in three places, and I startle myself by feeling a little happy.

Why not? It was not too long ago he was ready to imprison me. Drag me off by some aggressive and cruel means. Now he is not a threat. Now he is just a limp, unmoving body.

"Son of a *bitch*!" Yelling, again. "Move, move!"

"Carson's down! And Rico, too!"

"Dammit all, retreat!"

"What about the – ?"

"Leave it! They're picking us off like sitting ducks!"

The voices muffle as they get inside their vehicles, and a few heartbeats later they have abandoned me – the low grumblings of their vehicles growing fainter and fainter. I lower my hands, uncovering my head, but I do not feel completely safe. Not yet. An ominous silence sets in. The sand clouds my would-be capturers left behind obscure the stars in the sky. Just when I think I am alone, I hear faint moaning in the distance...and voices. Worried voices. Then –

"Are you all right?"

The words are soft spoken, yet I cannot help but jump. I spin around, get to one knee, and gaze up at the top of the crater. The clouds of sand and dust are still settling. I distinctly see someone inclining forward, standing at the crater crest.

They are trying to get a good look at me. I can tell by the way their head moves they are having the same problem I am and cannot make out my features and details. I crawl away, to the other end of my pit, and almost fumble over the dead body.

"It's okay," the voice continues. It is...it's a *girl's* voice.

"Farah!" a second voice calls behind her. "Get away from there!"

She doesn't. She doesn't even move. She just stands there and stares at me, continually leaning, swaying, moving, all efforts to look at me, to see me.

As the sand clouds continue to disperse and the moonlight sheds its light, I begin to see her more fully, her looking at me. Her hair is light. She looks small, petite. I even now am able to see her eyes, pretty eyes, confident eyes. I see concern in them.

Concern and compassion.

Yes, even in the night, with only the moon and stars as light, I see that the girl who stands above me is concerned and filled with compassion. I should move, tell her or signal that I'm fine – or, as fine as someone who just fell from the sky could be or should be. But I can't remember how to use my hands. Or my mouth. I can't remember how to do anything but stare. And that's what I do. I stare at the girl who came to see if I was all right.

Chapter 14 | Farah

I let out a thankful breath.

It's not Alex rolling in pain on top of the sand hill. He is there, however, and he applies pressure with both his hands on his fellow patrolman's leg. I watch, in shock, as Alex takes control of the situation, his movements fearless, confident. He belies the emotion I know he must feel. All the blood doesn't even faze him.

"Give 'em space," Lark says, pulling me out of the way. He's not gentle, but I let him move me so I don't have to watch any longer.

"Is he gonna be all right?" I ask.

Lark ignores me and orders for the first aid kit to be brought up from the trucks. This is my chance to help. I turn to act, but someone else is already halfway down the dune. I have to assist somehow. Be productive.

That's when I remember the person in the hole, the one the undergrounders were shooting at. I sprint away from Alex and the rest of the patrol. It's difficult to run too fast at this angle, and I have to slow down several times to avoid tripping over my own feet. Eventually the ground levels and I'm forced to squint through the swirls of sand clouds the Jeeps left behind. If I'm not careful, I might miss the hole and accidentally fall into it. Thankfully, I see it up ahead and slow to a stop as I approach.

Sure enough, the person is still there – curled up on the ground, hands shielding the back of their head.

"Are you all right?" I ask, and the person gives a start. I can't see much yet – if the person is visibly injured or not – but a second later they scurry off to the opposite end of the pit, exposing the form of a second body...it's not moving.

"It's okay," I say.

Someone calls out to me from behind, but I don't respond. I have to see if this person is okay. Alex doesn't flinch in the face of uncertainty. Neither should I.

I sit down on the ground, my legs dangling over the side of the hole, roll up my shirtsleeves and push off with my hands. I slide down the incline slowly, and reach the bottom a few seconds later. The hole is fairly deep, probably eight or nine feet, and I notice long streaks of black – like charcoal – stretching down the sides of the pit, where they eventually meet in the middle. Kind of like scorch marks. What happened here?

"It's okay," I repeat, standing up and wiping the sand off my hands.

The person hesitates, but then gets up and steps forward into the starlight. They're *naked*, but that's not what clogs the breath in my throat.

This thing that stands before me is tall, well over six feet, and its skin is clear. Like see-through plastic wrap. I see veins and streams of blood networking throughout its body, but nothing about its insides remotely resembles the makeup of a human. No, this thing's veins and organs and throbbing heart are almost square-like, with sharp edges and defined points. I'm reminded of a Rubik's Cube – Dad recovered one not too long ago.

This sight before me is more than enough to drive me away in fear. I should call out for help. I should scream. I should do *something*! But I don't feel threatened, not one bit, and I don't know why. The thing just sort of stares back. Its face is mostly humanlike, with two colorless eyes and a straight nose. Its mouth is currently closed – a straight line across its face. In the semi-darkness of the night, tiny cubes of blue and violet pulse in the thing's head, where a brain should be. The little cubes float, like dust particles suspended in air.

That's when everything starts to make sense. The light in the sky. The flash that prompted me to signal the twelfth alarm. The scorch marks in this hole – no, this *crater*. This thing...this being...fell from the sky.

It starts to move, and I flinch, but all it's doing is getting back to its knees.

"A-Are you hurt?" I manage to ask.

All it does is study me, resting firmly on both its knees. Its face...so expressionless. I can't even begin to read it. Although, something tells me this being is nervous. Apprehensive. And why not? I'm just as much a foreign creature to it as it is to me!

In this moment, looking at the otherworldly being

before me, my senses begin to catch up. My palms are sweaty. My heart is pounding. My breath is short. This is *really* happening. I'm *really* looking at...at an alien. I'm going to get one major I-told-you-so from Dad.

"What in the hell...?"

I stifle a gasp and turn around. Lark and three other patrolmen are standing behind me at the top of the crater, rifles drawn.

Chapter 15

I can't say anything. I can't reassure this girl's company that I mean no harm. The words are there, on my tongue, but the ability to speak is out of scope for me. Something's preventing me. Something I cannot control. I feel helpless. I *am* helpless.

"Get up here, Farah," one of the men orders, "slowly."

"Why, so you can shoot at it?" the girl replies defiantly, turning back to me. "You're no better off than the undergrounders."

"Farah – "

"Put your weapons down and I'll come up. We both will."

Why is she protecting me? In a short span of time, I've been attacked and almost forced into custody. I can only imagine how much suffering that would've led to. And yet, now, this girl – Farah – is standing up for me. She shouldn't have to. She shouldn't have to risk trouble with these men for my sake. But I can't defend myself.

"Do you realize how foolish you're being!"

"At the moment, no," she replies simply, her soft eyes locked on mine. "We'll go together," she tells me, drawing out her words and motioning up with her hands. I nod, indicating that I understand, but before I get to my feet again, a worried voice cuts into the night air.

"Farah! What are you doing! What is she doing?"

"Alex, stay up there," Farah responds, keeping her gaze on me. "I'm safe, and we're coming up."

" 'We're?!' " this person named Alex cries out. "What the hell is that! Farah, get up here!"

"Trying to – "

"W-Without that thing!"

"This *thing* is scared out of its mind, Alex."

"And I'm not?" he demands, pacing in between the other men. "You could get hurt! Give me your hand!"

"You know, if you're trying to keep it calm, shouting probably isn't the best idea," she says. I try to show a smile, assure her that I'm calm, but the muscles in my mouth are apparently still incapable of functioning.

Alex ignores her. "Don't touch it! Just, just lead it up here and we'll, we'll take it back to the Village for observation."

Observation? You plan on poking and prodding me? Farah doesn't like this suggestion either: her face shows it. I know, however, without having to think it over too much, that following Farah back to her "Village" is a safe choice. As long as she's around.

So, I get up from my knees and stand – towering over Farah, but keeping my head bowed a little. It's the only thing I can think of to show her that I intend to proceed with her, despite whatever Alex's ideas of examining me are.

53

"You understand us, don't you?" Farah asks quietly. I feel her watching me as I stare at the space of ground between us. I don't have time to give a response.

"C'mon, let's go," Alex continues, his voice calmer but still laced with anxiety. "We'll pull you up first."

"Then what?" she asks flatly.

A more serious, deeper voice replies: "Did I miss something here? Did I miss *why* we're having this conversation, Alex? Get her up here or we'll do it by force."

"Uncle – "

"Now." The man's words are statements. He's not inviting a dialogue. And yet, Farah takes a step closer toward me.

"We're climbing back up together, okay?" she whispers. "Let's go." She turns around and heads for the crater walls. I follow after, watching the men above us. There are some women, too. Most of them have young faces, especially Alex. But there's one among them who stands taller. His shoulders are broad. His head is clean of hair. He doesn't take his hate-filled eyes off me.

I mimic Farah and dig my hands into the soft, finite dirt and pull myself up in a staggered climb. We have to act quickly because the dirt slips down against us, almost instantly. Before long we pull ourselves over the lip, Farah getting help from Alex. We are out of the crater and the dead body it holds.

I inhale and exhale through my nose, hoping that finally the worst is behind me, when I see the bald man step forward quickly, raise his weapon high and bring it down into my face. I register the impact, the pain, then feel myself begin to slump...

Light fades, darkness remains.

Chapter 16 | Farah

I scream. "What are you doing!" I feel Alex holding me back as I try to rush over to the being's now unmoving form.

"Don't get too close, Uncle," Alex says behind me. Why is he condoning this behavior? They won't even give this being a chance! "Could be some form of radiation that's making it look like – "

"Whatever it has," Lark says, using his rifle to flip the being onto its back, "I'm sure we're all exposed to it now. No avoiding that."

Alex and a few other members of the patrol swear. It's the first time they're seeing it up close. Its body practically glows, giving off light by way of its exposed alien insides.

"What *is* it?" someone asks after a while. I push my way out of Alex's grip.

"My guess is that knocking it unconscious won't tell us," I say, kneeling down next to its head. I can't see any bruises or scratches on its translucent face. Least not yet...

"So...so what do we do with it?" another person asks.

Before I even open my mouth, Lark replies: "We're taking it with us. Alex is right, we need to have it examined. Then, it'll stand trial."

Trial? What's he talking about? Apparently, I'm not the only one confused, because I look up and see that everyone is wearing the same puzzled expression that I am.

"There's a dead body down there," Lark continues, pointing at the crater. "In case you didn't notice."

He can't be serious.

"That's an *undergrounder*," I say, "in case you didn't notice."

Lark hangs his rifle over his shoulder, smiling. "That's correct, Farah. Something happened that resulted in that man being killed – "

"We shot him, to protect whoever *they* were shooting at!"

"You know, I'm not certain that's how it transpired."

I don't even know how to respond. What's he playing at? Isn't *he* the one who fired the first shot?

"All I'm suggesting is the possibility of an alternative scenario," he says slyly. "For all we know, this thing" – he kicks its leg – "took one of their men down before we got here, which prompted them to open fire on it, starting this whole exchange of gunfire."

"Since when do you care that an undergrounder gets killed!" I say incredulously, standing up.

"When it plays a part in the death of one of my own."

I look from Lark to Alex, whose face drops. The patrolman, on the sand hill.

"Yeah, but..." I trail off, at a loss for words.

No, this being on the ground didn't directly result in

their fallen comrade, but this wasn't the time to argue that. We all stand there, naturally slipping into a moment of silence. Our Village is small, so while I may not know the late patrolman and his family on a personal level, I've most certainly interacted with them at some point, or at least seen them in the marketplace.

"Who?" I ask when enough time has passed.

"Morgan," Alex answers.

I shake my head, looking away. How hadn't I noticed before? Morgan's wife is the Village schoolteacher, and one of the sweetest ladies I know. She's going to be devastated.

"Trial or not, we need to get a move on." Alex clears his throat. "We can't give the undergrounders enough time to regroup and return."

I take a step back as two patrolmen use their faded bandanas to grab the being by its ankles. Like the thin cloth is going to protect their skin from whatever toxic emission they think they might catch. They drag the lame being across the sand and toward the dunes, and I start to follow, when –

"Hey, wait up." Alex stops me by the shoulder.

"You gonna yell at me some more?"

"I was gonna ask if you were hurt."

I try not to blush, but I definitely feel my cheeks getting warmer. "I'm fine," I say, and add, because I feel it's necessary, "sorry."

"Don't be. Look, I understand you wanting to help this...thing, whatever it is...but we have to play it safe. You could've been attacked or something."

Alex means well, I can tell by the sincerity in his voice, but I can't help consider this a lecture. We start walking, following the rest of the patrol back to the trucks.

"And since when did you get all reckless?" He doesn't say this angrily, but almost excitedly.

"I wasn't, you know."

"Hm?"

"Attacked. I wasn't attacked. Didn't even feel threatened."

He doesn't say anything back. We ascend the dunes, and twice I stumble and Alex has to catch me by the wrist and guide me until I regain footing. The patrolmen dragging the being carefully pull it up into Alex's truck and latch some handcuffs to its wrists. They're careful to not touch it, utilizing their bandanas as impromptu gloves.

I lean over the truck bed to get one last look at it before we leave for the Village, and notice something strange. The coin-sized cubes that float in its head aren't a purple and bluish color anymore, but rather red. A deep red, almost like blood. I'm not seeing things. I'm positive there's a change.

"What is it?" Alex asks from the other side of the truck.

I look up and meet his blue eyes. Either he's really good at reading my emotions, or I just wear them too thickly on my sleeve.

"Probably nothing," I mutter, knowing that what I see probably *is* something. Lark has injured the being

– more than he meant to, no doubt. When it regains consciousness, it'll likely be upset, and finding itself bound will add insult to injury. Who knows how it will react...

My guess? Not pleasantly.

Chapter 17

Conversations in a dark room. Multiple presences. I'm there, and I'm talking, but I can't see well. Everyone and everything's out of focus.

–Why? Why are you doing this?

Me: –Don't you turn your back on me now. After all of this work. This hard work.

–I'm not. I wouldn't. I just...why now? When it's not finished?

–You may not think it's finished, but it'll do the trick with the state it's in.

–How can you be certain? This is your life we're talking about.

I sound anxious: –Don't act like we haven't weighed the risks already.

–I'm not! But you're being hasty! What if it fails? What then?

–It won't, because you designed it. And you don't fail, so consequently it won't fail.

My emotions. They're pitted against each other. I can't remember if there's true confidence in my words, or if I'm challenging the one I am speaking with, as if to say, *Right? You did your best and I can trust you?*

More importantly, I can't exactly place what it is we're even arguing about.

It's well after midnight by the time we return to the Village, entering via the east gate. I'm shocked to see the main road packed with people. We slow down to less than five miles per hour and roll through the parting crowds as they stand on their toes and try to catch a passing glimpse at our cargo. Alex reaches for his walkie on the truck's dashboard.

"Uncle, come in."

A beat passes. Then, Lark's cocky voice cackles in: "Head for the storage units. Over."

"Did you call in ahead and announce what we found? Over."

No response. That tells us yes. I shake my head and look out the window, trying to spot Dad or Lois in the throngs of men, women, and children. Mostly everyone looks excited, but there are a handful of terrified looks, too. Lark shouldn't have said anything. Finding something like this life form required a level of discreetness first. All Lark did was stir up anxiety and uncertainty. But, then again, that's probably what he meant to do. For claiming to care so much about our Village and people, Alex's uncle sure has a stupid way of showing it.

"Please, return to your forts," Leader's voice

commands over the Village's loud speakers. "We'll have this all sorted out by morning."

I watch through my side mirror as people reluctantly turn away from our entourage and head back indoors. We turn off the main road and dead-end at the three storage buildings. The single story units are arranged in a crescent shape – more of a curved line then a true semicircle.

A few repurposed ladders jut out of the ground and serve as posts for gas lamps, which provide minimal lighting in this corner of the Village. In front of the middle storage building, I see a hunched form standing in the shadows.

"Dad," I say under my breath.

Alex parks the truck and I get out almost immediately, jogging over to where he's standing. I expect him to stop me so he can look me up and down and make sure I've not acquired any injuries. But instead he hugs me. He hugs me for the first time in so long I forget how to hug him back.

"It in there?" I hear Leader say as she and her armed guards stride over from behind one of the buildings.

Dad and I break away and watch Leader order for her men to open the storage unit nearest us.

"How'd you do?" Dad asks in my ear.

"I think I did okay."

He puts his left hand on my shoulder, and leans against his cane with his right one. Then he lets out a loud breath, smiling.

"So, found something out there, did you?"

"Some*one*," I answer.

We watch Lark park his truck, get out, and join Alex and Leader. They stand behind Alex's truck, and silence settles in as everyone takes in the view of the unconscious being.

"C'mon," I whisper to Dad, taking his hand and leading him to the truck. I feel the muscles in his fingers and palm tense as we get in between Leader and a member of her guard.

For a long time no one says anything. The life form actually looks rather peaceful, lying on its back with its hands chained. Seeing as how clear its skin is, I didn't think it would have any eyelids, but there's definitely thicker tabs of skin covering its eyeballs. Through the being's forehead I see its inner particles and rectangular strands float in slow rotations.

Its "blood" and "DNA" still emit a red glow.

"Well," Leader says at last, running a hand through her blond and grey hair. "Let's get a briefing, shall we?"

We listen quietly, huddled around the truck bed, as Lark recounts the events. As the oldest member of patrol, it's his duty. He tells Leader how we first spotted the gunshots in the air. How he engaged in assault because someone was potentially in danger. Then the undergrounders retreated. Morgan passed. And I found this...

To distract myself from the fact that everyone's staring at me now, I avert my eyes up a little and look at Alex, who is scraping something off of his hands. I realize, after a second or two, that it's dry blood. I hadn't seen it before, I was too wrapped up in everything else. He must be going through so much right now, even though he doesn't show it. Having had someone die in front of you like that, when you were trying so hard to save them...I shiver without realizing it.

"...right, Farah?"

"Hm?" I look up, eyes widening.

Leader half smiles. "You'll no doubt need to have a say in all of this, right?"

All of what? "Er...yes?"

Dad chuckles next to me. "Because you found it first, that entitles you to give input in the trial."

The trial. Lark still thinks that's necessary? I meet his eyes, and, surprise surprise, he winks.

"Of course," I say, unaware that my teeth were grinding slightly. Dad breaks from our huddle and limps away in his customary cane-assisted rhythm.

"Now," he says, pushing up his square glasses with his free hand. "It would probably be in the best interest of all of us to safely and kindly place this being in a situation where it won't feel threatened upon regaining its wits. I get this feeling that if it awakens and finds itself bound, with eight pairs of eyes staring down at it, things could, well, escalate."

"It's a passive, harmless thing," Lark says, spitting on the ground.

"Just because that's the only state you've seen it in,

doesn't mean that it's the only state it will remain in."

Everyone nods at Dad's words. Everyone but Lark.

"I, for one, am not fond of learning things the hard way," says Dad.

Two of Leader's men pull down the truck hatch, grab the being with gloved hands, and carry it off toward the open unit. We all follow ceremoniously and watch as the men eventually set it on the cement floor in the middle of the tall-ceilinged building. Rows of stacked crates and barrels surround us, and a few cylindrical fluorescent bulbs flicker above.

The alien life form lays there, legs crooked, head tilted back, body still. I can't help but feel enormously sorry for it. I'm sure whatever its reason for coming here, to our planet, it probably didn't expect to be captured like this. If it had a plan, some kind of agenda, we're hindering it. And we're definitely being unfair.

"It's only till Leader decides what to do next," Dad says under his breath.

That doesn't ease my upset stomach.

The two men who carried the being inside take two heavy sets of chains and clasp the metal brackets at the ends to its ankles. The chains are short, and they're anchored to the pavement via rusty stakes.

That's strange. I raise an eyebrow, leaning down to get a good look. This setup with the chains and stakes has been here for a while. There's no signs or hints on the floor that suggest it was arranged for this specific need of binding the being. No chunks or shavings of cement that would've been produced by pounding the stakes into the ground. No tools around: no hammers or chisels. What's this building really used for...?

"Three men will be assigned guard duty around the clock," Leader proclaims, ushering for us to leave. "I want the Professor roused from her sleep and brought in immediately to begin an assessment."

I look over my shoulder as we leave, and it takes a lot of resisting to not suggest that I stay with the guards overnight. Honestly, that's probably not a bad idea. When it finally regains consciousness, my guess is that having something familiar around will help.

And I'm that familiar thing.

"No way," Dad says next to me.

I swallow, turn my head forward, and continue alongside Dad until we exit the storage building. Someone behind us collapses the storage building's wide doors.

"It's going to be terrified when it wakes up and finds itself bound," I say, engaging in a battle I've already lost. "Who knows if those chains can even contain it?"

"There's potato and cactus soup on the stove," Dad says, not even bothering to counter. It's just as well, too, because at the mention of food my mouth gets instantly frothy. "There's also some unfinished homework sitting on the kitchen table that, I seem to recall, a certain teenager vowed to have completed before her night watching duties."

Wow.   Dinner.   Unfinished   homework. Responsibilities. Pieces of a somewhat normal life that

I haven't given any thought to since I first spotted the streak of light in the sky. It's going to require a lot of effort on my part to focus in school tomorrow, where a test that promises to leave me frustrated awaits.

Dinner is fast. I don't even use a spoon but just tilt my bowl back and swallow the soup down. Next, I try to focus on homework by candlelight, sitting on top of my covers with music playing through my headphones, but it's pointless.

All my attention and mind does are wander. Wander straight out of my fort, down the main road, and to the storage unit, where the life form we found in the desert is probably stirring and close to waking up. I hope it won't be scared, but I know that's foolish. Of course it will be scared. Suddenly, I find that I'm scared too, and so I just give up on my assignment and bury myself under the sheets.

The next morning Lois and Digs stop by my fort during breakfast, and they don't even wait until I finish chewing my oats before unloading a round of questions.

"Is it true?"

"You found an alien?"

"What's it like? I heard it's got like five testicles."

"You mean *tentacles*, moron."

Digs rolls his eyes and sits across from me at the kitchen table. "I know what I said." Then, after dropping his backpack on the ground, he whispers, "So?"

I swallow my food. I don't really know how to

respond. Lois and Digs watch me expectantly. I know how excited they must be at the prospect of what we've found, but I'm only filled with sorrow and pity as I think about the being's bound, unmoving form lying on the cement floor. Heavily guarded by the Village's finest. I still haven't had time to work out how I'm going to skip school to go to the storage unit. I decided, while brushing my teeth earlier this morning, that I owed it to the being to check on it first thing today.

"How about we let her finish her breakfast," Dad says, closing his bedroom door and limping over. He pours himself a cup of coffee and leans against the stove. "Can't let Farah be late today, she's got a test to fail."

I shoot him a scowl, but notice Lois's usually pink face pale. "There's a test?"

On our way to the underground schoolhouse, I give Lois and her kid brother a recap of last night's events. I walk in between them, and it's funny how they react to my story with gasps at the exact same time. I can't explain why, but I don't feel it's my place to tell them about Morgan's death. I just skip over that part, knowing that his wife – our teacher – will most likely be absent today, and so they'll find out soon enough.

"Well, the alien must be doing okay," Digs says when I'm finished.

"But we can't be for sure until – "

"Yes we can," he interrupts me. "The storage buildings haven't blown up or anything."

This brings a smile to my face. "Good point." We

turn off the main road and head through a crooked alleyway. "I should probably break away now, before we get closer to the schoolhouse."

"What?" Lois stops me, grabbing my wrist. Digs, who isn't paying attention, bumps into my backpack. "Break away?"

"I have to go check on it, Lois."

"And?"

I didn't think I'd have to defend myself, especially not to my best friend. She raises her eyebrows, almost like she's sizing me up for first time. I don't say anything for a moment, and she holds her ground – tucking strands of her black hair behind her ears.

"Look, I have a responsibility to this being," I say, well aware of the level of irritation in my voice. "At the very least I have to go check on it and – "

"Take me with you."

"I...what?" I certainly wasn't expecting that.

"Take *us* with you, she means," Digs says, his fists resting against his hips.

Lois snorts. "Yeah, like that'll – "

"Or, I tell Zane about your diary entries."

I stifle a laugh. You can almost smell the smoke coming out of Lois's ears. "I can't stand you," she says, her eyes forming into angry slits.

"Love you," Digs replies.

"How about this," Lois continues, reaching out and pushing her brother before he moves out of the way, "we go to class, check in for morning period, and then sneak off during lunch?"

I shake my head. "Lois, I don't think – "

"You're covering yourself this way," she argues. "Now, when your dad asks about school, you don't have to lie. You can tell him all about your morning and just conveniently leave out the second half of the day."

While she does offer a good point, I'm still not sold on bringing them along. But, before I'm able to present another option, the school bell chimes and Lois flashes a large smile. She turns around and continues up the alley toward our destination.

"Coming?" Digs says at my side. I shrug, and then just follow him all the same.

We reach the square opening in the ground on the west side of the Village and descend the spiral staircase. The single room schoolhouse is already bustling with the rest of the Village's kids and teenagers. Digs waves goodbye and joins his age group at the front of the room. Lois and I sit near the back, one row in front of the seniors.

The high ceiling is covered with salvaged portholes from submarines, and the substitute skylights let in pillars of early morning sunlight. I watch flecks of dust and sand spin around in the air, and I'm instantly reminded of the being. Did the fact that its insides change red truly mean it was injured? Was I just making that up? And, if Lark *did* hurt it badly, was it doing okay now? Recovering?

It's not until I feel Lois's elbow jab my ribs that I realize the entire room has fallen silent and everyone's staring straight at me. I scratch my eyebrow with my thumb, pretending not to notice, but who am I kidding? The awkward, uncomfortable atmosphere is practically suffocating. The whispers begin. *Did you hear what she found? Who hasn't? My dad thinks she could be contaminated now or something. Mine too – I'm supposed to avoid her or I'll get in trouble.*

Okay, that's as far as I let it go. I open my mouth, furious retorts close to spilling out of me, when the sound of footsteps pulls everyone's attention away from me and redirects them to the spiral staircase. I look up, too. It's Alex, followed closely by some shorthaired woman I've seen in the marketplace multiple times.

"Sleep any?" Alex whispers in my ear after taking the open desk behind me. He kisses my neck conspicuously before I can respond, and a flurry of chill bumps spread across my skin at the touch of his warm lips.

"Morning class," the shorthaired woman calls out, marching down the aisle and taking a place at the head of the room. She wears a blue button-up shirt with a large, white, oval brooch pinned at the neck in place of a tie.

"I will be taking over for Mrs. Patterson for the rest of the season," she says, looking out over the students.

More whispers. Everyone's wondering why, but I know. Lois gives me a sideways glance, and I play dumb. They'll find out, eventually, just not from my lips. When the interim teacher turns her back to write her name on the chalkboard, I look over my shoulder.

Alex is telling a joke to one of his friends, and I have

to hiss his name a few times before he notices me.

"What's up?" he asks, leaning forward.

"Are you, you know, doing okay?"

"What d'ya mean?"

Is he serious? A man died in his arms last night and he doesn't know what I'm referring to? He doesn't look fazed at all. I mouth Morgan's name, and realization slowly seeps into his face.

"Oh. That." He shrugs.

Before I can prod him more, I hear the interim teacher finish scratching her name in chalk. I give Alex a comforting look, and, before I turn back around, steal a glance at the long scar on his neck.

I know the patrol is trained well, and they're prepped for pain and loss, so Alex's sturdy resolve is no surprise. But cutting jokes? Showing uncharacteristic public affection? He's probably just overcompensating for his distress. That was, after all, the first time he has seen death so close and in such an intimate way. Right?

My thoughts are harshly interrupted by a loud, panicked voice screaming through a megaphone above the schoolhouse. It's the day watcher, sounding an alarm. The entire schoolhouse falls silent, and we look up at the ceiling just as the day watcher runs over the skylights on the surface.

"First alarm! First alarm!"

We all gasp, and I feel my breath desert me. First alarm. The undergrounders are at our Village's doorstep.

Chapter 19

More dreams. Dreams that are memories. My surroundings and company are still obscured by a hazy curtain.

Me: —I've fought. For too long, I've fought for this.

—The end result was never your ultimate goal.

—Wasn't it?

—You know this. It's your efforts and journey that will have the lasting effects they rightfully should. You will become a symbol now.

—Symbols are a fading thing. An ideal...now that's something.

—Yes, and then —

A louder voice creeps in: "How long has it been unconsciousness like this?"

"Lark says about a couple hours," a second voice replies.

Lark. I know that name. How do I know that name? Suddenly, light drifts in under my eyelids, growing brighter and brighter, and I start to come to. Slipping in and out of unconsciousness like this is becoming something of a habit for —

No. I didn't just "slip into unconsciousness." Lark did this to me. He took his weapon and smashed me over the head with it. I reach up to rub my eyes, but my hands are constrained. Chained together.

"Easy there, easy there," another voice says as my breathing quickens.

I move to stand up, but my ankles are bound too. What's happening? Where's Farah? She's the only one who will defend me. I try to use my mouth, try to call her name, but that invisible muzzle still keeps my jaw locked. I'm through with this.

There's just enough slack on my ankle chains to allow me to stand up. So I do. I look around, soak in my surroundings. I need to figure out the best point of escape. I'm through being imprisoned.

"What do we do!" a panicked voice yelps.

"Keep your rifles trained on it!"

"Will someone get the damn Professor in here!"

"You really think *she'll* know what to do?"

That voice. I recognize it. It's Lark. I squint, and, sure enough, see him emerging out of the shadows. I clench my fists, and I feel the muscles in my arms flexing and tightening up. He walks right up to me, leaving about an arm's length of distance between us.

"What seems to be the problem, boys?" he asks, not taking his eyes off me. I hold his gaze, refusing to blink beneath the room's flickering light. The space we're in is rather large, with various boxlike items stacked around us.

"It was getting up," someone answers Lark.

"I see that," he replies, his voice lazy. Uninterested. "Don't worry, though. It can't hurt you." Want to test that theory? I try to step forward, but all I'm able to do is rattle my chains on the cold floor. Lark grins and arcs an eyebrow.

"You should also," he continues, addressing his men, "make sure you don't show any fear, which, for you lot, may be difficult. Me, on the other hand," he says, lowering his voice and taking something out of his side holster. "Well, I'm not afraid...more curious than anything else."

Then, with near inhuman speed, he jabs whatever he's holding forward. In the split second that his hand is under the light, I see that he's wielding a dagger, and the blade catches the ceiling's reflection.

I react with an instinct so quick it's foreign to me. Like I'm watching myself from someone else's point of view. An out of body experience... I grab hold of Lark by the wrist with both my hands, stopping the tip of his dagger from puncturing my stomach. I jerk his hand up, just enough to cause discomfort, and he drops the dagger – gritting his teeth furiously. The dagger rattles loudly as it hits the floor, bouncing for a second or two before settling still. I don't have to hear the *clicking* noise all around to know that Lark's men have their weapons pointed at me and are a command away from inflicting pain. Yet, Lark doesn't voice any command. He just stares at me with his beady eyes.

We don't break from this moment. I keep Lark's wrist firmly clutched in my hands, and, even though I'm a foot taller than him, he still refuses to show hints of intimidation. I think this might go on for a while, when a man bursts onto the scene, panting crazily.

"Leader requires – requires all patrol present!" he shouts between breaths. "First alarm has been sounded!"

Lark's men react instantly around us, gathering in a group and preparing to leave. Whatever is happening on the outside, I can use it in my favor. It means I'll potentially be left alone. Lark jerks his hand back, but it's unnecessary because I've already begun to let go.

"Del," Lark says, turning around. "You stay here. If this thing so much as blinks, take out its legs." Then, he leads all his men but one out of the large room. The man I'm left with has a very wide frame and practically no neck. He cocks his weapon back idly and then sits on a nearby crate.

"I'd get comfortable," he finally drawls, more to himself than me. I assume he thinks I can't understand him. But that's one thing I've not had a problem with. For reasons I can't fully grasp yet, the beings on this planet leverage a language I completely comprehend. If only I could talk back.

Suddenly, the man named Del jumps up, his finger hovering over his trigger.

"W-What are you doing!" he stammers.

At first, I have no idea what he's referring to, but then I start to feel it. My lips have begun to peel open, but slivers of my skin resist. Like two sticky substances being pulled apart slowly. I feel air pass through the tiny strands of flesh that are straining to keep my mouth closed, and I can only imagine what this must look like.

Chapter 20 | Farah

Had Mrs. Patterson been at the schoolhouse this morning, she would have easily seized control of the situation, ordering us under our desks and telling Alex – the only patrolman still in school – to lock and secure the hatch.

But Mrs. Patterson isn't in school this morning.

Alex leaps up from his desk, tells the rest of the class and me to stay put, and bolts up the spiral staircase to the surface. It does no good. The four other seniors chase after him, and their respective younger siblings scream out in question. Then more people shout. Then just about everyone is shouting.

"Don't, it isn't safe," Lois says beneath the pandemonium as I eye the spiral staircase.

"It isn't safe if I don't have a plan," I say, meeting her eyes and smiling deviously. "Guess what though? I have a plan."

Lois shakes her head. "Since when did you become so – so – ?"

"Reckless?"

"I was gonna say fun."

I give her a playful punch in the arm. "Ha. Very funny. C'mon, we have to hurry."

"What about Digs?"

We both look toward the front of the schoolhouse. The interim teacher has finally maintained some semblance of control, and has successfully corralled the kindergarteners through fifth graders under their desks.

"He's safer down here than anywhere else," I say, reassuring my best friend.

She nods once and then we abandon our desks and backpacks. We hear the interim teacher call out to us, but her attempts at coaxing us back are futile.

When we reach the top of the staircase I close the hatch shut, hoping that no one will follow us. Even though you can only lock it from the inside, my thinking is that just seeing it closed will squander anyone else's plans of leaving.

"This way," I tell Lois, leading her down the same alley we took mere moments ago, before the first alarm was sounded.

We stop when we reach the main road. Two trucks zoom past us, heading for the east gate. Armed patrolmen chase after, running in ranks. A siren shrills in the distance, ordering everyone indoors.

Once the coast is clear, we cross the main road and round the mess hall, crouching to a stop beside the exterior stoves. I wait for a few seconds, though I don't know what I'm waiting for. I simply remain stagnant, hunched over on one knee beside Lois, who breathes silently through her nose.

"Now," I whisper to her.

I dart across the dirt intersection, exposing myself to

anyone observing from the rooftops, and reach the base of the Village watchtower. I climb the ladder as fast as my arms will pull, and I don't even spare a second to make sure Lois is behind me. I emerge through the center opening, wipe my hands clean of sand, and look out toward the east gate.

Leader has positioned patrolmen all along the eastern side of the Village. They stand on the catwalk that runs on top of the entire fence, rifles and pistols at the ready. Leader herself stands among them, megaphone at her side. Next, I see what it is they're staring at: Five gigantic diesel vehicles are lumbering toward our Village, slightly distorted by the morning heat haze. The biggest vehicle of the lot has the shell of a large, decrepit wooden ship, but the nautical skeleton doesn't cover the immense spinning tires. A black flag is raised near the back, and it whips in the wind dramatically.

"That's why they call themselves desert pirates," Lois says, holding onto the watchtower railing. I was too absorbed with the oncoming procession that I hadn't heard her come up.

Even though our Village probably outnumbers these approaching undergrounders five to one, I'm guessing they can do serious damage with that sand vessel.

Lois cusses under her breath.

"What do you think they want?" she asks.

I don't answer.

"Oh," she says, realizing. "Right. The alien."

"They were shooting at it, Lois. They wanted to hurt

it – or worse, kill it."

The undergrounders roll to a stop once they reach our gates, and I notice a stack of speakers at the bottom of their flagpole. The speakers are amassed in a haphazard pile, and none of them are matching.

"What is the purpose of your presence?" Leader says through her megaphone. A few moments later, a voice echoes back through the stack of speakers:

"Presents?" A cold, crazed laugh follows. "Who said anythin' about *presents*? What, you think we came bearin' gifts!" I shift my weight in the watchtower, uneasy about this whole situation. If the undergrounders truly believe they're entitled to take back the being, some twisted version of finders keepers, by what means will they try to accomplish this?

I watch, in horror, as a person dressed in rags emerges onto the deck. Their face is draped behind a veil of poorly stitched patches. I see that detail clearly, even from up here, and it tells me exactly who I'm looking at. A man I've only ever heard of in stories.

"Mr. Toff," Leader says, her voice unquavering. "We take your visit here very hostile. Please turn your battleship around and be on your way."

The covered form of Mr. Toff saunters toward the vessel's capstan and he climbs to the top of it, clutching a skinny microphone all the while.

"Now hold on, won't you?" he says, sounding pouty. I wonder how he sees because there aren't any visible slits or holes in his mask. "I've just come to engage in civilian conversation!"

I expect to see other undergrounders standing about the deck, maybe even pointing cannons at us. But Mr. Toff is the only person who has shown himself. It's obviously a statement.

Having hundreds of guns trained on him means nothing.

Leader: "What is it you wish to discuss?"

"Compensation, of course!"

"Uh oh," Lois says in my ear.

"I don't know what you mean," Leader replies, her free hand on her hip.

"My men found somethin' in the desert, somethin' rather special," Mr. Toff continues, his tone gleeful. "Then, *your* men showed up and attacked. Gave no warnin'! Now how's that fair? I lost three semi-capable bodies!"

"We, too, suffered losses."

"True," Mr. Toff said. "But would you have if your men *hadn't* initiated an attack?"

Leader lowers her megaphone as a short person standing next to her says something inaudible. It's her advisor – an older man I'm certain no one's heard talk except Leader.

"I'm still foggy on the details, to be honest!" Mr. Toff exclaims. Something about his constant mirth makes my skin crawl. "Like why my men were even fired on to begin with."

"Your men were attacking an unarmed – " Leader starts to counter, but is quickly interrupted by Mr. Toff's louder speakers.

"See, this is where I have a problem," he says, "because my men paint a different account. One in which your fine Villagers attacked for no reason, killed three of my men" – he holds up four gloved fingers, a poor attempt at humor – "and stole what they had rightly found. What *I* rightfully found."

I can't believe this monster thinks his claims will fly! Here's a man who travels the bowl for the sole purpose of raiding and plundering and leveling Villages where he sees fit. I've heard terrible stories of him leading the undergrounders on night raids where they slaughter men, women, livestock – even kids – just for the sake of slaughtering. They leave everything as is and don't bother collecting on their spoils. And now *he* wants to discuss compensation? Something other than disbelief wells up inside me.

Disgust and hate.

"So, was your plan to sit up here and watch this go down," Lois whispers, "praying that we won't get blown to bits if a mini war starts?"

She's right, and I'm running out of time. I take my eyes off Mr. Toff and his vessels and scan our Village. Because Leader has practically the entire patrol seeing to this situation, I'm hoping she chanced leaving the being on its own – chained up in the storage unit.

"From up here," I tell Lois, "I wanted to make sure we had a clear path to the storage units. If just *one* adult sees us, it's over. They'll insist we come inside with them."

Lois follows my gaze. "The Village is a ghost town.

No one takes first alarm lightly, so we should be fine."

Off to the left, Leader says something else into her megaphone, but I tune it out. Every precious second counts, and I have to use them wisely or I won't get a chance to see the being.

"After you," I say.

Lois gets down to the floor and starts climbing. I descend after her, and, a short while later we both hop onto the sandy ground. We zigzag around small forts, running in a crouch below window height. A handful of minutes have passed, and I'm starting to worry. Did we get turned around? Did I get us lost?

"There!" Lois yells, covering her mouth immediately. She's pointing at the three buildings.

"It's okay," I say, lowering her hand. "I don't think anyone heard you."

I stand up straight and jog to the middle storage unit. The side door is unlocked!

"I hope you're sure about this," Lois hisses. "Our safety, that is."

"Now you're checking?" I say, still grasping the handle. I hold in a chuckle and swing the door open.

Chapter 21

I hunch over, clawing at my mouth to try and break off the skin fibers clinging to my lips. Droplets of saliva run down my fingers. This isn't painful, it's just...awkward. It's like my mouth isn't meant to be open, like I'm fighting to tear apart a seal that isn't there.

I try not to make too many sudden movements. If Del feels threatened I'm sure he won't hesitate to follow Lark's orders and bring me down with his weapon. I pinch a particularly thick piece of skin between my lips and start to tug. This does no good! My body's actually working against me – attempting to patch my mouth closed permanently.

"Stop that!" Del shouts, and I hear him step toward me. "Whatever you're doing – stop!"

I try to respond now that I have a chance to talk, but I can't produce words. Instead, a low guttural sound comes out. Del fires his weapon and pieces of the ground spray up at me. A warning shot.

"What have you done!"

I freeze. That's not Del's voice. I look up and see Farah rushing toward Del. In a brazen act, she reaches out and lowers the tip of his weapon.

"Did you hurt it?" she demands.

Between my bizarre bodily changes and Farah's sudden appearance, I think Del's too disoriented to order her gone. Another girl appears behind them. She's dressed similarly to Farah but has darker hair and walks with a slouch.

"You've got to be kidding me..." the girl says, trailing off. She stares at me with eyes as wide as fists.

I lower my hands and shut my mouth. At this point I'd rather run the risk of resealing my lips than scaring off Farah and her company.

Wow, I think. Now that I have more than star- and moonlight to work with, I can really see Farah's features. Her full golden hair is done up beneath a bandana today, and a few loose locks dangle free next to her left eye. Her skin looks so smooth and fair, with an almost polished-like quality. And her green, unblinking eyes cut through the dimness with a beautiful radiance I've not seen on anyone else since arriving on this planet.

It's as though she doesn't belong here in this dirty, barren badland.

"I heard gunfire," Farah says, striding past her companion, who still stares – her mouth now agape. "Are you hurt?"

I shake my head, straightening up.

"You've got to be kidding me!" the girl behind Farah says, laughing. "It understands you?"

"Yes," Farah answers.

She walks up to me and stands on the tips of her toes, examining my forehead with a concerned expression. I see beads of sweat on her face, and the perspiration causes a unique shine. Her scent bears no bitterness or pungencies, the kinds that must come with living in this type of terrain. No, she smells of something sweet...something rather nostalgic...

"Are you sure?" she says, looking into my eyes. I just look back, wondering how someone's eyes can be so green. "Are you sure you're not hurt?"

I nod. She doesn't look convinced. She walks around me, examining my backside.

"You've *got* to be kidding me!" Farah's companion says again, gasping. "Farah – it's naked!"

I look down, remembering that I'm fully exposed as if all of the sudden. My body temperature gets warm ten times over. I hunch over, covering my genitals with my arms.

"Here," Del says, grabbing something off one of the nearby crates and tossing it to Farah. "Give it my duster. But then you and Lois gotta scram, got it? Lark would have my balls in a jar if he found you two here."

"Gross," the girl named Lois says.

"Lean up," Farah instructs me, her voice soft. "It's okay, this'll help."

She proffers up Del's large coat to assure me. Hesitantly, I obey and broaden my shoulders. Farah drapes the heavy coat around my back and fastens a few of the buttons so my mid-region is concealed.

I blink once, trying to show her thanks with my eyes.

"Has he been fed yet?" Farah asks, turning back to Del.

My insides feel as if they're skittering in loops, creating this indescribable sensation within me. For the first time, I've been referenced as a "he," not an "it." It's funny how I have all these questions pressing against me, threatening to break me like some powerful vice, and yet something so simple as Farah referring to me as a person fills me with ease.

"Don't believe so," Del replies. "Before you two got here, though, it started doing this weird thing with its mouth."

"What do you mean?"

Del never gets the opportunity to elaborate, because a large sliding door reels open, sending in a blast of powerful, blinding sunlight. A second later, the loud repetitive *clacking* noise I've grown so used to echoes loudly, and Del goes flying backward – spurts of his blood spraying all over the place.

Chapter 22 | Farah

In one moment Del is standing there, getting ready to answer my question. In the next moment, his blood is everywhere. He topples back, almost flying in the air, and smacks into a collection of steel barrels. I spin around, running for Lois, who just stands there – rendered motionless by shock. I grab her hand and tug her behind a wall of pallets.

"Let 'em go!" a hollow voice yells.

"But they'll warn the Village!"

"We'll be gone by then," the first man replies. "C'mon! We've only got about ninety seconds."

We huddle down, hidden in shadows. I silence my heavy breathing by covering my mouth with one hand, and with my other I have to stifle Lois's wild sobs. Her warm tears trickle over my knuckles, and that's when I see the spots of blood on my wrist. Del's blood.

I force myself to remain calm. "Go," I whisper to Lois. "You have to go to the east gate and alert everyone."

My stomach clenches, and I taste bile on my tongue, but I keep the vomit at bay. It's the realization that sickens me. The realization that Mr. Toff and his vessels were just a diversion, and that someone – someone from *our* Village – tipped them off about the being's holding location in a preconceived agreement.

How else did the undergrounders know to come here? And now our entire patrol is on the opposite end of the Village!

"Go," I whisper again. "I have to do something to stall them!" I expect Lois to argue, but instead she inhales through her nose – visibly righting herself – and lowers my hand. Next she peeks around our barrier, checking to see that she's clear, and then she squeezes my hand.

I give her a knowing look before she tiptoes in the opposite direction, making for the side door. I say a silent prayer for her and then creep up slowly to assess the damage. I peer around the side of the pallets cautiously. My head throbs and pulses so much that I'm certain the undergrounders will hear it and I'll be discovered. I swallow and inch further sideways, hoping that a plan will just materialize in front of me.

What I see is happening so fast that it appears to be going in slow motion.

Chapter 23

The first thing I'd do is cover Farah and her friend, Lois. Make sure they are safe. But the second Del's corpse crashes into a pile of cylindrical objects, Farah's leading Lois out of view. Good. Even with this much adrenaline pumping through my veins, I don't think I could rip these chains up from the hard ground.

"C'mon!" someone says to my right. "We've only got about ninety seconds."

A heavyset man stalks forward, silhouetted by the sunlight, brandishing a large axe. He drops the sharp tip onto the floor behind him, arcs it forward in the air, and I hold my forearms up. But the rounded blade makes contact with the chain binding my right ankle. They're here to take me away.

I do a quick body count. There's about nine or ten "undergrounders," and most of them stand guard near the retractable door.

A deep, memorable voice intones: "See what we're doing, you freak?"

It's the man from the crater. The man who said I was their "future." The man who ordered me bound. "We're setting you free, got it?" He stands in front of me, arms crossed. He has no hair on his head, like Lark, but has a full, gnarled beard.

The axe swings again, cutting through the links of the second chain tailored to my other ankle. The large man steps back, holding onto his precious weapon.

"Now," the bearded man continues, "Mr. Toff doesn't think you need to be tranqu'd. He thinks you'll play nice and come with us once we've set you free. Thinks you'll cooperate."

I hear a series of grinding noises as the men near the entrance cock their weapons. The man in front of me waves over three members of his guard, probably to escort me out.

"Please don't prove Mr. Toff wrong," the man says firmly.

But I plan to do just that. Summoning the speed I utilized when defending myself against Lark's dagger, I sidestep to my left and jab my fists into a forceful uppercut. Del's jacket slides down my backside the same time I make contact with the heavyset man's chin, which *snaps!* audibly.

The axe goes airborne.

I snatch the tool out of the air, clasping the hilt tightly, and spin – swinging vehemently. The tip punctures the bearded man's chest, and his eyes roll to the back of his head almost instantly. I don't pull the axe free, but instead push forward and run – using the man's broad body as both a shield and a battering ram.

I successfully knock over three men, wisps of air blazing past my ears. Only five of them left now. All I can think about is Farah. I hope she's fled as far from here as possible. I don't want her to see this, and I don't want stray firepower hurting her.

Either way, these men are a threat to her, and that kick starts a rage inside me.

Chapter 24 | Farah

From head to toe, the cube-like particles inside the being pulsate a deep crimson. Deeper than when Lark injured his head.

In a single move, the being yanks the axe out from the undergrounder's chest and ducks beneath a round of bullets. Then, he throws up the axe sideways, which collides with one man's nose. The being seizes this brief window to disarm the man, spin around him, and issue four deadly blows to the head in quick succession – felling the remaining undergrounders in less than three seconds.

Just like that, it's over.

I take a step forward, shivering in the carnage, and meet the being's pale eyes.

Don't look up.

Don't look down.

Just look straight ahead.

If he could do all this so fast, and while wearing handcuffs, I can't even imagine what he's truly capable of. Suddenly, in this moment of contemplation, standing in the middle of all these bloodied corpses, I begin to question my instincts. Was I too quick to deem him safe? Have I been acting foolhardily?

I should probably feel protected – the being *did* just

eliminate ten undergrounders in one fell swoop – but instead I'm afraid. I take a step backward beneath the flickering fluorescent light, my boots crunching over bullet casings.

The being starts toward me, his bodily glow resuming its bluish tints, and I shout, "Don't! Stay there!"

He obeys with hesitation, but he gets to his knees slowly. That marks the second time he's done this. First in the crater, when I found him, and now. He's telling me something, that part's clear. But what? Don't be afraid? I submit? You can trust me?

"Farah thank God!" Dad yells in one breath, waddling into the storage unit with his cane. He navigates around the bodies on the floor and then eventually reaches me, but this time I hug him. "What were you thinking?"

"I don't know, Daddy," I say, unable to fight back tears.

"What happened here?" he asks, breaking our hug sooner than I want.

He surveys the aftermath of the being's attempted capture, when Leader and a force of patrolmen run inside – trails of dust sweeping in behind them like an ominous fog.

The being keeps still as four rifles press into his back.

"Don't do that," I say before I can stop myself.

Dad puts a hand on my arm. "Farah – "

"He saved me," I say, feigning confidence and

striding toward Leader. "I came here to check on him, when the undergrounders appeared. They killed Del, and then tried to apprehend the being, but he fought back."

I feel the being's eyes on me, but I avoid his gaze lest my fear return. I can't let anyone think I'm scared of him, or my account might lose merit. It's crazy, I know. Who *wouldn't* be downright shaking after experiencing something like I just did? But I know how Leader operates. It's her job to question everything.

And after an incident like this one, she's going to have a lot of questions.

"Dammit," Leader says after a solid minute of silence. Her advisor appears amidst the wall of patrolmen and he pulls her aside. They converse for a few minutes.

"Give me your bandana," Dad says, walking up beside me.

I comply, and my hair tumbles down past my shoulder. Dad takes the blue, patterned cloth in one hand, leans his cane against his hip, and then grabs my wrist. He gently dabs my fingers and knuckles, cleansing my skin of Del's blood. Surprisingly, my hand is steady and no longer shaky.

For a while, the only sound comes from Leader and her advisor's whispers, and the electric hum of the fluorescent lights. Then,

"Everyone must be questioned and interrogated thoroughly," Leader says, standing in the middle of the storage unit. "I don't care if it takes the entire week.

I'm smoking out our traitor. We'll set up round-the-clock sessions at the barracks. I want both the east and south gates sealed. No one is permitted to leave. School, patrols, and trading with other Villages is suspended indefinitely.

"Thomas, are you still using your bomb shelter to stockpile junk?"

Dad hands me back my bandana. "No, and I wouldn't necessarily call my findings junk – "

"Good," Leader interrupts. "You have one of the most centralized forts in our Village. You and your daughter are practically equidistant from the Village walls."

Unlike the storage units, I think, which are backed up against the fence and rather close to the south gate. I understand where she's going with this before she even says it aloud:

"You and Farah will be housing the being until further notice." Dad's cane tumbles over and hits the pavement. He clears his throat and reaches down to pick it up, but I grab it for him. "I will handpick no less than twenty patrolmen to stand guard 24/7. You will cooperate with the Professor, who – once she's cleared – will pay daily visits to your fort to learn all she can of the being. Since the Professor has already confirmed there are no traces of radioactivity, or any other chemically harmful attributes, you should have no issues with this charge."

"No issues at all," Dad replies through gritted teeth. A blind man could see how much he opposes this. And what about me? Just when I'm starting to reevaluate everything – my feelings toward the being – I've now got to cope with him sleeping under the same roof as me?

"Look," Leader continues, holding her hands behind her back, "if this massacre is a product of the alien's combative skills, you two are officially the safest people in the Village."

Or the ones in most danger, I think.

Chapter 25

In a blur of bodies and movement, I am forced to my feet and escorted outside into the scorching sunlight. I can see the insides of my arms and hands, which are still chained together, reacting to the light. Streams of my blood and internal composition swirl in figure eights.

I hear Farah and her father talking at the head of our procession, but I can't see them. Ten members of the Village's patrol march at my pace, encircling me so that all I see are the tops of their heads and passing buildings. Faces press against glass. People stare and point as we head down this dirt road.

You'd never know there were so much order and control in Farah's Village by looking at the decrepit and crooked fortifications. And yet they have weapons and means of protection. They possess the intelligence to deem me physically safe for interaction.

What happened on this planet? Everything I've seen so far suggests these people should be prospering in far better conditions than these. Do the undergrounders drive them to live like this? Or did those cruel madmen simply rise out of the fear and ashes left over from some war or natural disaster?

I look up at the sky. It's strange seeing a starless

firmament. Only blue. Here and there a stroke of white.

We come to a stop as I look down, and the patrolmen have parted. A narrow path has been created, and at the end Farah and her father wait. I move forward slowly, apprehensive and even hateful looks follow me on both sides of the crowd. For an instant, I regret not taking the undergrounders up on their offer. At least they were seeking me out, whatever that reason may have been.

But that instant is a fleeting one, because when I stop in front of Farah, I realize there's no way I could leave. Not yet, anyway.

"Welcome to our home," Farah's father says, pulling a carabineer of keys out of his pocket. He fishes through the brass, searching for the right one. I look back at Farah, but she's still avoiding my eyes. Finally, her father procures the correct key and unlocks the door.

The space is somewhat crowded, but offers cool relief from the sun. There are piles and clusters and stacks of bizarre things all over the place. Old shelves and torn armchairs in two corners, a wide bench with a cluttered top in another corner, and an angular window built into the fourth.

Farah closes the door and then, wordlessly, leads me by the elbow into an adjacent room. I try not to focus too hard at the very first touch of her soft, warm skin, but that is not possible for me. She sits me down at a square table that seats two.

Her father walks in behind us. "Farah?"

"He hasn't eaten a thing yet," she says flatly, opening a cabinet and pulling out a bowl. "I'm going to warm him up some soup and – "

"What happens if he's deathly allergic to our – ?"

" – and in the mean time," she continues, completely ignoring him, "you're going to take off his handcuffs. When you're done with that, can he borrow some pants and a shirt of yours?"

"Farah."

"Your waist size looks similar, although the length might be an issue. I'm sure it'll be fine – "

"Stop," he says, firmly but gently.

He sets his cane against the table and grabs her arms, forcing her to stop what she's doing over the basin. Farah drops what she's holding and starts to cry. She doesn't weep or sob, she just...cries. Her father pulls her into a tight embrace.

This is my fault, I think as I turn away. I scared her when I took out all those men, but I did it to protect her. How can I possibly explain that? And what's more – I don't even know how I was capable of causing such damage. The fighting and attacking is rooted in some instinct I can apparently tap into.

It's possible that I'm some sort of soldier, or *was* anyway. But I can't remember. I can't remember much of anything. Only stars...and space...my prison...and then I willed myself to crash here, on Farah's planet.

Perhaps my past and secrets are buried in the

dreams I'm having. The conversations with other beings whom I can't see in detail. Of course, I'm banking on those being memories. They could simply be dreams –

"Hold out your hands."

I look up, my thoughts interrupted. Farah's father sits across from me, a tiny knife in hand. I obey him, watching curiously as he picks at the lock that binds my wrists.

"You know," he mumbles, "we could just request the key from the patrol."

"And what fun would there be in that?" Farah says, pouring a thick, hazel substance into the bowl and stirring it. "Don't pretend like this isn't the highlight of your day, Dad."

"I ever tell you how funny you are?"

"No – "

"Good, making sure."

I feel the muscles in my face form a smile in response to their banter, but I make sure to try not to open my mouth. There's a subtle *click*, and then Farah's father pulls the metal bondage through my hands. I rub my wrists, grateful for the freedom.

"Drink this," Farah says, setting a cup of water before me. "I'm warming up your soup right now."

I take the drink in both hands, hold it up to my lips, and slightly crack open my mouth. Except...I don't feel any restraint! I quickly set the drink down and open my mouth, prodding my lips with both sets of fingers. There are no strands of skin. I even stick out my tongue to be sure.

Nothing!

I ball my hands into fists and throw them into the air joyfully.

Chapter 26 | Farah

"What...er...do you think he's doing?" Dad asks me, like I'll know.

We watch as the being touches his lips and mouth repeatedly, occasionally sticking out his tongue, and then he throws his hands into the air.

"It's probably how his kind says 'thank you,' " I say with a shrug.

He eventually picks up the cup and downs the water in one gulp. I grab the bowl of soup off the stovetop with two mittens and carefully place it in front of him.

"Make sure and use this spoon," I instruct, handing the utensil to him. "The bowl is hot and you could hurt – "

The being sets the spoon down, grabs the bowl, and drinks the meal in a few swallows. I watch, in awe, as the soup passes through his mouth and slowly descends his throat.

I feel my face flush, so I turn the other way. I'd probably want privacy if anyone could see my food digesting.

"So," Dad says as I join him by the sink and set the mittens on the counter. "What are we going to call him?" We both watch as the being takes the spoon and uses it to scrape up the remainder of the soup, bright boxes and cubes flowing through him intravenously.

"Don't suggest E.T.," I say, even though it's one of the few salvaged movies in our Village's collection and I have watched it maybe a hundred times as a kid.

"I would like to point out," Dad replies, taking off his glasses and cleaning the lenses with his shirt, "that when you first raised the twelfth alarm, I suggested the possibility of a U.F.O."

"You gonna say 'I told you so?' "

"Just did, indirectly."

He puts his glasses back on and smiles. As I watch the being finish off the soup, I think of a possible name, which leads me to think that he probably already has one, as well as a home, an origin, and a story. He's already been among us for half a day, and there's absolutely nothing we know about him. We've got to find a way to communicate. The knowledge and wisdom he brings from his home is potentially limitless. Maybe that's his purpose here. His mission. To teach us, to help us.

"Rubik," I say, watching a series of cubes spiral up and down his right arm. "His name is Rubik, like the man who invented that toy you found." Dad nods, indicating that he likes this suggestion.

"Well then!" he declares, leaning on his cane. "Better get Rubik some clothes. I don't care if he is from another planet" – he stalks toward his bedroom – "I'm the only one who reserves the right to be naked in this fort."

I roll my eyes before realizing the being is regarding

me, his eyes soft and blinking slowly.

"It's rude to stare on this planet," I say, harsher than I mean to. He drops his gaze immediately, and that's when I think of something. "How is it that you can understand us? Our words?" I tap my chin thoughtfully. "Does that mean you can talk, too?"

He looks up again, watching me for a while, and then shakes his head.

"No?" I say, contemplative. "Maybe you can be taught how."

I cross our small kitchen and stand behind the other chair. I lean my arms on the backing, my mind racing as an idea begins to form.

"Rubik. Do you like that name?"

He smiles – he actually *smiles!* – and nods once.

"All right then, Rubik," I say, straightening up. "Would you like to learn how to speak our language?"

Again, he nods one time.

"Good. Stay here." I leave the kitchen, walk through Dad's work area, and crack open the door. "Excuse me," I say to the nearest member of the patrol. It's a young woman in her early twenties. She puts the water bottle she's drinking inside her pocket.

"Everything okay?" she asks, adjusting her rifle strap.

"Yeah, no everything's good," I assure her. "But, I'm going to have to leave for a minute or two. Just thought maybe I should tell someone."

"Where to? The Village is on lockdown – "

"I know," I say politely, "just going to the end of our

road. I need to gather a few things from the Bookkeeper."

If Rubik is going to be staying with Dad and me this week, I might as well try and make it a productive visit. Really, though, I'm hoping for a distraction. If I'm focused on teaching him things, I won't focus on the fear that's waiting and hiding in the deep recesses of my mind. That newly acquired fear I have for Rubik.

Chapter 27 | Rubik

The next couple of days whip past me much like the stars used to.

Farah's father – who insists I call him Thomas, even though I can't pronounce his name yet – provides me with a wardrobe of jean pants and solid-colored T-shirts. The bottom of his pants come up to about my shin area, so Farah rolls them up for me and calls them shorts.

We spend hours on the floor of her bedroom, sitting across from one another and poring over picture books. I find that I already know the names of most of the animals and objects she sounds out, and that it's just a matter of remembering.

The only explanation I can muster is that my home planet has ties or links to this one. But whatever that tie or link is, I cannot recall.

"*Truck*," I say, managing a full word for the first time.

It's strange hearing my voice out loud, which sounds hollow and deep. And yet, somewhat youthful. I start to wonder just how old I am, or rather, how young.

"Good," Farah says, lowering the picture book. Her face is painted with surprise. "You're getting better."

Only because she is helping me. I'm thankful for

this activity, which not only helps pass the time, but also allows for ample interaction with Farah. Something I'm enjoying quite a lot.

I expect to see Alex and Lois at some point, or even their leader, but no one comes to visit Farah and Thomas. I later learn, while inadvertently overhearing a conversation between Farah and her father, that the Village is still conducting interrogations.

"I haven't seen him in two days," Farah whisper yells, and I surmise she's referring to Alex.

"You'll live," Thomas replies in a deadpanned tone. "It's not for much longer."

"Am I allowed to send him a note?" she asks, a bit of sarcasm in her voice. "Or is that considered insubordination?"

The fact that she's so keen on reaching out to Alex bothers me. I refuse to accept that it's jealousy. Maybe it's just that she's arguing with her father? Regardless, I suppress the feeling and try to forget it.

On the third day, Thomas is permitted to leave the fort and collect food in the Village's marketplace. A member of the patrol has to stay inside with Farah and me to ensure her safety. I know they feel it's necessary, but I find a little humor in this. If I could defend myself against ten undergrounders, shouldn't they require more than just one patrolman to supervise me?

"I wanna show you something," Farah says in the middle of our lesson, taking me by the hand and leading me out of her bedroom. We pass through the kitchen, where the patrolman sits with his feet on the table, dozing off.

We enter Thomas's work area, and Farah digs through a collection of crates. She pulls various items out, handing them to me. I hold the ever-growing pile of plastic and metal objects in my arms while she carries on with her search.

"Found it!" she finally says, while I try to balance everything she has given me. "Oh, sorry," she exclaims, carefully returning everything, one by one, into their respective crates.

"Had to hurry," she explains, tossing the last object aside. Looks like it could belong to an engine of some sort, but I'm only guessing. "If Dad knew I was handling all this junk he'd flip out."

"Oh kaay," I say, embarrassed with how the expression comes out of my mouth. Still low and deep and drawn.

"This," Farah says, walking up to me and taking my hand. She turns it upright and places a small, colorful cube in my palm. "This is a Rubik's Cube."

Rubik. The name she gave me. I don't even try to pronounce it. I hold the item in my hand, bobbing it up and down slowly. It's very light. The colors are faded, but you can still see the greens, reds, even blues. Some yellow, white, and orange as well.

"It's a puzzle, see?" Farah takes it back and begins to rotate the planes, jumbling and mixing the colors more. "Never been able to figure it out though. I think Dad did once."

I watch her as she fools with the toy, one eye closed. I drop my gaze to her lips. *Never been able to figure it out though.* When Farah forms words, the muscles in her mouth work superbly. I doubt she fully comprehends her ability to take simple actions – like talking – and turn them into a beautiful, attractive –

She has stopped spinning the cube. I look up and find her eyes already on me. She seems expressionless, but I figure she's a breath away from scolding me for staring again.

I open my mouth, when there's a knock at the door.

Chapter 28 | Farah

Knock. Knock.

I break my stare from Rubik and find that my heart is fluttering in my chest. It must be intimidation causing this reaction. Rubik is so tall and lean, with defined edges around his humanlike face. I can see his toned stomach outlining the white T-shirt he wears. On his planet, he's either a warrior or an athlete – if his kind even has sports.

It's no wonder he took out all those undergrounders in such effortless fashion.

Knock. Knock. "Farah?"

Oh, right – someone's at the door. I turn away from Rubik, grab the doorknob, and say for good measure, "No staring, remember?" He swallows and looks away, despite my playful tone. I open the door.

It's Leader. "May I come in?"

"Yes, er, of course."

"Thank you." I stand aside and let her enter. "So, you two look like you're enjoying yourselves."

"W-What?" I stammer, closing the door. My ears and neck get hot. "Enjoying ourselves – ?"

"That's a Rubik's Cube, isn't it?"

I look down, realizing I'm still holding the square toy. "Oh, um, yes. I was showing him where I got his name from."

"His name?"

I feel embarrassed, but I press on anyway: "I named him Rubik."

Silence. Leader's mouth forms a crooked line. "I see." She pulls a water canteen out from her duster pocket and takes a swig, wiping her lips with the back of her hand when she's finished. Rubik stands still, like a statue, his arms, neck, and head shimmering vibrantly in our murky fort. Leader leaves me at the doorway, walking toward him slowly.

"You are a fascinating specimen, aren't you?" she whispers. Rubik looks down at the floor uncomfortably. "What's your secret, hm?"

There's a long pause. "H-He's learning to talk," I say, trying to relieve Rubik of Leader's extreme attention.

"That so?" she says, turning back to me. "Well done. The Professor's going to be pleased about that development. That'll help us in understanding why he's here. That's why I came, Farah. I wanted to tell you that, starting tomorrow morning, the Professor is going to begin a series of extensive testing."

This time I don't stutter. "What kind of testing?"

"Nothing to lose sleep over," she says, standing with hands behind her back. "Just minor blood and DNA samples. Cerebral readings and such. Look," she continues, changing her tone in response to my expression, "if Mr. Toff and his undergrounders staged an elaborate diversion to capture this alien, they must be aware of his value and worth – ”

"Or they know as little as we do," I offer, "and they just want him 'cause they can't have him." Leader sighs. I know she doesn't have to explain herself to me, or even entertain a conversation like this. But, because she *is* entertaining a conversation like this, I'm going to say my peace.

"We have a unique and exciting opportunity here, Farah." Leader crosses the room, ducks beneath a hanging lantern, and gently takes the Rubik's Cube out of my hand. "Your entire life all you've known is our Village. The sun, the sand, the heat. But I've seen more. Before the great wars, people could live where there were trees and grass. Forests! Green as far as the eye could see." She starts turning and adjusting the colorful planes on the cube. "Being forced to leave all that behind...the oceans, the gardens, the hills...it was crushing.

"Now, with this creature here, we could potentially have a solution to our problem. Maybe, he's here to help."

"But how?" I say, not convinced.

"That's what we've got to figure out, isn't it?" She turns the cube one last time and hands it to me. "They're calling him an angel, you know. A guardian angel who fell from the heavens."

"Who's calling him that?"

"The Village, everyone's talking about how he saved you." She pats my arm and then opens the door. "You and your father are the last to be interviewed. Two members of my personal guard will be here at eight tomorrow morning to escort you to the barracks, okay? Don't worry, it's just a formality. We've already narrowed down our mole suspects."

I want to ask whom that is, but I know it's not my place.

"You're to resume your night watch this evening," she adds. "The patrolman who's been filling in for you is scheduled for his round of questioning."

"Yes, of course," I say with a nod. Then, she leaves.

Before I turn around to address Rubik, I look down and see that Leader has completed one-sixth of the cube. Now, one side is completely white.

Maybe, he's here to help. Leader's words resonate in my head as I look up at Rubik. It's true, I suppose. For all we know he could possess the ability to work miracles. Wonders.

I toss the toy across the room and Rubik catches it in his right hand.

"How's that for pressure?" I ask him, folding my arms. "You...an angel. Possibly supplying a key to life outside the desert." I chuckle despite myself. "Life outside the desert. Imagine that."

It's only a few more minutes before Dad returns from the marketplace. I tap the patrolman out of his stupor in the kitchen, and he grunts irritably before realizing the situation. He offers an awkward apology to Dad before leaving.

Dinner that evening is short. We prepare lentil soup together. I show Rubik how to work the stove, and at the same time I tell Dad about Leader's visit. We create a half joking, half serious mole suspect shortlist. Lark makes it on both our lists.

I try to include Rubik in the conversation, but, by his timid looks, I figure he's not confident in full sentences yet.

After we eat, I compile a small stack of picture books for Rubik to go through in my absence, and he appears eager and ready to practice. I encourage him to work in the kitchen, as opposed to the shelter beneath our fort, which is rather damp and dirty. It's bad enough that he has to sleep down there.

"Hold on a sec," Dad says as I'm on my way out the fort. He takes off his glasses and gets up from his workbench.

"What's up?"

He picks up his cane and stalks toward me. "Just wanted to tell you to be careful."

"It's night watch," I say, smiling. "I've done it a hundred times – "

He cuts me off with a strong hug, and I'm taken aback. Dad and I have always been close, but there was definitely a season where we drifted apart after Mom died. Yet since Rubik has arrived, that's four times Dad's hugged me. More than I can say over the past year.

"I promise to be careful," I say as he breaks away. He smiles lovingly before turning around and resuming his dissection of some plastic device.

I step outside the fort, close the door behind me, and

inhale the cool night air. I'm actually really excited about spending the evening in the watchtower. I didn't know what going stir-crazy was until being confined to my fort for a few days.

I walk past the mini garrison guarding our fort and turn up the main road. Starlight and lanterns guide my path, and I look up at the buildings and forts as I pass them. Even though it's night, and this is when things wind down in our Village, you can still sense the tension in the atmosphere. Everyone's probably wondering who they can trust right now. I know I am.

Before Rubik crash-landed here, my Village only dealt with things like food rations, storm predictions, and the occasional thief in the marketplace. For whatever reason, the undergrounders never threatened our home. We've been lucky enough to only *hear* about them.

Now, in a brief span of three days, we've encountered them twice, and it's resulted in the death of both Morgan and Del. And then there's the mole the undergrounders have inside our Village. The thought is sickening.

I ascend the rope ladder to my watchtower after waving politely to the three patrolmen stationed at the base. Leader has really stepped up security. I wonder where Alex has been assigned, or if he's even on duty right now. I plan on stopping by his fort after my watch in the hopes that he's there. A lot has happened since the last time I saw him, which was back at the schoolhouse when the first alarm was raised.

If I can be inconspicuous enough, I'll try and check on Lois, too. She was pretty shaken up at the storage units. If I didn't have Rubik's lessons to divert my attention and energy, I'd probably still be recovering from that. Hopefully Digs has been keeping her on her toes.

When I get to the top, I close the hatch door and lean my elbows on the railing. The oil lamp hanging from the rafters is still lit, and I snuff it out by turning the tiny knob. Up here, I can see best with only the stars and moon providing light.

Through quick reflection I realize just how crazy things have been, and it all started on that chilly night mere days ago, when the biggest problem I faced was what role I'd choose in the Village. In comparison to recent events, that seems like a laughable, childish dilemma.

The stars. Hundreds of thousands of them, covering the massive desert like a great dome. If this is the most peace I'll ever experience during our hard times, standing atop the watchtower beneath the star-dotted sky, then I'll take it. And yet, this peace...this feeling of relief...I've experienced outside my watch, too. When?

With Rubik. These couple of days have been productive, and it has proven to be a sufficient distraction from the chaos at the storage units. But it has also been, what? Good? Yes, I've felt *good* around Rubik, not scared like I figured I would. He seems so eager to impress me, like everything he does is in pursuit of my approval. It's probably just the teacher/student thing we've established. He's bound to lose interest, and even get bored, once his otherworldly superiority kicks in. So what's he waiting for?

Something catches my eye, and my thoughts cloud over. It looks like a trail of dust, cresting a dune in the distance. I open the hollow compartment in one of the watchtower's pillars and pull out the spyglass. I extend the tool and peer through the lens.

At a modest speed, someone approaches our Village on a dirt bike. A second person sits behind the driver. The passenger holds onto the driver's shoulders, bouncing subtly in the bike's cadence. And behind them both, mounted to the vehicle's seat, is a tall flagpole. A long, white strip of fabric flutters above their heads. It's a sign. They're from another Village, and they wish to enter ours peacefully.

It could also be another trap, set by the undergrounders.

Chapter 29 | Rubik

I watch Farah disappear outside, and the front door closes behind her a second later. I'm left standing in the kitchen threshold, holding a stack of colorful books. Thomas fiddles with something at his workbench, his back to me, and he doesn't say anything. He doesn't hum or talk to himself. He just works silently, when –

"You're more than welcome to come in here, Rubik," he says, picking up a tiny tool from his supply bag. "In fact, why don't you pull up a seat? Could show you what I'm doing."

Intrigued, I set the stack of books on the nearest flat surface and walk to the other side of Thomas's workbench. There's already a stool resting in the corner across from him, so I drag it over and sit down slowly – careful not to nudge the desktop in the process.

"Is *tha-ght* bro*keyn*?" I sound out, watching his hands pull off a thin, grey covering.

He sniffs. "No, this is a typewriter. We use it to" – he cuts himself off with a chuckle – "you were asking if it was 'broken,' weren't you?"

He looks at me through his bespectacled eyes and I nod.

"Sorry, I'm always telling Farah that I'm as good as

deaf. Guess I've abused that joke so many times it's actually coming true."

I smile, knowing that it was really my lack of proper pronunciation and not his hearing that caused the mix-up.

"But no," Thomas continues, pushing up his glasses and resuming his dissection. "No, it's not broken. See, I have the most sought-after role here in the Village. I get to take the devices and gizmos that the patrol finds on scavenges and learn how they're built. What makes them tick. Then, I compile an instruction manual for each object."

I stare at the typewriter, and, as he pulls out a cylindrical appendage, I blurt out, "*Why?*"

Thomas almost drops his tool. "Why? As in, why do I do this?"

I nod again, regretful for asking the question. He's not mad, though, he's *excited*. Like he's been waiting for someone to ask this.

"Because," he explains, eyes alive and wild, "in the years to come, as we work toward rebuilding and reestablishing our society, people will need things like typewriters, and they'll need them to work. If they stop functioning correctly, they'll need something to reference – something to tell them how to fix it. That's where my hard work pays off, see?"

Yes, I do. It makes complete sense, but now I'm distracted. Thomas mentioned working 'toward rebuilding and reestablishing' their society. I had been wondering what caused them to live in conditions such as these, conditions where things like rebuilding and reestablishment were necessary. What had divided these people and created the evil band of men known as the undergrounders? In short, why were things the way they were here?

Now is my chance to find out.

Thomas is squirting a black substance into the belly of the typewriter, and I wait until he sets the tin can down before I incline forward.

"What hamp-*pinned* here?"

I don't have to elaborate. He knows exactly what I mean. I can tell by the way his eyes change – they grow darker.

"Good question, Rubik." Thomas takes off his square glasses, folds them, and sets them down delicately. "A lot happened..."

There was once a young man who had an idea. It started out simple enough, the idea, but it eventually grew into something special. Something coveted. As a result, the young man was targeted by news outlets and dubbed an extremist. So, naturally, the young man's fame widened. Strengthened.

"What w-was the i*dree*-uh?"

Thomas sighed. "The idea was really a plan. A plan for universal unity. Peace that spanned the globe."

The young man went by the alias, Ram, which supposedly referenced back to ancient symbolism. A new beginning, a new era. The things Ram wrote about and proposed ended up being perceived as threats. Threats on a grand scale. He was asked to kindly cease his "movement," or he'd be dealt with like a terrorist.

To the surprise of nations, Ram complied. He fell silent. Some speculated there was a payoff involved, but that was never confirmed. It did, however, seem like the logical reason, even though it went against everything Ram preached.

Regardless, shortly after Ram took his historic hiatus, things got ugly.

"I must've been six or seven when news broke of her murder," Thomas says, rubbing his eyes and straightening up. "You see, Ram had a wife. Wrote about her all of the time. She was young, like him, maybe twenty? They'd only been married about nine months when she was killed."

Ram and his bride were apparently traveling incognito by speed train. There was a bomb. Few survived. Ram was one of them. It could have been pure coincidence that Ram happened to be on that train that evening with his wife. But Ram didn't believe in coincidences.

While in recovery, Ram returned to the network. He called for justice, by any means, and slowly turned into a revenge-seeking, bloodthirsty madman. With the aid of his radicals, Ram staged a series of elaborate attacks across the world. Countries turned against one another. Treaties collapsed. Great wars began. Ram became the greatest terrorist in history.

"Somewhere in there," Thomas says, putting his glasses back on. "Ram was found and killed. Hung in a public square. But, by then, it was too late. Chemical warfare had begun, wiping out cities. Because of the residues leftover from the bio-weaponry, the Coasts had to be abandoned. Oceans were polluted. Trees, too. Really most forms of foliage were now considered poisonous. Toxic."

So that's why the desert, where everything here is practically dead already. I feel an enormous sense of pressure, as it occurs to me the people of this Village, of this world, are probably starving for something, anything, in which to put their hopes. They yearn for something new.

Even alien life forms falling from the sky.

"Don't do it," Thomas says ominously, yanking me out of my thoughts. "Don't you go feeling sorry for Ram. There's no room for sympathy or empathy in our story. The young man was a ruthless psychopath."

He's misread my face. I'm not thinking about Ram. I'm thinking about my quandary. I can't be perceived as a hero – a key to the problems on this planet. I'm no savior...I'm just lost.

For the first time since arriving on this planet, I figure out what I need to do: Get home.

"Make sure and go straight home."

"Why?"

"Sorry?"

"*Why* do I have to go straight home?"

"Because, er, it's not safe – "

I almost laugh, but I hold it in. "Really? Because it's 'not safe?' You have any idea what I've been through these past few days? You do? Good. So, you know that a civil dialogue can in no way be unsafe when compared to the week I've had."

The lead patrolman confers with his inferiors. "She's right, you know," one of them whispers.

"It'd be one thing if this was a parley," I add, unsure if I've fully won them over. "But it's not. It's two civilians from another Village."

We stand beneath the looming watchtower in a circle. After I signaled the patrol unit at the gate with my flashlight, I made my way down the rope ladder, where these patrolmen all but accosted me.

"Why is this even an issue?" I say, taking a stab at improvisation. "You do know the protocol, right?"

The patrolmen stop whispering and look at me, unable to mask their puzzled expressions.

"Of course we know the protocol," the lead intones

with a gruff.

"Good." I smile. "Then you know that the watcher on duty must accompany the patrol during civil dialogues to take detailed notes. Basically, this is part of my job. And I take my job seriously. You know it's almost my role, right?" I'm glad Alex isn't here because he knows the protocol like it was tattooed to the back of his hand, and he wouldn't hesitate to call me out. Plus he'd see right through that last part.

There's a pause. Once more, the patrolmen converse in whispers. "She's right, you know," someone says again. But before they're finished, we hear the east gate grating open.

"C'mon," I say, walking forward and forcing them to part. "I can't afford to miss anything."

I lead them down a low-lit back alley, and I'm sure any second they're going to stop me by the shoulder when they realize I was lying about the protocol. But they never do.

And since when did you get all reckless? Alex's words, right after I found Rubik in the crater. It was a good question, one that I never answered and still can't. Is it rooted in my desire to prove myself to Alex? Probably, but there's more to it than that. There's got to be. For one thing, Alex isn't here right now, as we make our way to the gate. Maybe it's just that I'm finally starting to act on my curiosity.

Curiosity is in my blood, sure. It's why Dad is so good at his role. You *have* to be curious to do what he does or else you'd go mad. Of course, some would argue that he already *is* mad –

"Stop," the lead says behind me as we approach the east gate. "We'll go together."

"Of course," I say. I hadn't noticed how far ahead I'd gotten.

We walk as a group to the gate, which is halfway open. The lead turns the corner first, and the rest of us follow.

Standing on the fringes of our Village is a tall man with dark black skin. He wears a clergy shirt, and next to him is a boy, probably my age, with a hawkish face and three or four bags over his shoulder. I see their parked dirt bike behind them, not too far off.

There's already a group of patrolmen facing them, rifles all but trained on the two visitors' chests.

"So then why come at night?" one of ours asks the tall man.

"Because," he replies, his voice deep and soothing, "well, technically we're not supposed to be here."

"You get so hung up on those technicalities, Father," the boy says impatiently, setting his bags down on the ground. "Look," he addresses us now with a big grin, "you want the short of it? Here it is. That's Father Cash – "

"Nikolaos, wait – "

"And I'm Nikolaos," he continues over the Father, bowing slightly. "At your service. Well, unless you take that salutation literally. Not good at service. In fact, I can get pretty lazy." He trails off, eyes distant. Then, with a single clap of his hands, "Anyway, we've traveled from three Villages over – near the outer rim of the bowl. I'm accompanying Father here on his ministry."

I look up and down the line of patrolmen. They're not convinced. Can't say that I am, either. Father Cash stares at the sand, a far off expression on his face.

"What do you mean you're *technically* not supposed to be here?" the lead asks, shifting his weight next to me.

Father Cash looks up.

"Our Village doesn't approve of ministry," he says painfully. "They say it's a waste of time and resources. God is *never* a waste of time, and he's my primary resource."

Nikolaos rolls his eyes, but catches himself – pretending to gaze at our fence, which stretches up toward the stars behind us.

"Also," Father Cash continues, "they weren't too keen on young Nick here abandoning his job."

Nikolaos perks up. "They'll find someone else to shovel shi –"

"You worked in the mess hall, *not* the compost field."

"I was referring to the food, *Father*."

"Okay, that's enough," the lead announces, raising his voice over them. "Here's what we can offer, take it or leave it: We'll escort you to the barracks, where you can rest through the night under our watch. Then, in the morning, you'll be taken before Leader, where she'll decide what to do with you."

There's something these two aren't telling us. You

can see it plastered all over their faces.

"Sir," I say softly, pulling the lead aside. "What if they were escorted back to my fort?"

"*What?*"

"I know how crazy that sounds, but hear me out. Because of the tension in our Village right now, Leader would want any visitors treated with extra precaution. She'd *demand* these two be placed under strict surveillance – treated as if hostile until proven otherwise."

I can see him putting my plan together.

"The alien," he whispers.

"You saw what he did to ten undergrounders," I reply, nodding. "While handcuffed, too. Add to the fact there's already a small army stationed around my fort, and you've got a place more secure than even Leader's headquarters." I add, for an extra nudge, "She'll praise your quick-thinking, you know."

The lead patrolman broadens his shoulders, looking past me at the two in question. Then, without acknowledging me, he marches forward.

"After having spoken with Farah," he says, "she has agreed to house you two over the night. This is the best way we can keep an eye on you."

A few members of the patrol murmur in surprise, but you can hear their tones changing slightly as they figure out why this decision is a good one.

Nikolaos reaches down and grabs his bags, and then he sizes me up with a quizzical look. You may really be tagging along on the Father's ministry, I think, but

there's definitely something you're not telling us, and I
intend to find out.

Chapter 31 | Rubik

Thomas fishes through his supply bag. After he finished telling me about Ram, neither of us said anything. Still haven't. I realize that Thomas probably lost a lot of loved ones during or after the great wars of which he spoke.

Have I, too? Lost loved ones in *my* past? It's time I start focusing all my efforts on remembering who I am. Where I came from. Why I was trekking through space for all that time, and how I ended up getting here. It's paramount that I understand these things, so that I can subsequently understand how I'm to return to my home planet.

The answers lie within my dreams. The ones I had during my stretch of unconsciousness. I need to figure out someway to summon those. If nothing else I can start to deduce if they're memories at all.

Satisfied that I finally have a plan in place, I open my mouth to thank Thomas for the history session, when the front door opens.

"Farah?" Thomas asks, twisting something into the typewriter with his back to the door.

She appears a second later, but she has company. A boy walks in after her, hefting a few bags, followed by a tall, dark-skinned man in a black shirt that has a white collar. A patrolman brings up the rear.

"I hope you have a few spare cots, Thomas," he says, keeping the door open.

I stand up slowly, and when the two newcomers notice me, their jaws drop – right on cue. Thomas sets his tool down and turns around. "What is this?" he demands, looking at Farah, who appears guilty.

I smile, knowing by that look she's responsible for these guests. Between these two newcomers and myself, she's accumulating quite the collection.

"These two are from another Village," the patrolman explains, motioning toward them. "Near the outer rim, so they claim. Since your fort currently has the highest concentration of my men, it makes sense for our guests to stay here with you, where a close eye can be kept on them."

"That is unacceptable," Thomas says, folding his arms. "I demand to speak with Leader."

"Sure. You want to be the one who wakes her?"

"I..." Thomas stops short. "Fine. While I'm at it, would you like me to lay out a bedspread for you as well? Why stop there? Let's get a few of your men in here, too!"

The patrolman smirks, and then exits.

"Farah," Thomas says flatly, turning to her. "This wasn't your idea, was it?" A pause. "Dumb question. Of course it was."

"I'll go get the spare sleeping bags out of the shelter," she says, weaving around the crates on the floor and heading for the kitchen. "Don't let them out of your sight, Rubik," she adds lowly, winking before she disappears.

The two hanging oil lamps give off thin lighting in Thomas's overcrowded work area, and as a result, the two guests are shrouded in long shadows. You can still see their expressions as if they were standing beneath afternoon sunlight.

"I told you I'd find it, Father," the boy faintly utters, stepping forward and almost tripping over his bags.

He gapes at me, eyes and mouth nearly the same circumference. Thomas picks up his cane and holds it out, stopping the boy by the chest.

"What happened?" Farah asks, reappearing in the kitchen threshold with two rolled-up fabrics beneath each arm.

She yelps when she sees her father holding the boy back with his cane. Without a second's pause, Farah drops the rolled-up fabrics and pulls something out of her pocket, pointing it with shaky hands.

I've seen it before, holstered to some of the patrolmen's hips.

"D-Did they try to hurt you, Dad?" she stammers, finger on the weapon's trigger. Thomas looks over, sees what she's holding, and almost drops his cane.

"Farah! Lower that at once!"

"It's fine," the boy says, his excitement audibly subsided. "It's just a flare gun."

"Wanna bet that it'll still hurt?" Farah asks, the tip of her weapon aimed at his leg now.

"Hey! Whoa!" he shouts, backing up. "All right, all

right. I'm back."

"Now," Farah says, her voice a little unsteady but hands under control. "You two are going to explain why it is you're *really* here, or I yell for the patrol standing outside the fort. They've lost two men this week, and they're *dying* for someone to take their frustration out on." Farah lowers her flare gun and stands next to me.

"Honey," Thomas says, turning on his cane. "What music have you been listening to?"

"Not now, Dad," she replies, folding her arms but still grasping the weapon. There's a period of stillness where both sides just regard one another. The boy's eyes linger on me the longest, and the dark-skinned man in the unique shirt still hasn't spoken.

"H-He s*eh*d he fow-*end* me," I sound out, feeling adolescent and incapable.

"*It can talk*?!" the boy exclaims, running both hands through his shaggy yellow hair.

"He is not an 'it,' " Farah says irritably, then, to me, "What do you mean? *Found*?"

"The young man told the Father here that he'd found it," her father answers for me, pushing up his square glasses. "Referring to Rubik, of course."

Farah holds her weapon out again. "Did the undergrounders send you?"

"*What*! No!" The boy's not lying. He looks disgusted by this accusation. "No one sent us, all right?"

"Then perhaps you'd better start talking," Thomas says, sitting down on his stool and laying his cane across his lap. "I can't claim responsibility for my daughter's actions."

"Nikolaos is correct." We all turn to the tall man, who finally steps into the light. His eyes seem very heavy. "No one sent us because, well, we don't have anyone."

"You said you were from the outer rim," Farah says, lowering her weapon again.

"We are," Nikolaos answers. "But we were banished from our Village." I hear the straining of wood as Thomas clenches his cane.

"Banishment is an unpardonable sentence," he says anxiously. "If your Village somehow catches wind of us taking you in, it could disrupt the peace. There hasn't been a civil dispute among Villages since the early days!"

"Why do you think we weren't so keen on mentioning that detail?" Nikolaos says, almost in a whisper. "Look, you want the short of it?"

"Last time you said that, a lie followed," Farah notes, and I wonder what she means. Nikolaos snorts.

"I didn't lie, all right? I just didn't give you the entire scoop is all." He kneels down and hovers a hand above one of the bags. "Can I show you something?"

"After you tell us why you were banished."

Nikolaos sighs and looks up at the man he calls Father. "Our Village outlasted two undergrounder raids in the last year," the old man says, his deep voice somber. "Our resources are limited. Tensions are through the roof. There's even been talk of relocating."

Beside me, Farah tightens up in response to that last thing he said. "Relocating" must be a serious, rare occurrence.

"So, things being what they are," the old man continues, "my work and ministry spiraled down the list of importance. Our Leader made it clear that he had no intention of extending continual support – going so far as to strip me of my title and role. He said he needed my help in more pressing matters.

"It's funny how times have changed... Used to be it was *only* when things got really bad that folks would turn to God. Those dark, desperate hours. Now it seems we can't even give Him that."

"So, then what?" Thomas says, clearing his throat. "Then you acted against your Leader's orders?"

"Told him God ordained me for this role. You can't simply *un*-ordain someone, can you?"

"What about you?" Farah says, looking down at Nikolaos, who is still on one knee next to his bags. "Guilty by association?"

"Hardly," he replies, grinning. "When I found out Father Cash was getting the boot, I saw it as my ticket outta there. I'd been looking for a way to sneak off for over a week! Father here was happy to oblige."

" 'Happy?' " Father Cash puts his hands on his hips and adds gravely, "We all have our crosses we must bear."

Nikolaos says, "That's very ominous of you, Father."

"But why?" Farah asks eagerly. "I mean, why did you want to leave your Village?"

Nikolaos grins some more. *"Now* can I show you what's in here?" Farah exchanges a glance with her father, who merely shrugs. "Where I come from that's a 'yes,' " Nikolaos says, unzipping the long bag. He sticks both his hands inside and slowly produces a thick, coal-colored shard of metal. He sets it on the dirt ground. There are faded glyphs in red lettering near the top.

"This," Nikolaos says proudly, standing up, "is a piece of your friend's spaceship."

It can't be. I was at the crash site, and we didn't see anything that remotely resembled what Nikolaos has brought before us. I turn to Rubik, but he doesn't appear to recognize the debris. He does, however, walk past me and around Dad's workbench. Nikolaos scurries backward slightly, clearly intimidated.

"I was there, you know," I tell him and Father Cash. "At the crater, where we found Rubik. There wasn't anything like this."

"No, there wouldn't be," Nikolaos replies, watching as Rubik runs his fingertips over the metal. "At least, there *shouldn't* have been, based on what we saw."

"What do you mean?" Dad asks, getting back to his feet. He leans over Rubik's hunched form and studies the metal as well. I stay right where I am, unconvinced until Rubik offers confirmation.

"Can we clear a wall?" Nikolaos says, looking around the room.

"Why?"

"I've got some footage to show you."

Turns out Nikolaos and I have something in common: We both don't really care for our jobs. His is dishwasher. And, while I find solace in music, he maintains his sanity with cameras.

"This is video taken a week ago," he explains, fast-forwarding the footage. We've moved to the kitchen, where Nikolaos rigged up a digital projector. It rests on the table, pointing a fuzzy, pixilated square image on my closed bedroom door.

Rubik and I occupy the only two chairs, sitting on either side of the projector, while Nikolaos stands behind us, operating the playback. Father Cash and Dad stand near the stove, sipping on hot tea that I prepared while Nikolaos got to work setting everything up.

"You just happened to have a camera set up that night?" I ask, looking over my shoulder. "Pointed at the exact spot in the sky where the flash occurred?"

Nikolaos has the tip of his tongue clamped between his teeth as he focuses on the sped-up playback.

"We have several cameras set up," Father Cash says. I turn to him, watching the blue light from the projector bounce off his and Dad's face. "They run simultaneously, 24/7. Young Mr. Nick here wired the whole thing when he was just thirt – " He stops, voice caught in his throat, and then says, quieter, "My word, you are a marvelous creation."

I follow his gaze to Rubik, whose inner network of floating cubes is on full display in the semi-dark kitchen. Father Cash is right – Rubik really *does* look marvelous. I've grown so accustomed to him that I've forgotten what it was like to truly *see* him. To see his translucent skin. To see his alien blots of blood, dancing up his muscled arms. To see –

"Farah?"

I flinch, turning from Rubik to Dad. "Hm?"

"Father Cash asked about his name," Dad says, drinking his tea. "How you came up with it."

"Oh, right," I say, blushing. "It...I got the name because of his – "

"Here it is!" Nikolaos interrupts excitedly, pausing the footage.

We all redirect our attention to my door, where the video of the purple flash in the night sky is frozen in place. Nikolaos walks around the table and stands near the edge of the image, pointing.

"Look here," he says, his arm and hand now bearing part of the stagnant footage. "Do you see it? The breaking point?"

"What?" I squint, leaning forward. Beside me Rubik gets up, steering clear of the projector's line of sight.

"I see," he says quietly, and that's when I do, too.

Near the top of the picture, in the vicinity of where Nikolaos is pointing, is a trail of dots. They're distinguishable from the stars because of the flash, which illuminates from an unseen source.

"Here's what we're thinking," Nikolaos says, looking back and forth between Dad and me. "Rubik fell from the sky, but what caused the flash *wasn't* him penetrating our atmosphere. It was him getting ejected from his spaceship or pod. He then crash landed where you apparently discovered him, but only after leaving bits of his disassembled 'vehicle' in his wake. One of which landed in our Village square. The one I showed you earlier."

Dad whistles. Despite all this evidence, I'm still rather leery, and I cannot explain why.

"If you could take me to the crater," Nikolaos says eagerly, "then maybe we could use it as a starting point for gathering up the rest of Rubik's ship."

"What you're talking about is practically *impossible*," I blurt out. "Those pieces are most likely scattered all across the desert, if they're even still there!"

"What do you mean?"

"You think the undergrounders would pass up a piece of alien machinery if they came across it?" I say, reaching up and brightening the oil lamp that hangs in our kitchen. I then flick off Nikolaos's projector and say, before he can object, "We need to conserve energy. In *this* Village, we have limited use of generators."

Nikolaos blinks. "I, er, okay – ?" He turns to Dad, who I can feel watching me.

"Suppose the undergrounders *haven't* collected up the scattered wreckage," Dad says, setting his mug down on the stove.

"Wait," I flatten my hand and hold it up. "You actually think this is a good idea?"

"Guess I'm playing the role of impetuous teenager now!" he jokes, but when I don't laugh, he clears his throat. "Anyway, let's suppose the debris is still out there. Imagine what we could learn from the technology, Farah – the advancements we could glean from. Not to mention it'd be my biggest, most challenging task yet: Reassembling a U.F.O...."

I roll my eyes. "So this is about you now? *Not* Rubik?"

"It's precisely about Rubik," he says, leaning on his cane. "This could be his only chance at getting home!" There it is. What I was thinking all along, but refused to admit. I turn to Rubik, who is completely ignoring us and looking out the kitchen window. The desert sky is packed with its usual host of stars.

"Going out past the dunes for exploration purposes is suicide," I argue, taking a different approach. "We'd be completely exposed to an ambush."

"Of that your daughter couldn't be more correct," Father Cash interjects, turning to Dad and sighing. "Yet, her earlier point should be considered more seriously. What *if* the undergrounders have already discovered parts of the wreckage? My guess is that they'd find some way to weaponize it. However, if we were to find just some of it, it could potentially make it harder or even impossible for them to do so."

I swallow, fighting off a chill. I hadn't considered that. It's a possibility for sure, one that is so scary and frightening it cancels out any objection I – or anyone else, for that matter – might have about searching the bowl for pieces of Rubik's ship. Father Cash has just made this a critical mission, whether he realizes it or not.

"God chooses our paths, Farah," Father Cash says, looking from me to Rubik. "No life form is excluded from that truth. You think it's a coincidence that Rubik ended up here, in the only Village that has a dissector? Your father could be the only person on the planet who can solve the mystery of Rubik's ship."

Again, Father Cash is right, and this pattern is starting to annoy me. Nikolaos coughs into his fist, obviously uncomfortable, and then starts to disassemble his equipment.

"I'll lay out your spreads," Dad says, hobbling on his cane toward the front room. "If we're going to present all this to Leader tomorrow, we'd better rest up and be on our game."

Right now Rubik is impossible to read. Is he excited? Is he scared, like me? Or is he just hopeful? That's when it dawns on me: He's probably got someone he cares about...someone who's worried, wondering if he's safe. Why *wouldn't* he want to get home then?

Tired and frustrated with all these unanswered questions, I rise and bid goodnight. I avoid Rubik's eyes. I can't let him see my concern, and, yes, dread. I'd want him to be confident for me if I was in his shoes.

Before I head for my room, I notice something strange and...familiar.

"Father Cash?" I say, my heart *ka-thumping* loudly. "May I ask you something?"

"Of course," he says, setting his empty mug in our basin.

"How did you get that scar?" I ask nervously. It's in the exact same place and has the exact same shape as the one along Alex's neck.

Father Cash's face grows aberrantly grim. "Goodnight, Farah," is all he says.

Chapter 33 | Rubik

I don't have any dreams tonight, because I don't get any sleep.

I lie on my cot beneath the kitchen in the room Farah and her father refer to as the bomb shelter. The lantern above my head is creating patterns on the walls, and I watch the yellow shapes do nothing but glow.

When Nikolaos produced that piece of wreckage from his bag, delight should have flooded my system. Yet instead, all I felt was confusion. Why didn't it look familiar? Why is my entire existence one seemingly unsolvable puzzle? Should I accept the fact that maybe I experienced irreparable damage to my head when I landed on this planet?

That's a terrifying thought, because if Farah's Village is able to recover the bits of my ship that are scattered about, I'll know about as much as they will in terms of how to reassemble it. In other words, I won't have a clue. I may well be stuck here until the fates decide what to do with me...

When I emerge from the shelter the next morning, I find that Farah and Thomas have already left for their scheduled "interrogation." Father Cash is reading at the kitchen table, and he acknowledges me with a single nod. I see Nikolaos in the front room, sitting on the floor and surrounded by various pieces of his recording equipment. He cleans them with a tan cloth.

"That's one of the many problems with living in the desert," Nikolaos says when he notices me. "Everything's always dirty."

I don't respond.

"So," Nikolaos continues, picking up something else and spitting into his rag. "Being cooped up like this must suck, right?"

I assume his slang is referring to undesirable. I can't imagine he meant anything else. I nod my head. Someone raps on the front door a moment later. The patrolman who dropped off Nikolaos and Father Cash appears. Today he wears a red bandana around his neck and a wide brimmed hat.

"Looks like you've settled in," he says to Nikolaos, wiping the sweat from his forehead and upper lip. "Too bad, 'cause you're being transferred."

"To where?" Father Cash asks, appearing behind me. He holds the tome he was reading under his arm.

"A holding area," the patrolman replies, shutting the door and ridding the room of most of the sunlight. "Once Thomas and his daughter are done with their interrogations, the two of you will be called before an assembly."

"Good! Not wasting anytime, that's good," Nikolaos says as he collects his things.

The patrolman, thrown off by Nikolaos's giddiness, narrows his eyes suspiciously. "You'll be stripped of all your possessions before entering the assembly hall," he says, folding his big arms. "I hope you have strong stomachs – you'll be cavity searched."

Nikolaos almost drops one of his devices. "*What?*"

The patrolman smiles, satisfied. "Be ready to move in ten minutes." Then, he leaves.

"Can they do that?" Nikolaos demands, turning to Father Cash.

"We're here on their terms, Nick. Don't you forget that."

"So, what, we're supposed to just bend over for them!"

"In a matter of speaking, well, yes."

Nikolaos makes a gagging noise, but resumes gathering all his possessions. Father Cash only has one bag – one so small I didn't notice him carrying it in last night. That's really all he chooses to travel with?

"Here," Father Cash says, setting his bag on the kitchen table. I approach him curiously. He opens the top and pulls out a necklace with a cross made of two nails. "For you. It was my daughter's." He holds it up, and I receive it with both hands. It's simple, really, but has a lot of weight to it. I run my index finger over the long groove in both nails.

"Trying to convert aliens now?" Nikolaos asks, walking into the kitchen with his bags over his shoulder. "Man, there's nothing you won't corner, is there?"

Father Cash reseals his bag, sighs through his nose, and heads for the front room. But, on his way through the threshold, he reaches out and smacks an unsuspecting Nikolaos behind the head.

"You promised you wouldn't do that anymore!" Nikolaos says, wincing.

"Oops," Father Cash responds from the other room. "Forgive me?"

A few minutes later I hear the door open, and several voices echo from the front room as Nikolaos and Father Cash are corralled outside. I stand in the kitchen, unseen, holding the keepsake in my hands. Why give me this? Was Nikolaos right? Is this an attempt at conversion? With no disrespect to the man named Father Cash, religion is the absolute *last* thing on my mind.

The front door shuts, I set the nail necklace down on the table, and then turn into Thomas's work area — planning to review Farah's picture books to pass the time.

But, with a start, I find that I'm not alone.

Chapter 34 | Farah

I sit on an uncomfortable bench in the white, windowless holding area outside the room where my Dad's being questioned. I can't complain too much. The fans in the ceiling work perfectly in keeping me cool. Better than the one's at our fort.

I glance over at the patrolman who's standing at attention across the room, rifle at ready. He's older, in the neighborhood of Dad's age, and doesn't even acknowledge me.

Okay. Need to focus. I need to psych myself up for the next hour of questioning – ensure I have all my facts straight about everything. Even though Leader assured me this was just a formality, I can't help but feel a little nervous.

Yet all I can think about is my exchange with Father Cash. Or lack thereof.

At first I scolded myself for jumping to conclusions. It's most likely a coincidence that he has a scar like Alex's. What, are they the only two people in the bowl with scars on their necks?

But scars with *identical* shapes and locations. Not to mention Father Cash responded the same way Alex does anytime I bring it up: He avoided the question all together. What kills me is that I was just starting to accept him and Nikolaos, even if I don't agree with their plan to search the bowl for Rubik's wreckage. Now I have to start from scratch and second-guess just about everything Father Cash says.

Or, at the very least, I have to keep an eye on him.

A voice cracks in through the patrolman's walkie: *"Fitzhugh, come in."*

"This is Fitzhugh, over," the patrolman replies, holding his walkie in front of his mouth. I tuck a dangling strand of hair behind my ear and perk up.

"You're needed at the south gate. We're initiating your shift change now. Over."

Patrolman Fitzhugh's face drops. Probably he doesn't want to leave the cool waiting area and head into the sunlight.

"Affirmative. Over."

Fitzhugh clips the walkie onto his belt and crosses the small room to the door. The next moment, there are three repetitive knocks, and Fitzhugh unlocks the deadbolt, exchanging places with –

"Alex!" I say, leaping up and throwing my hands around his neck. I hadn't realized how much I'd missed him until I saw his wind worn, suntanned face. He wears his customary desert goggles on his head, and he smells of heat and outside. But I don't mind.

"Hey stranger," he says, chuckling while he hugs back. He kisses my neck before breaking away.

I smack him on the arm. "Where have you been? You haven't visited *once.*"

"This place has been on lockdown – !"

"So?" I fold my arms. "You're a patrolman, aren't you?"

"Yeah, but that doesn't mean I get special treat – "

I pull him in for a kiss. Things have been pretty intense this week, even by bowl standards, so it feels good to escape all of that in this moment and just be sixteen – stealing a kiss in a quiet room. I probably should have reamed Alex some more, but I prefer his moist lips.

"*Wow*," he says when our moment's up, and I flush despite myself. "I should ignore you more often."

"So you *did* do that on purpose!" I smack him again.

"I'm kidding," he says, laughing. "So, how long has he been in there?" He gestures toward the closed door, behind which Dad is talking with Leader and several of her officials.

"Close to an hour," I reply, consulting my wristwatch.

"Means they're probably wrapping up," he says, voice serious now. "Look, we don't have a lot of time if you're on deck for questioning. I would've been here sooner, but I had to pull in a few favors to swap places with Fitzhugh."

There's urgency to his tone. I wanted badly to bring Alex up to speed on the week's goings-on, what with Rubik learning to speak, the arrival of Nikolaos and Father Cash, and now the proposal to leave the Village and seek out remnants of Rubik's ship.

But it looks like all of that will have to wait.

"Here, let's sit." Alex leads me to the waiting area's

lone bench, and we take a seat simultaneously. "A lot's happened in the past week. I don't even have clearance to know what I'm about to tell you, but members of the patrol talk, and, thankfully, I'm in the right circles."

I chance a glance at his scar when he looks away, but hold my tongue. That's for another conversation. It sounds like the secrets he's getting ready to share have been threatening to bubble out of him for days.

"What's up?" I whisper. "Did they find the mole?"

"Never thought I'd says this, but the mole is the Village's least concern right now..."

That can't be good. Alex lowers his voice even more, and I have to focus to absorb every word: Apparently, when the undergrounders' mission to capture Rubik from the storage units failed, Mr. Toff went off the deep end. That same night, he left a message graffitied to a portion of our fence that read, *One Village A Day*.

At first, Leader deemed this an empty threat, and ordered the graffiti removed at once. But, later in the morning, just to be sure, she radioed in to all twenty-four Villages in the bowl. All but the south-most Village responded.

"The undergrounders could have just knocked out their tower, right? To trick us into giving in?"

"Well, yeah, that's what Leader was hoping for," Alex answers, but then shakes his head. "Except, the next day, another Village went off the grid. And the next day, another."

Six Villages in all, starting at the lower rim and going up, have been unresponsive to radio contact since

Mr. Toff's message was discovered. At this daily rate, twelve more will be offline in twelve days, with our Village geographically set to be the thirteenth. Goose bumps spread across my entire body.

"Leader's been keeping this under wrap to avoid panic," Alex explains, "but word is she's going to finally call a meeting and announce the situation to the Village."

"She waited *six days* before taking Mr. Toff's threat seriously?" I say, appalled. To this Alex only responds with a dark look.

"What?" I demand, realizing there's something he's holding back.

"I..." He clears his throat. "Nothing. Look, I wanted you to know first. There's a good chance Leader will call a vote for relocation."

My mouth falls agape. Since our Village was established in the early days, we've not once relocated. It's a process that requires a lot of effort, coordinating, and strategizing. It also puts us in a terribly vulnerable state. Women and children, trekking across the desert for weeks with limited rations of water and food, while the undergrounders are on our tail... It's a setup for failure – no, for annihilation.

"W-What's the alternative?" I say, trying to banish the graphic images from my mind. Images of my Village getting massacred en route to a new site in the bowl.

"Full-out war with the undergrounders," Alex says matter-of-factly. Before I can even process this, the door next to the bench opens, and Alex rises to his feet. He bows curtly as Leader appears.

"Mr. Windsor," she says, looking him up and down. "You relieved Mr. Fitzhugh?"

"I did," he responds, eyes downcast. Why's he acting so strange? Is he afraid he'll get reprimanded for swapping places with the other patrolman?

"*That's* convenient," Dad says, walking out of the interrogation room slowly, the tip of his cane thudding on the ground with each step.

"Indeed," Leader replies, tapping her right boot a couple of times. "Come, Farah, let's get started. You and your boyfriend can resume your conversation when we've finished."

Alex finally looks up, but only to escort Dad off. I stand on wobbly knees, pretending to smile. But what is there to smile about? If Alex is right, and the undergrounders have initiated a historic wave of carnage, we're as good as doomed. Relocating? War? Whatever we do, how can we *possibly* get through this in one piece?

And, amidst all of this, one pressing question moves its way to the forefront of my thoughts: Why do the undergrounders want Rubik this badly?

A round, rather portly woman stands on the opposite end of Thomas's work area, wearing a long white coat over the desert garb I've seen on everyone in Farah's Village. She is between two patrolmen, who have their respective rifles clenched in tense hands.

"H-Hello there," the woman stammers. "Are you ready to resume?"

I cock my head like I didn't hear the question. She shuffles her feet, probably contemplating if she should step forward or not. What is she referring to though? Resume *what*?

"B-But of course: You were out cold the last time," she continues, more to herself than to me. She gives the stack of folders in her hands to the young patrolman on her left. He lets his rifle hang by its strap and receives the stack, which is bound by twine.

"I'm the Village Professor," the woman explains, moving toward me cautiously. "Though, I hate that job title. I don't *profess* my findings to a lecture hall full of students. I just...learn things. Observe. Take reports.

"Anyway, you can call me Moira."

I stare at her, and she stops in the center of Thomas's work area.

"You *can* understand me, can't you?" she says, her

head of red hair a stark addition to the dim room. I remain stagnant in the kitchen threshold, unsure of what to think or how to respond.

"According to young Farah, you've begun to talk, correct?"

I swallow. "*Yes.*"

"Fascinating!" she replies, eyes watering. "Leave it to that girl to discover a way to teach and instruct you. She always shows such promise on her classroom visits to my lab."

That puts me at slight ease. If Farah can vouch for this woman, I should have nothing to worry about.

"My, my," Moira says, gawking at me. "You really just *glow*, don't you?" I should have grown accustomed to all of this staring and marveling, but it never ceases to unsettle me.

"Douglas!" Moira snaps joyfully, sweeping around to face the two patrolmen. "Please wheel in my supplies, would you?"

"Er, it's Roy, Professor. My name's *Roy.*"

"Of course it is," she booms, turning to Thomas's workbench. She begins to clear the surface, setting the assortment of tools and knickknacks in the windowed corner. If Thomas were here, he'd probably be cringing and –

The front door opens, but it's not the patrolman leaving to fetch Professor Moira's things. It's Alex. He enters and steps aside, making way for Farah's father, who, by the assistance of his cane, walks inside.

"I don't need my own door opened for me," Thomas is

saying in an agitated voice. "Or an escort, for that matter."

Alex sighs. "Yes, Mr. Miles."

"And further more – " Thomas stops midsentence when he notices the two patrolmen and Professor Moira, the latter setting a large apparatus on the dirt floor.

Thomas turns. "C'mon, Alex," he says. "We've got the wrong fort."

"Oh don't be so dramatic, Tom," the Professor says in a bubbly way.

"I *know* those aren't my tools on the ground." Thomas stops by the door, raising his voice. "I *know* the privacy of my fort hasn't been disregarded."

Professor Moira ignores him and turns to me. "Come, have a seat. We're behind schedule."

Hesitantly, I step toward the workbench, but freeze when Thomas's voice has risen to new heights.

"Stay there, Rubik!" He waddles toward Moira, wagging a pointed finger furiously. "My workspace is *not* your laboratory! You can't just barge in here without permission and setup shop!"

Moira makes a *tsk tsk* noise. "Oh, Tom. You used to be all for working together to reach a common, productive objective."

"I – you – I *still* am!" Thomas is shaking now. I can't help but find some humor is this exchange. Clearly Farah's father and the Professor have a history. I look away, wondering if Alex is having the same reaction, but I find that he is glaring at me through narrowed eyes.

It's the same look his Uncle Lark gave me back at the crater, right before he knocked me unconscious. And at the building where I was bound, right before he attempted to stab me with his dagger.

"Well, that's good to hear then," Moira is saying. She looks at the patrolmen and nods to the door. Reluctantly, one of them leaves to retrieve her supplies.

"Where's he going?" Thomas fumes. "Get back here, boy!"

"First you want us gone, now you're summoning him back?" Moira says with a chuckle. "Tempered *and* indecisive? Tom, you must not have had your tea yet."

"I – he – *you* – !" Farah's father can't even produce complete thoughts now.

"Ray, dear," Moira says calmly, addressing the other patrolman, "bring my folders and reports here and kindly make Tom some tea before he has a hernia."

The patrolman doesn't even correct the Professor this time. He shakes his head dejectedly, but obeys, setting her folders down on the workbench and striding past me into the kitchen.

"Stop – don't touch anything!" Thomas's attempts are pitiful now. Behind me, Roy fills a container of water from the basin. At the same time, the other patrolman returns with a cart full of wires and monitors and bulbs.

"*What is all that?*" Thomas demands, taking his glasses off. "Get it out of here – !"

Alex moves to assist the patrolman, and together

they roll the cart to Thomas's workbench, where Moira is already leafing through her documents.

"Tom?" she says absentmindedly, digging through reports. "Close the door, would you? The cool air is getting out."

Red-faced, Thomas sets his jaw. But a moment later he limps to the front door and closes it firmly, mumbling a collection of derogatory phrases. Then, he slumps into the leather armchair by the door and pulls a tiny wooden box out from beneath the seat.

I watch as he slowly produces a pipe, still grumbling under his breath. Next, he pulls out some flint and a pouch that bears a familiar scent.

Moira sniffs. "Tom!" she says, looking up from her papers. "I thought you'd given up on tobacco!"

"I *had!*" he barks, lighting the bowl of the pipe with his flint.

Chapter 36 | Farah

I follow Leader into the interrogation room.

The walls are dark grey, made of cement, with no windows – just like the waiting area. In the center of the room is a long table, behind which three women and two men sit, including Leader's advisor. Leader takes her seat beneath a chandelier of lanterns and motions to the wooden stool opposite them.

This doesn't seem like a formality, this seems like an interrogation.

I inhale through my mouth and take my seat, facing the row of Village officials. I try not to slouch, but the nonexistent backing on this seat makes that near impossible. Probably meant to be uncomfortable.

"So," Leaders says, fingers interlaced and resting before her. "Let us begin. Can you state your full name, for the record?" After she says this, the old man at the end of the table begins punching keys into a loud typewriter. His dangling jowls literally jiggle with each letter.

"Um, Farah Marie Miles," I answer, feeling awkward. The woman next to Leader has perfect posture and a scowl that seems so natural I can't imagine her smiling. She reaches forward and sips from a lacquered mug, using both hands to do so.

Where have I seen her before?

"Thank you, Farah," Leader says over the typewriter. "Now, also for the record, please recount – using as much detail as possible – the events that led up to the being's would-be kidnapping at the storage units. Start from the moment you arrived, and take your time."

She orders this in an almost *bored* way. Like she's just going through the motions. Perhaps she really did mean for this to be a formality. Hopeful now that I can get through this quickly, I clear my throat, sit up, and dive right in.

I tell them how I left the schoolroom against the interim teacher's instruction, and "coerced" Lois into joining me. I have to make sure they're both left out of this as much as possible. I'd never forgive myself if they were somehow punished for my actions.

I explain how I used the watchtower to map out our path to the storage units, but don't elaborate on how much we heard of Mr. Toff's exchange with Leader. Then we entered the storage building through a side door, shared a few words with Del, and were ambushed by the undergrounders.

"That's when Rubik saved me," I say in conclusion, trying to fight back the memories of the scattered corpses. "And then, you arrived."

Leader nods, looks up and down her row of officials, and then pauses. The old man finishes typing a minute or two later, and then pulls out the sheet of paper. He files my account in a manila folder, and, wordlessly, seals it.

That's when he and the rest of the officials stand up and file out of the interrogation room, leaving only me, Leader, and the scowling woman.

"Um, are we finished?" I ask, confused. Leader didn't dismiss the others when she was questioning Dad – I would've seen them in the waiting area.

"Not quite," Leader says, rather coldly.

"Why is everyone leaving then?" The door shuts behind the last person and I gulp.

"Because," Leader explains, rising to her feet, "this isn't for the record." She walks around the table and faces me, half sitting on the desktop informally.

"How long have you and Alex been dating?" she asks, arms folded.

I'm unable to mask my surprise. Why does she want to know *this*?

"Leader asked you a question," the woman sitting behind the table says, setting her mug down. That's when I realize who she is. I've only met her once, a year ago, and she mostly works from home and avoids the marketplace. Yes, working from home as a consultant and high-ranking Village official.

"Mrs. Windsor?" I say, tilting my head.

"Don't address me, *girl*," Alex's mom says, eyebrow arched. "Leader has asked you a question."

"We've been seeing each other for a year," I say, puzzled gaze locked on Mrs. Windsor. She knows how long her son and I have been dating. Why couldn't she have told Leader this? And yet...maybe she *doesn't* know.

Alex rarely talks about his parents, so, likewise, maybe he rarely talks about me? It's not like we hang out much at his fort, and anytime we do, his parents are sequestered in their respective offices, buried in official paperwork. If I remember correctly, Alex's dad is on the agriculture board.

"Leader, what's going on?" I ask, turning to her.

"And, in that span of a year, have you noted anything peculiar or strange?" Leader goes on, completely avoiding my question.

"Yeah," I say, "he has to be forced into taking me on dates." I get out the smart remark before I can help myself. I just don't like being in the dark. Especially about Alex.

"Don't be cute," Mrs. Windsor snaps, practically spraying her words.

"Then why don't you tell me what's going on!" I stand up, inadvertently scooting my stool back. Leader regards me, arms crossed over her chest.

"Tell me, Farah," she says calmly. "What were you and Alex talking about before you were summoned to questioning?"

That's what this is about? So Alex filled me in on the string of undergrounder raids. Big deal. He said Leader was going to announce that soon anyway, right?

"Everything," I say, fists clenched at my side. "We were talking about *everything*." There are such bigger things at play here – such as impending war – and I'm fed up with discussing this. You want to get Alex in trouble for telling me something he shouldn't have? Fine. You can even reprimand me, too.

Let's just get it over with so Dad and I can go before the assembly and discuss what matters. Rubik. Father Cash and Nikolaos's proposal. Plans of relocating. And, possibly, war.

"I see," Leader finally says, sighing as she does so. She looks over her shoulder at Mrs. Windsor, who's shaking her head.

"My brother was right," Alex's mom says angrily. Ah. So Lark's from *your* side of the family. That explains the ugly facial expressions.

"What does any of this matter?" I say, un-balling my fists. "You think Alex is the first person to share something he didn't have clearance to?"

"You poor thing," Mrs. Windsor says, her scowl somehow managing to harden. "He really *has* gotten to you, hasn't he?"

And what is that supposed to mean?

"Farah," Leader says, standing up. "If this were merely an issue of sharing classified information, we wouldn't be making such an ordeal. Alex would be suspended from patrol and required to serve probation – all before he could make a case before my officials to be reinstated."

"Then what *is* the issue?" I ask, not sure I want her answer. My head's swimming. Have I missed something? And why is Alex's mom acting so, well, unmotherly? You'd think, by this conversation, she and her son *weren't* related.

Could it be...? No. Alex isn't the traitor, the one who passed on Rubik's location to the undergrounders... He can't be.

"How well do you know your American history?" Leader says, pocketing her hands and walking forward. I always grow panicky when she gets this close.

"I...it's one of my best subjects." I look past her head to Mrs. Windsor, trying to figure out where this is going.

"Good," Leader replies. "Then you recall the Operation Northwoods incident, correct? During the Kennedy administration?"

I bite my tongue, trying to rack my brain for that lesson. It's ringing a bell, but for some reason I can't recall much. It's probably because I'm on the spot, standing a few small feet from Leader.

"It was a proposal," Leader continues after a moment of silence, "or rather, a collection of proposals, to stage false acts of terrorism. Why? To gain the nation's support and declare war against Cuba."

My lungs close up. My temples pound. I sit back down, feeling dizzy. They're accusing Alex of somehow being involved in attacks. Attacks against other Villages in the bowl – all to garner consent for war against the undergrounders. There was no note left by Mr. Toff? The undergrounders aren't wiping out Villages one by one?

It was all a farce?

"We've figured he's been involved in this for some time now," Alex's mother says, disgusted. Her voice is distant, like it's coming from underwater. "Leader just needed to catch him in the act. That boy may not be *the* traitor we were looking for, but he's *a* traitor, and you just helped us implicate him."

Impossible. There's no way. I know Alex, and it's something he's not morally capable of. He tells me everything – between us, there are no secrets.

Except, of course, if you count that *damn* scar on his neck.

I sit across from Professor Moira at Thomas's workbench. There are several wires taped to my bare chest, and they snake across the tabletop to the Professor's cart, where they're connected to a series of odd machines that blip and beep.

Thomas still lounges in his chair, puffing on his pipe and mumbling things to himself. Shortly after the Professor got situated and finished setting out her workstation, a patrolman – who appeared to have a high ranking – showed up and summoned Alex away, stating "urgent matters."

Alex was sure to throw a glare my way before allowing himself to be led outside.

"This is fascinating, truly fascinating," the Professor says, monitoring a flat display and taking down some notes.

I should probably feel more nervous and uncomfortable than I do, but I reassure myself with something Thomas said earlier. If I'm anything like my pod or spaceship, which he said could potentially contain technological advancements, then it stands to reason I, too, could contain unique and genetic material. Who am I to withhold that from Farah's race? It could very well be the only contribution I give on this planet.

So, I sit.

"What's fascinating?" Thomas eventually asks. I'm glad he does because now I don't have to attempt pronouncing "fascinating."

"These readings," the Professor replies, not looking up from her notes. "Based on what I'm gathering, it looks like our dear Rubik here possesses identical structure to ours. Same D.N.A. Same brain. Same heart. Except, of course, it's not identical, is it? It *looks* wholly different."

"Meaning...what?" Thomas asks, exhaling dual puffs of smoke from his nostrils.

"Glad you asked," she says, setting her pen down and turning to face him. "I'm working on a theory. We're going to have to continue tests, such as these, to be sure, but I believe this being is *adapting*. Somehow, his cells and organs and – well, just about everything – are rapidly shifting and changing to mirror our race."

If what she's saying is true, I'm not controlling it. Is that why I had such a hard time breathing when I first crashed here? Is that why my mouth wouldn't open fully until hours later? On the surface, her theory makes sense, but it paves the way for more questions. Just what *am* I?

Wish I could say.

"Well, that *is* fascinating," Thomas says, nodding.

"Glad you agree," Professor Moira says, spinning back around and adjusting some knobs and dials. Are her cheeks red?

A shadow passes over the windowed corner, and the next instant Farah steps inside.

"*Dad!*" she yells before she even closes the door. Thomas, startled, practically juggles his pipe nervously.

"Honey – I – !"

"What are you doing?" she demands. "You said you quit!" She slams the door shut, and then notices the Professor, who is rising to her feet. Farah's expression instantly changes.

"Professor Moira!" she strides across the room and they exchange a hug. "Sorry for, er, shouting and all."

"You are your father's daughter," Moira says sweetly. "Can't fault you for that."

"What in the bowl is *that* supposed to mean?" Thomas says, putting out his pipe. Farah shoots her father an angry look, as if their roles have suddenly switched and it's now her duty to divvy out disappointment.

The Professor says something else to Thomas, probably another clever insult, but I don't catch it, because Farah turns to me, her face suddenly grave, and mouths, *We need to talk.* She's worried. Did something bad happen during her questioning? Is she in trouble?

"Professor," Farah says, looking away. "Could you maybe take a break? Unless Rubik fed himself, I don't think he's eaten at all today."

The Professor beams. "Of course, dear." She begins to remove the wires from my skin gently. "In fact, I'd say we're just about done for the day. I have *a lot* to go over in my lab now."

Farah takes my hand as I get to my feet and she leads me into the kitchen. Behind us, Thomas and the Professor resume their bickering, so there's no chance we'll be overheard.

"What's wrong?" I ask, surprisingly well. We converse beside the stove.

"It's Alex," she responds, folding her arms. I can feel my muscles tighten.

"Did he *herrt* you?"

"What?" She shakes her head. "*No*, of course not. I think he's caught up in something bad though."

I know I should care. If Alex is important to her, then by all accounts I need to help her where I can. Any animosity toward her boyfriend is unfair.

Right now I don't feel like being fair. "What's wrong?" I ask again.

"He was just arrested." She tells me this in a calm way, almost as if it's not a shock. "Leader and the Village officials think he's involved in some elaborate plan to stage attacks on other Villages, and then make it look like it was the undergrounders."

Farah walks past me and stands in front of the kitchen window.

"Did he dee-*nigh* it?" I ask, joining her in front of the glass. The afternoon sunlight flows through the square opening and sets Farah's skin aglow. Don't stare, I scold myself.

"He hasn't had a chance to deny it," Farah replies,

putting her hands in her pockets. "They locked him up. No visitors. I don't know when I'll see him again."

We watch a group of kids outside kick a brown ball in the road. They laugh, taunting one another as they pass it back and forth. The ball rolls near our fort, and a patrolman standing guard breaks rank momentarily to kick it back in their direction.

"What troubles me, Rubik," Farah continues, "is that I'm not sure he's *not* involved."

"Why?"

"Can I tell you something if you swear not to laugh at me or think I'm crazy?"

I could never do those things. "Yes."

Farah turns from the window and drops her voice: "A while back, Alex showed up at school with a strange scar on his neck."

I blink once, thoughtful. I haven't noticed what she is referring to, though I've only ever seen Alex in poor lighting.

"He also had a couple of bruises and a swollen lip," Farah says, head shaking. "I asked him about it at lunch that day, but he wouldn't talk about it. He wouldn't even address it."

Farah moves to the kitchen basin and pours herself a jar of water – sipping it briefly so she can continue. "And then, when Father Cash and Nikolaos showed up, I saw the exact same scar on the Father's neck. In the same place, Rubik. If I'm not stretching here, and it's *not* a coincidence, what could that mean?"

I feel like shrugging my shoulders, using the gesture

I've seen these people use to show indifference, but I stifle the urge. Yet it's not that I'm indifferent, it's that I really don't know what to make of all this. Is she positing that Father Cash and Alex were attacked and branded by the same person or persons? Is the scar a mark, a warning?

Either way, I feel my heart warm at the realization that Farah chose me to discuss this with. Not her friend, Lois. Not her father. Me.

"I don't get it, Rubik," she says, sighing. She walks over to the table, pulls out a chair, and sits down – bowing her face into her palms. "Why keep something like that from me?" Her voice is muffled behind her hands.

"And Fah-ther Cash?" I say, staying by the window.

"Don't you remember?" She looks up at me. "I asked him last night, and, go figure, he ignored the question."

"Oh," I reply, feeling rueful for not paying better attention. In my defense, my head was practically in five different places.

"It's not that I think that stupid scar is related to all this," Farah says, taking another drink of her water. "It's that it's something Alex won't explain to me, you know? We're supposed to be able to talk about everything."

I'm not sure how to console her. She has every right to be upset, and every right to question what she thinks she knows about Alex. But that's probably the last thing Farah needs to hear.

She gives a chuckle. "You know, about a month ago,

Lois snuck some liquor out of her parents' room. We tried it together. Repulsive stuff, really. Even when it's mixed. Not to mention it all but knocks you out... Well, anyway, I could *definitely* go for some of that liquor right about now."

That's when the idea begins to form. "Lee-core?"

"*Ih*," she says, helping me. "You've got to emphasize the 'i' after the 'l'. *Liquor*."

I try it a second time, and Farah nods approvingly.

"I need liquor," I say, crossing the kitchen to the table. I lean over the chair, and try to stress urgency. "Can you heh-*lp* me get some?"

"What?" Farah straightens up, and I can tell she's attempting to hold back laughter. "You trying to get...drunk?"

"I need to be *knock'd* out. Sleep. I need heh-*lp* sleeping."

"Why?"

"To dream. Th-aght is where my mem-*or*-ies are."

Chapter 38 | Farah

Memories? In his *dreams*? What's he talking about? Before we can discuss this further, I hear the front door opening, and bits of sunlight trickle into the kitchen. Professor Moira's leaving, and voices other than hers and Dad's fill the air.

"C'mon," I tell Rubik, pushing my chair out and standing. "We'll figure something out tonight. If Dad still has his pipe, he probably has some liquor around here, too."

We walk into the front room together just as Dad is "welcoming" a Village official inside.

"Thinking about starting a bed and breakfast, Farah," he says, leaning on his cane as the Village official stands by the door. "Ever hear of those? A bed and breakfast? Could be a lucrative business for us, honey!"

I roll my eyes at Dad's sarcasm and turn to the official, who's a younger man with a crew cut. He wears a tan duster and has a strapless patch over his right eye, and I remember his name because he spoke at the schoolhouse about safety measures and ambush protocols.

"Mr. Strauss," I say, dipping my head down respectfully.

"Farah," he replies in his characteristically soft voice. He addresses Dad next, "You and your daughter are free to come before the assembly now. The Father and the boy, Nikolaos, have been cleared, and they're being transferred to the hall as we speak."

"Rubik needs to come, too," I say, and, beside me, Rubik gives me an expressionless look.

Mr. Strauss clears his throat. "Beg your pardon?"

"Sorry, *this* is Rubik." I put a hand on Rubik's arm. "It's his name now, and he needs to come before the assembly."

Dad slides his glasses on top of his head and rubs his eyes. "Farah, *honey*, this newly acquired impulsive behavior of yours is starting to grey my hairs."

"Why?" Mr. Strauss asks. "Why does, er, Rubik, have to accompany you?"

"He's the reason Dad and I put in a request this morning, before our round of questioning." I drop my hand and take a step forward. "Rubik is why we're going before the assembly."

Mr. Strauss looks from me, to Rubik, to Dad, and then eventually shrugs his shoulders. "Just make him presentable. We need to leave in five."

I give Mr. Strauss an appreciative smile and nod. "Let's get you a shirt," I tell Rubik. He looks anxious, most likely at the prospect of facing our Village assembly, but he has to be there with us. Nikolaos is going to propose the plan to search and recover Rubik's ship. Dad will second this, and so will Father Cash. I have to agree as well, because ever since the Father stated the possibility of the undergrounders weaponizing Rubik's technology, I can't pretend this proposal isn't critical.

Having Rubik there will merely reinforce the entire agenda.

After helping Rubik into a white T-shirt and one of Dad's ripped dusters, the three of us march outside in the thick heat behind Mr. Strauss. We're escorted by Leader's personal retinue, and the men hold up a few parasols to block out the painful sunrays. I'm grateful for the shade, but this draws the eyes of every single person we pass.

"Maybe we should take Rubik with us everywhere we go," Dad says, waving at a few kids who have stopped in the road to gawk at us. I laugh inwardly, turning to Rubik. He is looking all over the place – from the ground to the sky, and everything in between.

"This is probably the strangest place you've ever seen, hm?" I ask, pulling my bandana out from my back pocket and wiping my face.

"I don't *re-mem*ber," Rubik says, watching a worried mother order her kids inside as we stride by. "But *I* am prob-ablee the strang-*ist* thing *they* have seen."

"Nope," I say simply. "Lark holds that honor. Trust me."

Rubik gives me a sideways glance, and then smiles. His pale eyes tarry on me, so I face forward and command myself not to blush. Thankfully, in the desert, it's impossible to differentiate between blushing and heat redness.

"Pretty hypocritical, huh?" I say, noticing just how many people in my Village have stopped what they're doing to watch us. "I tell you not to stare, and yet all anyone does here is stare at you."

Rubik says nothing in response. I see one of my classmates helping her father fix a fan, and they both stop to observe us. If I'm not mistaken, I catch a hint of jealousy in her gaze. What? You think I *want* to go before the stern-faced assembly? You think I *wanted* to see Morgan and Del get killed? You think this is all a privilege?

I clamp my teeth down, turning as we veer west. I guess I did this to myself. I did choose to leave the schoolhouse that day. I put my best friend in danger. And now I have to support a plan that will put lives at risk. I have to sit idly and wait as Alex faces trial. I have to accept that if he's guilty of lying and helping stage false attacks, *that* will be dubbed good news, because it means the undergrounders aren't days away from obliterating us. I'll be forced to break up with him.

My life has turned into one great sandstorm, and no matter how tight I hold on, I *will* get swept violently away, as dust in the wind...

How fast things can change. One day you're putting off homework, listening to David Bowie, and dreading night watch. The next day, an alien falls from space and sets you on a different course. I never could have imagined facing new problems with so much weight that I'd long for my old ones.

"This way," Mr. Strauss commands, walking behind a two-story fort. We approach a pair of wide, steel cellar doors in the ground, and the two patrolmen standing on either side reach down and pry them open.

Leader's retinue stands around the entrance with parasols raised, and we descend the stairs single file – Mr. Strauss, Dad, me, and Rubik.

I've never seen the assembly hall, so this is new territory. When we reach the bottom of the stairs, the cellar doors close above us, and hanging torches offer flickering light. We move down a narrow hallway, and I start to feel claustrophobic. I glance over my shoulder. Rubik, who has to hunch slightly beneath the low ceiling, is alight with his iridescent cubes.

We eventually slow our steps, and I start to wonder what section of the Village we're underneath. The barracks? The marketplace? Regardless, the air is satisfyingly cool down here, so much so that I almost shiver. The hallway widens into a circular, modest-sized room, and the torches have been replaced with lanterns.

Father Cash and Nikolaos sit at a table, two water-filled jars between them. Behind them are three armed patrolmen.

"Wait here," Mr. Strauss instructs. "Have some water. You'll be summoned in a moment." Then he exits through the room's lone door.

"Pull up a chair!" Nikolaos exclaims, holding up his water. "Your patrolmen were just about to give us a deck of cards."

"No we weren't," one of them replies, sounding annoyed.

"Oh." Nikolaos sets his jar back down. "Well that sucks." Father Cash stands up, offering Dad his seat.

"Thank you," he says, letting out a groan as he flops down.

He leans his cane against the table. Rubik and I follow, and Father Cash insists we take the remaining two chairs — though he's intentional in avoiding my eyes while he speaks. His scar is near impossible to see in the minimal lighting.

"Could you drink this for me?" Nikolaos asks Rubik, sliding his jar across the tabletop. Rubik cocks his head, confused by the request, but he sips the water all the same. Nikolaos leans his chin on his fist, watching with unblinking eyes as the clear liquid runs down Rubik's throat.

"*Whoa,*" one of the patrolmen says, and another one whistles.

Nikolaos mimics the whistle and says, "…Is right."

"Proof of life outside our galaxy," I say, shaking my head, "and him *drinking water* is what astounds you?"

"But it's so cool!" Nikolaos says, taking back his jar and regarding it like a holy relic. I roll my eyes, turning to Dad. He's watching Father Cash with a certain look I can't decipher.

He pushes up his square glasses. "So, Father, this must shake things up for you, huh? Rubik being here has got to have you questioning a lot."

Father Cash shrugs. "God is limitless. No being or

form of creation is a happenstance." He reaches down and picks up his water off the table. "If anything, Rubik here is merely a testament to God's scale. His fingerprints are all over the universe, and we now know this for a fact."

"Sure," Dad says, uninterestedly. "If that Bible of yours is the only lens you look through. And a 'god' that has fingerprints? Makes him sound awful human when you put it like that."

"It's only a figure of speech," Father Cash replies, chuckling. "And yet, we *were* created in His own image."

"Course we were."

Father Cash and I give Dad the same look – a look of surprise. Where's this coming from? Dad never discusses religion with me, and, apparently, that was on purpose. Mom used to pray for me at night when she'd tuck me into bed. That's all I've ever known of God – you say prayers to Him in hopes that He'll watch over you.

Does Dad blame *God* for mom's death? If he does, he's never said it out loud.

"Uh oh," Nikolaos says to Dad, interrupting my thoughts. "You've officially made it to the top of Father's prayer list, Mr. Miles."

Dad almost appears...angry. He opens his mouth, but is stopped short when the door on the other side of the room re-opens.

"The assembly will see you now," Mr. Strauss says, lingering by the threshold.

180

We all inhale – practically at the same time – and gather our wits. I meet Rubik's eye line and give him a reassuring smile. It's okay, I mouth, but instead of nodding or acknowledging my consolation, Rubik is the first to stand. Surprised, but without delay, we all follow suit and make for the door.

The assembly hall is mind-blowing, unlike anything in my Village. It must have once been a place of magnificence, because the tall walls are covered with massive stain glass windows. Images of saints and majestic angels. Except, those images are diluted now: many are missing panes or sections of glass, where dirt has pushed through and now leaks into the room. Small dams constructed of scrap wood are stationed all along the sides of the hall to cease the influx of sand. The result is that it appears how stagnant jets of water might look in a frozen fountain.

How did this hall get underground? Some powerful storm bury it?

"Let's go, hon'," Dad says next to me, nudging me along. I hadn't realized that I'd stopped in place.

We amble down the long aisle that splits the rows of pews, and I'm astonished by how many people are here – sitting on the stiff benches and watching us go by. The hall is nearly full!

"*This* many people from our Village get to watch assembly proceedings?" I whisper to Dad. He doesn't say anything back. Instead, he pretends to be focusing all his energy on striding with his cane. Like it's the first time he's ever used the walking assistance.

He's just as nervous as I am, I think.

Ahead of us, a patrolman guides Rubik, Father Cash and Nikolaos to our designated seating section. It's where the front row would have been, only here the pew has been ripped up. Instead, there's a table with five chairs on one side, pointed at the altar.

Father Cash sits at the far end, then Nikolaos, Rubik, me, and Dad. The stage before us is lined with ten armchairs, all of which are currently unoccupied. Organ pipes web up the angular wall behind the armchairs and reach the ceiling, where scores of hanging lanterns dangle by cords.

A door off to the side of the stage opens, and Leader walks through, followed by Mr. Strauss and eight other assembly members. We can do this, I tell myself. We can convince this hall of people that finding Rubik's ship is of the utmost importance –

My heart seems to freeze. The final member of the assembly has entered, closing the door and taking the last seat. He scans the crowd of people, finds me, and blows a kiss.

Lark's a member of the assembly? This just got a lot more complicated.

Chapter 39 | Rubik

Farah's Leader raises one hand, hushing the chattering crowd behind us. I see Farah stiffen out of the corner of my eye. I look forward, following her gaze, and realize why she's tense. Lark is among the seated assembly. He crosses his legs lazily, fiddling with a zipper on his cargo pants.

The part of my head where Lark knocked me unconscious feels like it's throbbing in reaction to his presence.

"...Will come to order," Leader is saying, lowering her hand. "We have two guests who have traveled from the outer rim, where their Village is located. They have requested a platform in which to offer a proposal. Will the guests stand and state their names?"

Father Cash rises first, then Nikolaos. They both introduce themselves before taking turns explaining their background and history. I take this opportunity to watch Lark. I can tell by Farah's body language his being here is most unexpected. Something they hadn't planned on. That means this is the very first time Farah and her father have been present during one of these assemblies.

As if their plan of convincing the Village to leave and find my ship wasn't going to be difficult enough.

My ship. It's strange thinking within a possessive context. I don't own anything here – not even attire. No possessions, no plan, no direction. Just a few dreams that could potentially be memories, and a desire to return to my home planet. And now Nikolaos has proof of something that *is* mine. A piece of my ship with inscriptions I can't decipher, and moving images of my crash landing. What he refers to as "footage."

An excitement starts to surge through me. What if the assembly approves this? What if they agree to send a team out into the badlands and they actually recover my ship? Maybe then, when I see my galactic vehicle, I'll finally be flooded with remembrance. I'll finally remember who I am, where I am from, and why I –

No. That excitement is almost instantly replaced with fear. Beneath the table I feel my hands begin to tremble. How could I have so easily forgotten? It was among the stars...in my pod or spaceship...that I felt *trapped*. Imprisoned. I had to wrestle my conscience...convince myself that being in space wasn't natural.

What's really going on here? No matter which corner I turn, more and more questions confront me, consume me. I know this much: whether or not I return to my home planet via my prison of a spaceship, we still have to recover it. It's literally the only place I might find answers.

"...Which is why Thomas and Farah were kind enough to request this platform on our behalf," Father Cash is telling the assembly. He and Nikolaos sit and look past me at Farah and her father.

"So," Leader says, hands in her lap. "Let's have it then. What exactly is your proposal?" There must be some protocol I'm missing. Can guests not offer proposals in Villages that aren't their own?

Thomas clears his throat, and then he uses his cane to stand up. "Leader, assembly, hall of attendants. Last night, upon our guests' arrival, my daughter and I were shown something very...exciting. However, it was both exciting *and* pressing. Something that can't be ignored."

While he says this, two Village patrolmen work to configure Nikolaos's recording equipment at the foot of the stage. I catch Lark yawning, then he turns to the skinny woman to his right. He whispers, she stifles laughter.

I grind my teeth together.

Eventually, the patrolmen finish, and they point the cued up image at a white board that sits on an easel. It's the image Nikolaos found and showed us last night. The image of the flash in the sky, with fragments and elements of my ship trailing behind.

A creaking noise spreads throughout the hall as people shift their weight in the benches or stand – both in an attempts to get better looks. Thomas explains what we're looking at and how Nikolaos was able to come across the footage. Leader and the assembly members take turns stepping down from the stage to inspect the image closer.

Lark opts to remain put.

"By way of inferring," says one of the assembly members, a tall man with a beard that reaches his stomach. "Are you suggesting we need to scour the bowl for this being's wreckage?" He points at me from his armchair.

"I would change 'suggesting' to 'stressing,' " Thomas says, leaning on his cane. "It's already been, what, a week since Rubik here came to us?"

"A week indeed," the bearded man says, chuckling. He then uses the very argument Farah had earlier: "This is an impossible feat. The manpower and resources alone would be as big an economical gamble as relocating!"

The hall fills with murmurs of agreement.

"Not necessarily," Thomas responds. "Nikolaos believes that he can use the crater – where Rubik was discovered – and this footage here to map out the coordinates of the scattered ship. If he could pinpoint the exact places in the bowl, the team we'd send could be quite small."

"But the crater is only *one* reference point," the skinny woman next to Lark says, shaking her head. "You'd need more than one to narrow down the possible coordinates!"

"Actually, we have three reference points," Thomas corrects. "The crater, the perspective of this footage, and – well, perhaps you'd better see the third one."

Gasps fill the air as the same two patrolmen who set up Nikolaos's equipment reveal the black, metal debris with the faded glyphs. The patrolmen walk it down the row of armchairs, then place it on a table before the hall. Thomas describes to the assembly members how this part fell from my descent and landed in the Village of Father Cash and Nikolaos.

It looks like we've got Lark's attention now as he gapes at the wreckage with eyebrows raised. Beside him, the skinny woman tosses her hair back – surprised, but appearing to accept this new development.

Next we hear the argument that offers the possibility of the undergrounders finding my ship's remains first. It's the perfect segue.

"Yes, see, that's why this is so pressing," Thomas explains, addressing the grey haired man who stated the argument. "What *would* happen if the undergrounders discovered Rubik's technology before us? Based on their track record, I don't feel it's out of the realm of possibility that they'd try to weaponize it."

More gasps. Leader raises her hand again, trying to settle the attendants with their worried whispering, but it spreads throughout the hall. Having such a large audience here is boding well for this proposal.

Lark puts his hands on his armrests, looking like he's about to stand. This is it. Here comes the big counter to Thomas's entire presentation. I suddenly feel compelled to do something. I have to help.

So I stand first. Lark freezes, and the hall goes instantly quiet. Eerily quiet.

"I have to find my ship," I say, using the best articulation I have since Farah taught me how to talk.

I look straight at Leader, and I feel the eyes of dozens of people looking straight at me.

Farah stands, too, coming to my rescue. "T-This is about protecting our Village," she says nervously. "But it's also a way we can learn more about Rubik and his race. Maybe, even, to help him get home."

Silence. I turn to Farah and she smiles, placing a hand on my arm. Beside her, Thomas nods at me. Good job, he's saying, even though I didn't really do anything. It's true, sure – I have to find my ship. But I hate that it's the Village's problem. It shouldn't have to be this way, and yet, it is. Nothing can change that.

"Quite a proposal," a voice says. We all look back to the stage. Lark is standing in front of his armchair, arms folded. "Let's summarize. You think it's in the best interest of our Village to send a team out into the bowl, where they will use coordinates comprised of the crater and wreckage trajectories to find the being's dispersed spaceship? And you're proposing we do all this quickly, right? So as to avoid the undergrounders beating us to the race?"

Thomas grips his cane, but answers calmly: "Yes, that pretty much covers it."

Lark scratches his head, face unreadable. "I think it's brilliant." Did I hear him correctly? Or am I just hearing what I want to hear? Farah and her father swap glances.

"Leader," Lark continues, the chatter in the hall resuming. "I move for this proposal to be called to a vote."

"Did we really just convince Lark?" Farah says under her breath. I know her question is rhetorical, but I respond anyway.

"I don't know," I say, confused. This was supposed to be a challenge. Are we missing something? I know little to nothing about Lark, but I know enough to understand that with him, nothing is as it seems – with a man who acts as violently as he does, how can it be?

Leader swallows, looking somewhat apprehensive.

"You're *sure* you want to call a vote, Lark?" she asks, eyeing the rows of attendants. Some people are shouting now, though I can't tell if it's in opposition or agreement. All I do is watch Leader and Lark's exchange. Something about it seems...off.

"Do I seem unsure?" Lark replies, almost in a whisper.

"It's your first motion," the bearded assembly member tells Lark. "Leader wants to make certain that you – "

"It may be my first motion," Lark interrupts. "But the late assembly member whose role I have filled *did* offer up many motions in his term. Don't regard me, members of the assembly, regard the position I've filled. And, as acting patrol contributor, I move for a vote."

So Lark's a replacement on the assembly? I turn to Farah, but she's not watching. Her and Thomas have leaned back and are exchanging excited words with Father Cash and Nikolaos. No one is watching, it seems, but me.

"He's right," Mr. Strauss says next to Leader. "Even though Lark has replaced Morgan on this assembly, the role of patrol contributor has remained intact. We should treat this motion with the same respect Morgan would've received."

"Lark is still new to the role," Leader says curtly. "What, we're supposed to disregard who is actually sitting in that seat, so long as it's occupied?"

"But I'm not just a body in a seat, Leader," Lark replies slyly. "I am now the senior most patrolman. All high-level threats to our Village are my responsibility. And the possibility of the undergrounders weaponizing the being's technology is a *high-level threat.*"

Leader sits back, tapping her chin. All of this politicking is almost making me lightheaded, but I've drawn enough from the heated conversation to conclude that Lark is now more powerful in his new role on the assembly. The confidence in which he politicks appears to fluster Leader. There's a subtext to all of this I can't decode.

"Shall we vote?" Lark says, raising his hand. This action quiets the hall. To my right, Farah and her father stop conversing to watch the vote.

Leader stands, and everyone in the assembly hall mimics. "All in favor of sending a search team out to recover the alien ship?" She and one other member are the only two who don't raise their hands.

Eight to two. We've just gotten one step closer to finding some answers in the form of my ship. This is a victory, but I didn't expect to feel so worried. Uneasy.

What is Lark's game?

The assembly hall fills with partial applauding, and partial shouting. Leader looks irate, and she orders for Nikolaos's equipment to be stripped down. Farah and her father hug, relieved.

"Well," Nikolaos says to me. "Hard parts over now, huh?"

I'm about to reply, maybe even agree with him, but that's when Lark offers a second motion. One so unexpected that Farah and Thomas drop back down into their chairs, leaving me standing with Nikolaos and Father Cash.

We've been blindsided.

Chapter 40 | Farah

This was Lark's intention all along.

To put us in danger.

He wants *us* to lead the search team. Me. Dad. Nikolaos. The assembly will never agree to this. There's no way. We're just...pedestrians. The bowl is too dangerous for pedestrians. I should stand back up, show that I'm confident and ready to object. But I can't move.

"It makes sense, when considered," Lark says above the shouts. "So consider this: Thomas here is a dissector. He'll need to be present to help ensure the pieces of the wreckage are handled carefully and properly. Because of his *crippling* setbacks" – he nods to Dad's cane – "he'll need his daughter at his side, offering assistance. This boy, Nikolaos, is a given. He's already mapping out the coordinates of the lost wreckage, so it makes sense for him to accompany the search – his contribution would be invaluable."

Beside Rubik, Nikolaos opens his mouth, then pauses. "Wait. Invaluable is good, right?"

Mr. Strauss shakes his head at Lark, flipping the back of his duster up and sitting down. "That's asking a lot of these three, who aren't trained or equipped to survive the harsh terrains of the bowl."

"Leader's instinct to send Farah with my patrol last week paid off," Lark says, meeting my eyes. "She's the definition of untrained and unequipped, and yet she did *wonderfully*."

I can't believe what I'm hearing. He knows I was terrified. He knows I stood there in shock as Morgan died in Alex's arms. I'm so angry and scared a muscle starts to twitch in my forehead.

"This is different," Leader says, hands on her hips.

"How?" Lark challenges. She doesn't reply.

I keep waiting for Dad to stand up and tell the assembly how bad of an idea this is. He just sits there, like me. Other members of the assembly begin to whisper amongst themselves.

They're actually considering this? Someone needs to object! There's no way Dad will last long out in the bowl – not at his age, and with such a bad leg. Not even if I'm there to see to his every need.

"The difference," Mr. Strauss says after a while, "is that this time they could be out there for days…maybe weeks. It's not safe."

"Either way lives are at risk," Lark says quickly, like he was waiting for this argument. "Whether it's this lot, or another search team altogether. Why not set ourselves up for the best possible way to succeed?" His point is actually a good one. I can't believe how quickly he's turned this proposition from crazy to somewhat logical. Lark is not just the sadistic, impulsive man I've known since I was a little kid.

He's someone far more calculating. Far more

dangerous.

"We'll send them with our best patrolmen," Lark continues, projecting out to the crowd. "Meanwhile, we could further our research of the alien. Run more tests. Prepare ourselves for the search team's findings."

"You speak out of line," Leader says, and the assembly hall dips into an awkward silence. "You may offer up this motion before the assembly and its attendants, as it includes patrol involvement, but suggesting anything further – such as research and tests – is outside your scope."

"Of course, Leader," Lark says, backing down.

He takes his seat, unfazed by the chastising. He knows he's all but won. And with Dad and me gone – out of the picture for weeks – Lark will be free to manipulate the assembly into doing God knows what to Rubik.

But there's still a chance we could get out of this. The assembly has to vote. I come to my senses, getting ready to stand up and offer a case for Dad, Nikolaos, and me to stay behind, but Rubik is quicker.

"I will go too," he says, shocking everyone – most of all me. Not surprisingly, Lark stands again to voice disagreement, but Rubik continues: "I have to help them."

"Rubik's not bound by our ruling," Dad says, coming out of his daze. "Being from another planet affords him that luxury. If he wants to leave, he should be free to do so."

Why is Dad doing this? He's acting like we *have* to

go. No one's voted yet! I try to get his attention, but Rubik has more to say.

"I will *all*-so pro-teck them," he says, addressing no one but Leader. For a minute or so, she says nothing. Lark looks furious, but he holds his tongue. There's so much going on I want to scream. Press a reset button or something.

"Well," Leader finally says. "Then let's vote. All in favor of sending Nikolaos, Farah, Thomas, and the being with the search team?"

My mouth goes dry as the assembly members raise their hands. It's a split. Five hands are in the air, five are not. Leader did not vote in favor of this.

"A tie vote," she says, looking up and down the stage. "This prompts an executive ruling." The assembly members that voted lower their hands as Leader steps to the edge of the stage. She sighs as she regards me, Dad and Rubik. I can't figure out what she's thinking. Her expression is neutral.

Behind her, Lark is glaring at Rubik – apparently he ruined some master plan Lark had. Before I can relish in that thought, Leader announces her decision.

It's exactly as I feared. She's had a quick change of heart. It looks like we're heading out into the bowl. It's no wonder Dad and Rubik were acting the way they were. Preparing for the worst. Although, I feel as if there's nothing I could've done to prepare me for this...

The walk back to our fort is long, without conversation, and somber. We have the rest of the afternoon to prepare for the journey, which begins at dawn. The sooner the better, right? Can't say I disagree with that, except for the fact that "sooner" is referring to my departure.

You've done this before, I tell myself as we head down the main road. I've been out there, near the dunes. At least this time we'll have a more clear objective, plus Rubik as added protection.

The sun's new position tells me how long we were down in the assembly hall. Close to two hours. I check my wristwatch, confirming this. So much has already happened today. My round of questioning. Accusations about Alex, and then his incarceration. Now this.

At this point I don't know how much more I can withstand.

Dad unlocks the front door to our fort, and I walk inside first, followed by Nikolaos, Father Cash, Rubik and Dad, who collapses into his chair after locking the deadbolt. Rubik relieves himself of the duster, hanging it near the kitchen doorway. I lean against a stack of crates, and Nikolaos does likewise. Father Cash loiters by the door, a thoughtful look on his face.

After a few beats, Dad lets out a collection of cuss words so passionately, I blush.

"My thoughts exactly," Father Cash says, and Nikolaos and I burst into laughter. I'm so tired and angry that I feel delirious, so I just let this reaction play out. Nikolaos is doubled over, wiping tears out of his eyes. Rubik looks around the room, hoping someone will explain. Soon Dad and the Father are even chuckling, leaving Rubik as puzzled as ever.

"I should have known Lark was up to something," Dad says when our laughter fades.

"You mean that assembly member?" Father Cash asks, taking a seat at Dad's workbench. "You think he's intentionally putting you in danger?"

"Yo, Father," Nikolaos says, hands in his jean pockets. "Were you at the same assembly proceeding as us? You could almost *smell* the bad blood between these three."

"Four," Rubik says, exposed arms and neck pulsating. "He tri-*ed* to stab me."

"Wait what?" My reaction is instant. "When?"

"He was prove-*ing some*-thing," Rubik replies. "That he is not scared of me."

"Yeah, well I'm about to prove something to him," I say, marching toward the door. Dad holds out his cane. "Drop it, Dad."

"And just what do you plan on doing, hon'?"

"I'm going to report him to Leader!"

"You're going to report him to Leader," Dad repeats back to me. "Farah, it's Rubik's word against Lark's – "

"So you think Rubik's lying?"

"Did I say that?"

Practically. "Lark can't get away with this kind of stuff!"

"Look, what Lark did wasn't right. None of this is right." Dad lowers his cane, his tone growing serious. "But we – you and I – have to focus on what we can control, okay?"

This is no time for a lecture, I think. I stomp away from the door, turning on the fans in our fort to keep myself occupied. I'm this close to quoting Dad's collection of cuss words.

"So what's Lark's deal?" Nikolaos asks Dad. "I mean, why do you think he wants you guys outta the Village so badly?"

"We're basically Rubik's only support system," I say, running a hand through my hair. "Take us out of the equation and Lark can propose just about anything to the assembly. I wouldn't be surprised if he wants Rubik for a soldier!" I'm almost panting with fury. Rubik looks slightly pleased with himself, like he appreciates me getting so upset for him.

"Doubtful, honey," Dad says, crossing his legs. "If I recall, Lark wanted Rubik here to stand trial, remember? And now we're finding out that he's attempting to stab him? No, if Lark wants Rubik as an ally, he's doing a poor job of showing it."

Dad's right. I had almost forgotten about that stupid trial. Lark was so intent on recommending it when Morgan was killed, but what about Del's death? As far as I can tell, Lark hasn't followed up with that initial request, and he never saw a need for Rubik to stand trial when Del was murdered. Maybe he didn't suggest it because both Lois and I were clear witnesses at the storage unit?

But if there's one thing I've learned about Lark today, it's that he's more cunning than he leads on. So what am I missing? I need to try and figure out Lark's agenda so I can get one step ahead of him and steal the advantage.

It's just one more thing on my ever-growing list of predicaments.

"We should probably get all of our stuff together," Father Cash says, rising from the workbench. "I plan on doing a lot of praying before our caravan rolls out in the morning."

"You don't have to go," I say, confused. "You weren't part of the vote."

"Nikolaos is my responsibility," the Father replies, adjusting his clerical collar. "I made a promise to his mother I'd keep a close eye – "

"You did *what?*" Nikolaos palms his forehead. "I can't even run away without her babying me!"

The next couple of hours we work in silence. Dad packs in his room with the door shut. Father Cash reads in the kitchen, sipping a mug of water. Nikolaos is escorted off to collect the video equipment he lent out during the assembly presentation. I pack lightly, stuffing clothes into a duffle bag, and various things to keep me occupied in my backpack: CDs, books, and old magazines.

Rubik sits on the floor beside my dresser, watching me pack. You know you don't have to come with us, I mean to tell him. I'd rather you weather more testing here at the Village than go out into the bowl and risk the undergrounders attempting to capture you again.

I never say any of this though. Truth is, I'm glad he's coming. He may have frightened me back at the storage units...killing all of those undergrounders with such fluidity...but at the end of the day, it was to *protect* me. I can't deny that. Leader said that people in the Village were referring to Rubik as a guardian angel. The more I think about it, the more I realize that's pretty accurate.

We pull a couple stools in from the front room and sit around our small kitchen table for dinner. Father Cash asks if he can bless the meal, but Dad ignores the request and begins sipping his soup. So, Father Cash bows his head and prays to himself.

I turn to Dad, but he's avoiding all eye contact. He stares across the room as he swallows his mouthful. When the timing is right, I've got to ask him where this loathing is coming from. I can't stand to see my own Dad upset about something as simple as prayer.

Rubik is the first to retire. He sets his empty bowl in the kitchen basin and goes down the steps into the bomb shelter. I have so much I want to talk with him about, but I let him go. If he's only half as nervous and scared as I am, he needs time to himself. He has no idea of the dangers we're about to face – traveling through the bowl with such a large entourage. But, well, I guess he'll know soon enough.

Nikolaos leaves the table next, heading into the front room to charge his cameras. I wish there was something I had that could absorb my time and focus – something that would help me fall asleep. I chuckle inwardly. Sleep: don't think I'll be getting much of that tonight.

"I heard the patrolmen talking," Father Cash says, wiping his mouth with a cloth. "Earlier. When Nikolaos and I were waiting for you to arrive before the assembly proceeding. They said your Village's security was compromised this week. Something about a surprise attack?"

"The undergrounders showed up in their desert vessels," Dad replies, leaning back in his chair. "They drew our men to the east gate, creating a diversion."

"So they could sneak into our Village to try and capture Rubik," I add, putting my hair up with a band.

"How did they know you had him?" Father Cash asks, rubbing his chin.

"It was the day after we found Rubik," I answer. "He was being shot at in his crater the night before. We saved him from the undergrounders. And then a traitor within our walls tipped them off..."

"Interesting," the Father says, standing and walking to the window.

" 'Interesting?' " Dad echoes, laughing. "Wouldn't call the undergrounders opening fire on an alien life form *interesting*. Or the fact that they have a weasel infiltrating our Village. No, I've got some choice words for that."

"That's not what I mean," Father Cash says, looking through the glass at the sunrise. Lanterns are starting to flip on outside. "It's the time line of all this."

"The time line?" I ask, curious as to where this is going.

"The undergrounders were at our Village roughly a

week ago," Father Cash says, his back to us. "Remember how I said we endured two raids in the past year? The second one was very recent."

"I didn't think people survived raids," I say, voice almost trembling. I can't stand the fact that we might face the undergrounders in the bowl.

"Normally, they don't," Father Cash says, turning our way. "Only, in the case of our raids, they did more than just set fire to our forts and destroy our resources. They actually *raided* something. Our archives."

I pause, turning to Dad. "Yours is the Village with the archives?" he asks Father Cash, who nods his response.

"What are the archives?" I say.

"In the early days," Dad tells me, "one Village was selected, in secret, to bear the responsibility of protecting military, religious, and political documentation that was salvaged after the great wars. High-level information that only leaders and generals would have had access to in the past."

"I'm betting the undergrounder raids we've come to fear *were not* as random and reckless as we all assumed them to be." Father Cash inhales heavily, looking worried. "They were searching for the Village with the chamber of archives. And, once they found it, they returned with double the manpower."

"What did they take?" I ask, sharing in the Father's worries.

"That wasn't released to the public," Father Cash replies. "Could have been everything. Could have been

202

one thing in particular they were searching for. At any rate, what's interesting about all of this, is that you're saying your patrolmen had to fight off the undergrounders from Rubik's crater. On the same night they were plundering our archives."

"And? So?" Dad doesn't see where this is headed anymore than I do.

"The undergrounders could've had other troops of men," I offer, "who happened to be in the area around the time Rubik crashed in the desert."

Father Cash raises his eyebrows. What? Just say what you're thinking – I'm too overwhelmed by today's events to muddle through hints right now.

"You think they were expecting Rubik?" Dad whispers, inclining forward.

"Why else were they in the area?" Father Cash says. "From what I've gathered, in relation to other Villages, *yours* is the closest to the crater. There isn't anyone around for miles..."

"Hold on," I interject, my thoughts shooting off in different directions. "If the undergrounders were expecting Rubik, why shoot at him? I was there – they wanted to harm him!"

"Perhaps Mr. Toff didn't explain to his minions what exactly they were waiting for." Father Cash takes his seat again. "Perhaps he just told them to wait, and – "

"This is a wild, speculative theory," Dad says, taking off his glasses and rubbing his eyes, "with a lot of perhapses. Besides, let's say you're right. With something as important as an alien life form, you'd think Mr. Toff would have personally seen to the apprehension."

Father Cash folds his arms. "Hadn't thought of that."

"But..." I say, realizing something. Dad and the Father turn to me. "But Mr. Toff did go through the effort of planning a huge diversion. It's something Leader pointed out to me, and I didn't think much of it at the time. She's right, though. That's a risky and bold endeavor Mr. Toff embarked on...he must know something we don't." Enter the latest question I'm faced with. Another strand to this complicated thread.

Were the undergrounders purposefully near the crash site, waiting for Rubik's arrival? I never considered just how fast their response time was. And what exactly did the undergrounders steal from the chamber of archives?

"Recovering that ship is important," Father Cash says, taking his mug of water. He hovers it in front of his mouth. "But keeping Rubik out of the undergrounders hands now transcends all else."

I turn to Dad. He meets my gaze, and there's a pregnant pause before he says anything. "Better get some rest, hon'."

I don't know how that's going to happen, but I stand anyway. I take my bowl and spoon to the basin, set it down, and think of something. No matter how scary this may seem, I have to accept it as a possibility: I might not survive the bowl. We could get ambushed. Killed.

Tonight may be my last chance to see Alex. I have to try and sneak into where he's being held captive.

Chapter 41 | Rubik

I lay in the rigid cot Thomas lent me, looking up at the closed shelter door. The cool room is almost pitch dark. I hold out my arm in front of my eyes, watching the purple and blue cubes burn like the embers of a dying fire.

Professor Moira said that I'm adapting. My body is transforming into something new. Do I *want* that? Obviously the will to survive is innate. That is true of any living creature. My body is proof of that. But...this process, whatever it is...is it irreversible? Does this mean I'm stuck here, or will my body merely readapt to fit my home planet's atmosphere?

I suppose that will be a good problem to have, because it will mean I'd found a way back.

My head feels as if it's being suppressed by an immense amount of pressure. Everything that has happened this week spins around me in a whirlwind of dizzying questions. Has Farah and her Village smoked out the traitor yet? Why are Father Cash and Alex hiding their scar's origin from Farah? Speaking of Alex, is he really caught up in a political maneuver to justify war with the undergrounders? And, most importantly, what is Lark's next play? He's clearly begun to shift the pieces of some intricate scheme. So what is it?

I'm so expended by these thoughts that I don't realize I've fallen asleep. The voices are back. The blurry, out-of-focus veil has not been dropped. I still can't see to whom I'm talking.

Me: —I'm going into hiding.

—Why? You can't do that. Not now.

—I never meant for this, any of it. I pause. —Your actions can never be undone. Doesn't that frighten you?

—My actions? What frightens me is that you would foist this upon my shoulders! Are you forgetting who we serve?

—I didn't ask for your servitude or loyalty!

—No? Perhaps not. But you didn't turn us away either. And you also didn't deny us our suggestions or plans.

—What do you want from me! I can't stay here, it's not safe. Going into hiding is the only option I have left.

—Then we'll follow you. Into hiding. All of us.

—No. With the way things are, it wouldn't be wise. We need to scatter.

The voice laughs back at me. —Scatter? You would risk that?

—What do you mean?

—The only reason there's some semblance of control is because you are the beacon! Snuff that light out and yes, we'll scatter, but then what? Chaos. Together there is order. Apart there is chaos. More chances of you being found.

—And if I want to be found?

—You don't mean that. Those who hide don't wish to be found.

—Fine. I may not want that, but I do want closure. In some form or fashion. You're right. I shouldn't hide...I should ascend. Ready the Leaper.

—Why? Why are you doing this?

—Don't you turn your back on me now. After all of this work. This hard work.

—I'm not. I wouldn't. I just...why now? When it's not finished?

—You may not think it's finished, but it'll do the trick with the state it's in.

—How can you be certain? This is your life we're talking about.

—Don't act like we haven't weighed the risks already.

—I'm not! But you're being hasty! What if it fails? What then?

—It won't, because you designed it. And you don't fail, so consequently it won't fail.

—Don't do this...I'd rather you go into hiding.

—You preach loyalty. Now act on it.

Chapter 42 | Farah

I wait until the lantern in Dad's room dims before sneaking out my window. My sneakers hit the ground softly and almost completely soundlessly. I pivot around, shutting the window, and crawl to the back of our fort – just in time to avoid three patrolmen marching by.

I noticed it the third night after Leader stationed her men outside Dad's and my fort. There's a gap in their shifts. About thirty seconds to a minute where the patrolmen swap posts and leave the sides unguarded. I use this flaw to my advantage.

Moonlight casts long and wide shadows, giving me many opportune hiding spots. I crouch in darkness, count to ten, and then scurry to the next unlit portion behind our fort. I do this several times, until I've finally made it past the perimeter of security.

I stand upright, rolling my head and loosening my joints. Okay. How am I going to do this? Sneaking out of my bedroom was the easy part. Next I've got to sneak into the barracks, where the underground prison cells are. I feel a pricking in my heart. Even though there's a slight chance Leader's accusations are founded, and Alex is guilty, I don't like the thought of him shivering in a damp cell. I care about him too much. He deserves the benefit of the doubt, which is exactly what I intend to give him.

I press my back flat against a fort wall and peek around the corner. The main road is empty. In the center, where the marketplace is, there are a few lights on in the shops' second story rooms. That gives me an idea.

I turn the corner and jog up the road, checking over my shoulder periodically. In a few beats I reach the roundabout and veer left, approaching the first storefront: the boot doctor. Lois's dad has run this repair shop for years, and he and his wife always work into the late hours of the night. I creep up the wooden steps and peer through the glass door. Sure enough, Lois's parents sit at the back of the store. They're hunched over a workstation, peeling off boot soles by lamplight.

Good. It means they might not hear this next part. I hop off the porch, snag a couple of rocks off the dirt ground, and head to the back of the shop. I find Lois's bedroom window, take aim, and toss the first rock at the glass. Nothing. After the second rock makes contact, a light inside flickers on, and Lois's head appears a second later.

"Farah!" she hisses after opening the window. "Is everything okay?"

"I don't even know how to begin to answer that," I whisper back. "Throw down your ladder."

She disappears into her bedroom. A few years ago, Lois and I "borrowed" a rope ladder from the supply bins on the south side of the Village. We needed it for important occasions. Talk of breakups. Various gossip. Sleepless nights.

Wow, I think. This is actually the first true emergency.

A few moments later Lois reappears, tossing the ladder into the air and allowing gravity to unfurl it. I manage to catch the bottom before it can swing back and smack into the side of the shop. I've had a lot of practice over the years. Lois latches her end onto two hooks beneath the sill and I tug, testing the tension.

I climb up the ladder quickly and duck into my best friend's room. It's similar to mine: small, simple. There's a twin sized bed and a wooden dresser. She has a vanity with exposed, balloon-like bulbs outlining the mirror. I remember when her dad built it, he used salvaged magazine clippings as a reference. Lois loves it, even though the bulbs don't work.

I pull out the vanity bench and turn it, facing the window.

"So what's up?" Lois asks, tugging the ladder back.

"A lot," I reply, and before I sit down – before Lois even finishes rolling up the ladder – I walk over to her and give her a hug.

"Farah – ?"

"Thank you."

"For what?"

"For alerting my dad and the patrolmen when I was in danger." I pull away, smiling, and then go back to the vanity bench and sit down. Lois finishes gathering up the rope ladder and stores the bundled pile beneath her bed.

"I didn't have to do much, you know." She sits under the open window and pulls her knees behind her baggy T-shirt. Just like old times. "When I left you that day, I ran up the main road, and apparently Mr. Toff had just turned his vehicles around, because Leader and the patrolmen were already flooding back into the Village.

"All I had to do was call them over."

I nod, whispering serenely, "Well, *thank you*." I hug my arms, rubbing up and down. "We named him, by the way. Rubik. His name's Rubik."

"The alien?"

"Yeah. And, he's learning to talk. He has trouble with multiple syllables, but he's got the basics down."

"Seriously? That's...wow." Lois shakes her head in disbelief.

"It's almost like he's recalling, not learning. You know? Like he somehow knows the things of our planet already, but just needs help remembering."

"Well, maybe now that he's talking, he can explain how."

"That's the frustrating part," I say. "I don't think all of that has caught up with him yet. Like where he's from. How he got here. *Why* he's here."

Lois scratches behind her neck. "Maybe if you guys find his ship, you'll find these answers, huh?"

I straighten up. "You heard? How?"

"Mom was summoned to the assembly this afternoon

by post," she replies. So that's how they choose attendants? It's all random? Lois continues, "I overheard her telling Dad the juicy parts when she got back. How are you doing?"

"I'm terrified, Lois. I barely made it to the dunes and back!"

"But this time you'll have your guardian angel," she says, cracking a smile. I blush without realizing it. "Uh oh. He's got you blushing even when he's not around?"

"Lois – I – what are you talking about?"

"You hadn't heard that they're calling him that now?"

"Well, yeah, but – "

"And you didn't notice how Rubik was looking at you?"

My face goes blank.

"You know," she says, "that day? At the storage units?" I can tell, even in the minimal lighting, that her face loses a little color at the mention of "storage units."

Lois forces a chuckle. "You're either really oblivious, or just a good actor."

"You think he...?"

"Yes. He *likes* you, Farah. He couldn't stop staring at you."

No, Rubik doesn't like me – not in the way Lois is suggesting. He's just attached to me because I'm the first one he saw after we fended off the undergrounders. Rubik lacks our social awareness.

It's why I constantly have to remind him not to stare. Right?

"Lois, you're being ridiculous," I finally say, a little snap in my voice. "We're two different species. Don't you get that?"

"Sure, yeah," she says, looking away. "Sorry."

I sigh. "No, I'm sorry. I didn't mean to get irritated." She closes her eyes. "How are you holding up? Since...that day?"

"Since we saw Del get shot?" she says flatly, looking back at me. "You can say it, you know. Doesn't make it harder for me or something."

"Okay," I say, adding carefully, "I didn't mean that. I – let me know if you ever want to talk about it."

"I will." I can't tell if she means that, or just wants to move on.

"So, I need your help with something." I get off the bench and kneel in front of her. "Alex was arrested this morning."

She gets an immediate look of concern. "*What?*"

"Yeah, I'll explain later. But I need your help trying to see him. It could be my last chance, since I leave in the morning."

"I...what can I do?"

"Well, not exactly sure. But I thought I'd come here first, see if we could put our heads together." I sit on the hardwood floor beside her, leaning against the wall. "I'd probably just walk up to the barracks and get caught before I knew where to start."

"Maybe that's your best option."

"Hm?"

"Walk up to the barracks, get caught sneaking in, and tell the patrolman some sob story about never getting to see the love of your life again."

I consider this for a second, then shake my head. "Too risky. I don't know that I can summon tears at will."

"Shame. It's how I get Digs grounded. Works like a charm."

I laugh. "Maybe your brother could have a suggestion? He's smarter than the both of us."

"We talking about the same Digs?"

"I don't know any other Digs," I reply. It's true, though: Digs is clever, and it might be worth waking him up. Before I can suggest this, Lois snaps her fingers.

"Got it." She stands up, takes off her night shorts, puts on a pair of jeans and shoes, and retrieves the rolling ladder.

"What?" I say, rising.

She stands where I was sitting and attaches the ladder to its hooks. Since I'm not down there to catch the ladder this time, she does her best to drop it without making too much noise.

"Let's just say you're going to owe me big time after I help you tonight." Lois sticks her left leg out first, straddling the sill.

"Why don't I feel good about this?"

She swings her other foot around and descends the rope ladder. I follow, plopping onto the ground next to her a few seconds later. Above us, the stars are slightly obscured now, like a giant brume is attempting to swallow them gone. Thankfully, the moon is almost completely full, and we don't have to rely on starlight.

We head to the back of her parents' store, keeping our eyes wide so as to not trip over something hidden in the shadows. It's a difficult task because the stores in the marketplace are among the tallest structures in our Village – even though they're only two stories – and they do a good job blocking moonlight.

"This is oddly familiar," Lois says under her breath. We walk side by side down a long alley, cutting through this section of the Village to bypass the primary entrances to the barracks. "First we're sneaking in to see your alien, now your boyfriend."

I hadn't thought of that parallelism yet, but I don't address her comparison. "He's not *my* alien, Lois."

"Of course," she responds in a ribbing tone. "You gonna explain why Alex is locked up?"

I tell her the short version. "...And I haven't even had a chance to talk with him since his arrest. Everything's been going a million miles an hour."

"You've got to be kidding me," she says softly, and I see her shake her head out of my peripheral. "Do you think it's true? That he's helping plan those fake undergrounder attacks?"

It can't be true, Lois – there's no way. Only, I can't say this to her and completely mean it, can I? I know Alex has his secrets. Who doesn't? But, really, he's not in a position to have secrets right now...not with the situation he's landed himself in.

Add to the fact that something about my relationship with Alex seems off lately. For starters, how come he didn't try to see me during our Village's weeklong lockdown? He said he couldn't, but I'm not letting some rules stop *me* from sneaking in to see *him*. And, why wasn't he there, at the storage units, when Lois called everyone over for help? Even Dad, who's crippled, found a way to get there – and quickly.

The only explanation I can form is that something has been preoccupying Alex's time. What that is, I have no way of knowing until he tells me.

"What's your big plan?" I say a while later. Lois takes the hint and doesn't push me further about whether or not I believe Alex is innocent.

"Well, it's genius, really," she answers as we turn a corner. "I'm going to do the same thing the undergrounders did last week. Create a diversion. Maybe get into an argument with a patrolman. Then, you sneak in unnoticed."

I chuckle and say, "Actually, that's probably the best chance we have."

"I know," she says importantly, and I can clearly make out the wide smile on her face in the poor lighting. I'm getting ready to thank her for sticking her neck out for me again, when we hear voices up ahead. I grab Lois's hand and lead her forward, eventually ducking behind a steel barrel at the end of the alley. We have a clear line of sight to the barracks' rear entrance. Two lit lanterns hang on either side of the double doors, where a group of three patrolmen converse.

"...And I never disregard orders," one of them is saying. He's a short man with long hair in a ponytail. "Especially not when they come from this high up."

"What? Does this get you off or something?" A second patrolman rears his fist back, like he's going to swing at the shorter one, but the third patrolman restrains him.

"Better hold him back, Jon," the patrolman with the ponytail says, folding his arms. "Or he's gonna end up like Alex."

Lois and I exchange a look.

"What you're doing is wrong!" the patrolman being restrained yells. Alex is in more trouble than I feared. That much is blaringly obvious.

"Get him inside, Jon," the patrolman with the ponytail says, leaving them and walking toward a parked pickup truck. The vehicle is pretty close to us, so Lois and I instinctively lower to the ground. But not before I catch a glimpse of a bound person sitting in the backseat of the truck.

Alex.

"At least tell us where you're taking him, Everett," Jon says, opening the double doors and forcing his partner inside against his will.

"The storage units," the patrolman named Everett answers, opening the driver's side door. "Lark said to deposit him there, and that he'd take care of the rest."

I let out an involuntary scream because it doesn't

218

take me long to connect the dots. The storage units. Where Rubik was being held. Where the chains and shackles nailed to the pavement were waiting like coiled snakes...

Lark means to torture his nephew. Alex. My Alex.

I stand up against Lois's pleading and walk around the barrel, just as a flashlight pours over me and voices order me to remain still.

Chapter 43 | Rubik

The setting's changed. In my dream. I can only tell because the voice is now a female's. Kind, soft. *Wonderfully* soft.

–You are a traveler, she says lightly. –I can tell.

Me: –Oh? Then can you tell I despise it?

–Traveling?

There are loud noises behind her. Grinding, churning. Machines or monsters of some kind.

She adds, –I love discovering new places.

–So do I, but it's the traveling part I can't stand.

–That's half the fun!

–Well, see, therein lies the problem. I suppose I don't know how to have fun.

I can tell I've made her uncomfortable. I'm not carrying myself well during this exchange. She makes me nervous, whoever she is. If I could just sneak a glance at my home planet – or at least to whom I'm speaking with – so much clarity could be obtained.

But the veil will not be penetrated. My mind can't even process if we're talking in my native tongue, or if my subconscious is utilizing the language Farah taught me.

I ask, –Where are you from?

–Far away. A pause. –Came here to start over.

–Ah, so you're running.

–I never said that.

–I was implying. Filling in the blanks.

–You shouldn't do that, she replies, sounding agitated. –There's a reason they're blank.

–Look, I –

–You know, you're not very good at this.

–At?

–Carrying on a casual conversation.

I hear her stand up. Do I hold out my hand? Try and stop her? I can feel that she's still near. Hasn't left.

Me: –I'm sorry. I...I'm not the best at making friends.

–What a surprise.

–I guess you could say that *I'm* running. From what, I'm not really sure.

–Your past? Your family, maybe?

–Perhaps, but I don't know where they are now. We haven't spoken in years.

There's an even longer pause. Neither of us say anything. Then,

–You should lower your expectations, she whispers. –You don't have to make friends with everyone you meet. Sometimes you can just talk.

My heart doubles its rate. Her words are right in my ear. Her breath is warm, tingling. She must be leaning down...speaking right up to me.

–Think that's my problem? I ask.

–Yes. Don't overcomplicate it, just talk. The rest

221

will work itself out naturally.

—I like talking to you.

—Guess I do too.

Her words are playful. I can feel her sitting back down.

—That's probably why I agreed to see you again, she says. —Even if you lack tact.

I've met her before? Where? Then I should know her name. Why can't I hone in on details!

—So is this the 'rest working itself out?' I ask. —Are we…friends?

—What'd I just tell you! Her voice cracks and she begins to laugh. —You're hopeless.

She's on the verge of saying my name. I can tell. Somehow, I don't know why, I can just tell. But I'm shaken from the dream before another word is spoken. A light covers me from head to toe. I sit up in the cot, eyes squinting.

It's Father Cash. He stands at the top of the stairs, morning sunlight leaking in behind him.

"Good. You're up," he says.

I swing my feet around and touch the cold floor. "Is it time for our *de*-part-shure?"

"Yeah," he replies. "But you might wanna see this first."

Chapter 44 | Farah

"What are you doing!" Everett, the patrolman, yells. He slams the truck door shut and marches toward me – Maglite in hand. I see Jon, the other patrolman, jogging over anxiously.

"Let Alex go!" I yell back at Everett, taking a step forward. Lois grabs my T-shirt before I can advance. She mutters something along the lines of, Let's get out of here!, or Are you crazy?, but I'm too irate to tell exactly.

Everett shakes his head, his stupid ponytail swinging behind his back. "You have any idea how much trouble you can get in for being out this late?"

I hear Alex's muffled voice call out to me from behind the truck's windshield: *"Farah! Please – get home, I don't want you to see me like thi –* !"

"I'll escort her home," Jon tells Everett, speaking over Alex, which only makes me angrier.

"No you won't." My teeth are chattering I'm so upset. This is the last straw. Lark will not get away with this. No way Leader knows he's conducting these clandestine torture sessions. Once she finds out, Lark's done. Finished for good.

Jon stalks forward without waiting for Everett to take action, and he grabs both Lois and me by our arms. I yank and struggle, but it's no use – Jon's got at least a hundred pounds on me. He's one of the larger-built patrolmen. It's only a few seconds later that I hear Everett closing the driver's side door, the engine rumbling to life, and his vehicle lumbering off in the opposite direction.

The last thing I hear is Alex's faint whisper of a shout: *"Fare! I love you!"*

Under normal circumstances, hearing Alex say those three words for the first time might have changed things between us. Elicited new excitement, longing, maybe even some confusion.

But the circumstances aren't normal.

"Lark can't do this!" I whimper, tepid tears leaking down my cheeks. Jon ignores my cries, towing Lois and me down the moonlit alley. If I don't wake half the Village with all this noise, I'll be surprised.

Let them wake up, though. Let them storm the main road to see what's wrong. *I'll* tell them what's wrong. I'll tell them what Lark means to do to his own nephew!

"W-We have to tell Leader!" I yelp, kicking in my heels. It does no good. Jon lugs us along like two inanimate objects. "Let go of me!"

"Farah," he finally says, keeping pace. "You weren't supposed to see that back there."

"Well I did! Now let us go!"

"I can't," he says evenly, pulling us down an adjacent alley. "I'm taking you home. You can argue with your dad." He's not worried that I'll tell my dad what's

224

going on? Shed light on their whole operation?

"He's going to tell you the same thing," Jon continues. "There's nothing we can do."

"We can tell Leader!" I shout.

"If Alex is a traitor, like she thinks he is, then Lark has the right to institute his own interrogative tactics." Jon's grip tightens around my arm. He's not happy about any of this, either. "Basically, he's in charge of stuff like this. No matter how sick and wrong it seems."

"And if Alex isn't a traitor! Where's the proof! He deserves a trial!" I'm so furious that words are just spewing out of me. I can't contain myself. This is all so horribly wrong.

"Are you listening to yourself?" Jon says, his voice growing louder. "Who are you to question Leader's judgment? She's *Leader*! If she has enough proof to arrest him, all we can do is wait and – "

"That's not good enough!" I scream, and Jon startles me by tossing me onto the ground. I grunt, falling sideways and rolling over.

"I don't think Alex is guilty anymore than you do," Jon intones through gritted teeth. "But I have a place in this Village. So do you. It's time you learn yours." A door opens behind me, and a second later I see Dad's upside down face in the darkness.

"What the hell is going on here?" he demands, helping me to my feet.

"These two were out past curfew," Jon explains, still grasping Lois. "Sneaking around the barracks. Better

225

deal with your daughter. Leader won't be pleased with this kind of behavior during a lockdown." And with that, he stomps off, ushering Lois away angrily. She doesn't resist, or even try to glance back at me over her shoulder.

I turn to Dad, who didn't even have time to put on his glasses. "Inside," he whispers. "*Now.*"

"Dad, I – !"

"I'm not asking you again," he says firmly. I turn away, looking at the patrolmen on guard outside our fort. They seem downright shocked and are probably wondering how I snuck past their perimeter. They watch me, exchanging hushed sentences.

"Look somewhere else," I say to them, my sobs returning. I push past Dad and go straight to my bedroom, slamming the door shut. If I thought falling asleep was going to be difficult before, now it's going to be unachievable. I kick off my shoes and pace around in my socks. I try to harness my emotions, but the tears won't stop.

Alex is suffering right now. He's being subjected to his uncle's grisly methods. At this point, I want him to admit anything – even if it's all lies – so he can just face lifetime imprisonment and avoid torture.

And why did he have to say he loved me? Why *now*? Didn't he realize that would only make all of this harder? I should have yelled it back, but everything happened at breakneck speed...I never even had a chance to digest that he *actually* said it. I love you.

Do I love *him*? All I know for certain is that I wish

226

he was safe. I wish there was something I could do.

I can't tell if it's minutes or hours later, but I eventually collapse facedown into my bed. I soak my pillow with tears, and the energy I put forth with all this weeping finally knocks me out.

In the morning, I wake up with both my eyes and mouth dry. It's time to leave the Village and begin the expedition into the bowl. I'm sitting on my sheets, knees pulled up to my chest, when Dad opens the door to fetch me.

I don't say a word. Instead, I just tie on my boots, put on my backpack, and grab my clothes-filled duffle bag off the floor. I follow Dad into the kitchen, and I don't stop to accept the breakfast he offers. I keep moving.

In the front room, Rubik, Father Cash, and Nikolaos wait. Only, their backs are to me. They're staring at something through the window. I drop the duffle bag, announcing my arrival, and they all turn and look at me.

I forego asking what's outside and just see for myself. In front of our fort, stretching out into the road, are piles and piles of food and breadbaskets. It's an offering of sorts, in the highest regard. Food is such a special and important commodity in our Village, and leaving it at someone's doorstep indicates thanks and respect.

All of this doesn't make me feel any better about our situation, because acts like these are usually reserved for funerals.

I turn from the view as Dad enters the front room. He has a rucksack on his back, and he's swapped out his cane for a walking stick. He wears desert goggles with assisted lenses in place of his glasses.

Nikolaos chuckles. Then Father Cash. I even catch Rubik smiling out of the corner of my eye.

"What?" Dad asks, fiddling with his goggles.

"Nothing," I answer for the group.

This is no time for laughter, don't they get that? We're practically marching to our deaths. But if I find out that Alex didn't make it through the night, I can't say that I don't deserve this sentence. If I'd kept my big mouth shut in front of Leader and Mrs. Windsor after my round of questioning, Alex might still be free. He might even have come with us on our mission. His being locked up and tortured is my fault, and now he's either a bloodied mess, or lying in a body bag.

I shiver, walking from the window and grabbing my duffle bag. "We should go," I tell the room pointedly. Dad moves first, striding toward the door and opening it. Father Cash follows, then Nikolaos.

"Are you *oh*-kay?" Rubik asks, falling in behind me.

"Yeah." I don't say anything else. The early morning sunlight wraps around me, instantly triggering goose bumps. Leaving our cool fort and standing in the heat always has this effect on me.

Three grey vans roll up the road and park in front of us. Two patrolmen get out of each vehicle and work to collect all of the baskets.

"We'll stick together," Dad says, hobbling to the

228

large van at the head of the line. I jog ahead of him and open the passenger door, then relieve him of his rucksack. He leans his walking stick against the door and climbs in, grumbling while I help him. Beside us, Nikolaos opens the side doors and hops in, then Rubik and Father Cash. The vehicles are still running, and the air conditioning is turned up all the way.

"You good?" I ask Dad, and when he nods, I hand him his stick and rucksack. After I close the door, I pass my duffle bag to Father Cash, who leans back and stows it beneath a seat. I step inside, sitting behind Dad and next to Rubik.

"This is cozy," Nikolaos says behind me after I shut the doors. "Beats your dirt bike, Father."

"That's a fine vehicle," Father Cash snaps.

"Maybe, but riding it for miles while hugging a grown man isn't necessarily my ideal traveling situation."

Right now, Nikolaos's candor annoys me. I try to tune everything out and focus on the large task ahead of us. Once the patrolmen finish loading up all the excess food, I'll play some music. That always helps me level myself. I know I'll have to use my batteries sparingly, but all I want to do is listen to something on a constant loop to avoid having to make small talk.

"Hope your Leader caught the traitor," Nikolaos says, unzipping a pouch in one of his bags. "If they're still running around, who's to say they won't contact the undergrounders and give them a heads up about our little trip here?"

"I'm sure Leader's weighed the risks," Dad replies, looking in the rear view mirror. "That's what her advisor's for – "

"Leader's not perfect," I blurt out. "She's human. She makes mistakes." I look down at my boots, knowing everyone is staring at me quizzically – most likely wondering where this outburst came from.

Dad: "Honey, you have to – "

Thankfully, his attempt at consolation is cut short when the driver's side door opens, and a patrolman with olive skin climbs in. He wears aviator sunglasses, and the customary cargo pants, plain T-shirt, and boots of every member of the patrol.

"Name's Sam Pujol," he says in a thick Spanish accent, closing the door. "You can just call me Mr. Pujol, unless I say otherwise."

"How about Señor Pujol?" Nikolaos asks. Mr. Pujol lowers his sunglasses and gives Nikolaos a blank stare through the rear view mirror. Nikolaos swallows, sitting back in his seat, and Mr. Pujol pushes his sunglasses up.

"Once we reach the crater, we'll set up camp," he says, putting the van in drive and easing forward, "and you'll have the rest of the afternoon to map out our next set of coordinates."

I've met Mr. Pujol on a few other occasions, mainly in the mess hall during Village feasts. He's a no-nonsense man, and having him as our driver alleviates a small bit of anxiety. I know every decision he makes will be in our best interest.

We cruise down a back road, exiting the residential fort section of the Village. The place seems eerie, still. No one is outside. The marketplace is bare. Everyone was fine dropping food off, but it's like they don't want to see the recipients of their gifts. It's just as well. Seeing their worried faces might bring my dinner up...

We reach the east gate. It gradually swings open, but Mr. Pujol never has to brake because he slows down and times his turn perfectly. Behind us, the two other vans follow suit, and before it dawns on me that this is *actually* happening, we're speeding across the bowl. I turn around. Through the back window, I see my Village shrinking and shrinking.

"Here we go," Nikolaos says, sighing. I can hear Father Cash mumbling fast words under his breath. Praying. I turn to Rubik, who has his face pressed against the side glass. He stares out at the infinite sand hills.

I start to wonder if our journey will take us through another Village. I'm sure most Villages are similar to ours, but I'm still curious. I've only ever known my home, and it'd be interesting to see how other people are living in the bowl.

Up front, Dad and Mr. Pujol engage in conversation. Listening in, I learn that the other two vans are stocked with supplies. There are five other patrolmen – two in one van, three in the other. They're all specially trained in hand-to-hand combat, and possess weapons expertise. I should feel safe, then, if we come across six to ten undergrounders.

And if we come across more than that?

I turn left, watching Rubik. He's still fascinated with the outside, even though it's nearly the same view three hundred and sixty degrees around. His miniature cubes flash and pulse up his arms, neck and head. Always glowing. Always beautiful.

Yet such beauty can inflict such damage. I think back to that morning, when he saved me from the undergrounders. He was able to act quickly, like a skilled soldier, because the enemy was in such close proximity. What happens when we're out in the open?

"What *hamp*-pinned to your mom?" Rubik says quietly. I see half his face in the reflection of the window.

"She killed herself," I reply, just as equally quiet. "Five years ago, when I was eleven." No one should be able to answer a question like that so simply, and yet I've had more than enough time to accept my mother's mistake. She loved me, I've no doubt about that, and she just had a lapse in judgment. A very big lapse.

Rubik looks away from the window and meets my eye line. "I'm sar-ree."

"Don't be," I tell him. "I felt sorry for too long. I can't blame myself – can't even blame her, to be honest. Hurts too much. I focus on the good, and that helps me love her."

Rubik has nothing to say to this, for which I'm grateful. I'm okay to talk about my mom, but only in short spurts. Anything longer than this and I start to feel uncomfortable.

I glance over my shoulder. Nikolaos is almost asleep with his head tilted back, and Father Cash is writing in a leather bound journal. In the passenger seat, Dad reads from a thin book, licking his finger before turning the pages.

Rubik leans his ear against the window, like he's absorbing all the nuances the van is putting off. He closes his pale eyelids, inhaling through his translucent nose. I reach down and grab my headphones and CD player out of my backpack. With everyone doing their own thing right now, this is my chance to seek solace in my music.

An hour passes slowly, like the sands tumbling down an hourglass shoot are met with resistance. Like the hands of a clock are fueled by nearly spent batteries.

The second hour is just as slow. Nikolaos is passed out. Father Cash's eyes are closed, but I can tell he's alert because of his breathing pattern. Meditating? Rubik still gazes out the window mysteriously. Dad's moved onto a second book. Every so often he slides up his goggles, rubbing the redness around his eyes and nose. Mr. Pujol chews gum, both hands on the wheel.

We should be approaching the crater soon. It was about two hours when we traveled to the dunes last time. I lean forward in my seat, and, sure enough, I can see the pointy hills – disfigured by the heat haze. I hope Mr. Pujol and his men can assemble the tents quickly, because the temperature's bound to be soaring right now. I unclick my seatbelt and stretch out my legs. I start to wrap up my headphones, when Mr.

Pujol curses loudly.

"What's wrong!" he yells into his walkie. I spin around, looking through the rear window. The van directly behind us is swerving crazily, as if the driver's lost control.

Mr. Pujol's swearing and Farah's subsequent gasp jerk me from my thoughts. In the front seat, Thomas sets his book aside and strains his head back – looking out the back window. I copy him, seeing the vehicle behind us veering all over the place. The tires shoot dirt and sand into the air, like the driver is giving wide berths to giant, invisible pillars.

"Pull over!" Mr. Pujol shouts into a communication device. Nikolaos grabs one of his cameras and begins documenting the scene. The van jerks left, and then complies with Mr. Pujol's orders and skids to a stop. We brake as well, and so does the van at the end.

"Wait here," Mr. Pujol commands, unfastening his seatbelt. "There's a pistol underneath each seat, just in case." Then, he leaves us, locking the doors. We watch as he jogs in the sun to the middle vehicle, pulling a gun out of his belt and slowing his approach.

The side doors open, and Mr. Pujol climbs inside cautiously. We all look on silently...each second that ticks by quickens our breathing. A tiny red dot flashes on the side of Nikolaos's camera, contributing to the dramatic uncertainty.

What could possibly be going on in there?

"Mr. Miles," a voice says in our van. We all jump at

the unexpected sound, especially Nikolaos, who nearly drops his camera. I turn and watch Thomas grab the communication device Mr. Pujol was talking into earlier.

"Er, yes, this is Thomas."

Static on the other line, then, "Situation's secured. Apparently, we have two stowaways. One of 'em sneezed, startling my men and creating the ruckus."

"*Stowaways?*" Thomas repeats, meeting Farah's gaze, and then Father Cash's and Nikolaos's.

"We're bringing them over." More static. "We'll figure out what to do after setting up camp."

Thomas shakes his head, setting the communication device down. We all turn and watch as Mr. Pujol reappears outside the second van, and then he reaches in and grabs a young boy beneath his armpits, setting him on the sand. Next, he helps a girl with a familiar face.

"Lois?" Farah says beside me, gasping. "Digs?"

"You know them?" Father Cash asks.

"This is unbelievable." Thomas sounds furious. "That's Farah's friend, Lois, and her kid brother. This is unbelievable." He faces the front, folding his arms across his stomach. Nikolaos turns off his camera and puts it away.

"I had nothing to do with this, Dad," Farah says, and I believe her.

"No?" he responds, chuckling. "This isn't what you two were doing last night? Planning this?"

What's he talking about? I give Farah a sideways

look, but before she can argue further, the side doors to our vehicle open. Mr. Pujol steps aside.

"Get in," he says firmly. The boy, Digs, clambers up first – eyes downcast. He wedges himself between Nikolaos and Father Cash.

"You two have a lot of explaining to do," Mr. Pujol adds while Farah slides closer to me, making room for her friend. The doors slam shut. Mr. Pujol gets behind the wheel. We start forward again.

"Wicked..." a tiny voice declares behind me. I peer over my shoulder and catch Digs gawking at me. His curly hair is wild, messy. I try to make light of the situation.

"Hell-*low*, Digs," I say softly. The boy starts, stifling a yelp.

"He knows my name, Lois!" he says excitedly. "He knows my name!"

"Farah probably told him, moron," his sister replies. She and Farah resume a whispered conversation. Digs's face drops faintly, but it's only a second later that he recovers.

"You're an alien," the boy tells me with absolute awe.

"And you're sitting on one of my camera bags," Nikolaos tells him irritably. He reaches down and pries his bag out from beneath Digs's rear.

"Sorry about that," Lois says, motioning to her little brother with a nod. "He tends to find himself in places he shouldn't." To this Digs scowls at Lois angrily, all but sticking his tongue out.

"Hey no worries," Nikolaos replies, locking eyes with

Lois, and then scratching behind his ear nervously. They regard one another for a long beat, and this extended moment makes me slightly uncomfortable, so I face forward.

We've changed course. Now we're cruising north, along the expanse of the dunes. Trying to find level ground. About a half an hour later, we do, and then we backtrack southeast, toward the crater.

A full hour has lapsed since we picked up Lois and her brother. Mr. Pujol finally eases our vehicle to a stop as we near our destination. We all pile out, instantly taking direction from Mr. Pujol and unloading the cargo and supplies. His men set to work assembling a few tents – ones so tall, we'll be able to stand up inside.

I leave the group as Father Cash begins to hand out water canteens. Ahead of us – maybe twenty yards or so – is the crater. It looks different in the sunlight. The black scorch marks are more contrasted and defined. I stand with my toes just over the edge, wondering how I survived a crash like this...the hole is so deep and wide. If Nikolaos's theory pans out, and I truly was ejected from my ship, then my body is what caused this.

And somehow, I lived to tell the tale.

"Seems like forever ago, hm?" Farah asks, swinging a pole at her side as she strides up to me.

"Yes, it does."

"You know, at first I thought I was helping you because I wanted to prove myself to Alex," she continues, coming next to me and gazing down at the crater, "prove that I was capable."

I don't know what to say, so I just let her go on.

"But then, at some point, it became more than that." She sighs, eyes glazing. "You're so different from us, Rubik, and I don't just mean in the obvious ways. You didn't have to save me when you did, at the storage units."

"You saved me." I point. "Here."

She laughs. "I *found* you. There's a difference."

I suddenly feel compelled to take Farah's free hand in mine, offer her reassurance. I resist with much restraint and just say, "Not to me. You fow-*end* me, you saved me."

Farah turns, meeting my eyes. Strands of her yellow hair stick to her forehead in perspiration. Even though she talks to me in her soft voice, she looks so strong. Determined.

"I dreamt," I say, looking away. "Last night. I think they were more mem-*or*-ies."

"Tell me about them tonight, okay?" She takes the pole in her hand and runs her thumb down the side. A circular covering blooms. It's for protection against the sunrays.

"This is a *parasol*," Farah tells me, noticing my expression. "We had some when we were escorted to the assembly hall, remember?"

I nod, and as I'm about to attempt pronouncing the device, Farah's mouth lowers in astonishment.

"What?" I ask, concerned.

"This is the longest you've been exposed to our sun, isn't it?" She grabs my hand and pulls it toward her, stretching out my arm. My transparent skin has an almost gold-like appearance, but not as intense. It's more like...sand. My square-like cells have even lost their bluish properties.

"C'mon," Farah says, raising the parasol and leading me away from the crater. "Let's get you inside. They're prepping lunch."

We walk to the tents and enter the largest one of the four. The space inside is surprisingly large, equivalent to Thomas's work area. There are a few small tables set in the middle, where our company already indulges in a meal. The patrolmen set up maps on easels and carry disassembled cots to the other tents.

Farah collapses her parasol and sits beside Lois. I move to the back of the tent, studying the maps. The bowl — what I've heard Farah refer to this land as — appears massive in scope. Tiny black diamonds represent other Villages, and jagged lines are drawn to depict known dunes and canyons.

I hope my ship didn't scatter into too many pieces, or we may be in the badlands for quite some time.

"Now," Mr. Pujol says, walking into the tent. The door flap swings in his wake. "I hope you two are comfortable, because you've got a lot of explaining to do." He towers over the tables, eyeing Lois and Digs.

"Perhaps we should get started with our task," Father Cash says, wiping his mouth. He stands, gesturing for Nikolaos to grab his bags.

240

"I'm not finished with my sandwich!"

"Bring it then," Father Cash says, picking out a parasol from a community bin. "You can eat while we work."

Nikolaos grumbles to himself, grabbing his unfinished food. He takes up his things and follows the Father outside into the near-suffocating heat.

"Do you realize how much of our progress you have annulled?" Mr. Pujol asks, pacing around the tables. I stay by the easels, pretending not to listen. "We now have to find a way to get you back, which will cost me a van and at least two men!"

"Then don't send us back!" Digs pleas. He is sitting next to Thomas.

"I don't have enough eyes to spare," Mr. Pujol answers, taking off his sunglasses. "I already got enough liabilities on this trip."

"Gee, thanks," Thomas says, taking a bite out of his food.

"We'll help," Lois offers. "I promise you won't even know we're here."

Mr. Pujol barks a laugh. "I don't see how that's possible. And, besides, what help can you offer?"

"For starters," Digs says, mouth full, "I can load the batteries into the portable fans. It's hot in here!"

"*We're in the desert*," Mr. Pujol says, teeth clamped down. "Of course it's hot!" He then mutters in another language I don't understand, most likely swearing.

"See," Lois says, leaning over the table and scolding her brother, "this is why you should've stayed back!"

241

"You're in just as much trouble as I am, genius."

"All right enough," Mr. Pujol says, tossing his sunglasses onto the nearest table. He ruminates for a second, rubbing his neck. "What am I going to do with you two?"

"There's no way to send them back, is there?" Farah asks. Lois shoots her a hurtful look. "Not without putting us at risk?"

"No." Mr. Pujol shakes his head. "No, I don't guess there is."

"How did you even manage to sneak onto the van?" Thomas asks, sipping his canteen. Lois finishes swallowing before she explains: She noticed the vans parked outside the shop next to her parents' while the engines were getting serviced. Lois then acted on impulse, throwing a few things into her backpack and heading out the door, at which point Digs saw her. He threatened to tell on her if she didn't allow him to tag along.

"We emptied two bins full of food, and reorganized the canned goods beneath the back seats," Lois says in conclusion. "Then, we each hid in one bin. Worst two hours of my life."

"Agreed!" Digs exclaims happily. "I actually faked that sneeze, hoping you guys would hear us and we could finally get out and stretch! Paid. Off."

Lois squints one eye, looking utterly appalled. "You did that on purpose?"

"They were gonna find us sooner or later!" Digs says in defense. "I prefer the 'sooner' over the 'later,' you know?"

"I know I could strangle you right now!"

"Hell, you two!" Mr. Pujol curses. "That's going to have to stop. Got it?" They both nod in submission and return to their food. Mr. Pujol checks his wristwatch. "You've got ten minutes to finish. Then, I'm patching you through to your parents so you can tell them what's going on." He storms out of the tent, talking in his fast language again.

Digs heaves a big sigh, taking another bite out of his food. "Mom's gonna flip."

"No kidding," Lois says in agreement. I take a seat at the table next to them, and Farah hands me an unopened bag of food. I catch Lois watching me, and she immediately feigns a cough and swigs some water down.

"Seriously though," Farah says to Lois and her brother, "what were you guys thinking?"

"That we wanted to help." Digs chews his food. "When is helping someone a bad thing?" The young boy's sincere point is met with silence. Thomas appears as if he's holding back a counter argument, and he just continues with his meal. Farah shrugs, clasping her canteen in both hands.

"Helping's not a bad thing," she says, though she sounds unsure of herself. "It's just – "

"You don't think we can help," Lois interrupts. "You're not any more prepared for a mission like this than we are, you know."

"I didn't say that!" Farah looks flustered. "And

besides, it's not like I want to be here right now. None of us do."

"So, what, you didn't mean to propose this whole mission?" Lois asks snarly, setting her utensil down. "This *wasn't* your idea?"

"Y-Yes!" Farah yells. "And no. I mean, I didn't want to come, but this has to happen! We have to find Rubik's ship!"

. "Girls, I'm sorry," Thomas interjects, dabbing his mouth with a napkin. "But what exactly are you arguing about?"

"Just stay out of it, Dad!" Raising her voice like this — and toward her father, no less — is very uncharacteristic. Farah pants, glaring around the table, and eventually gets up and leaves the tent.

"Let her go," Thomas tells me, just as I've begun to rise. "She had a tough night. Needs space right now." I give him a puzzled look, then turn to Lois. Guilt and embarrassment cover her face, so she resorts back to finishing her food.

"It's Alex," Digs explains in a lowered voice. He picks up his meal and joins me at my table. "He was arrested yesterday. Then, Farah and Lois tried to sneak in and see him during the night, but I guess they showed up as he was being transferred."

Transferred? To higher-level security? They must really think he's a threat. He's barely a young man though. Farah's Leader must have a lot on him.

A few minutes later, Mr. Pujol returns and collects Digs and his sister. They head to another tent, where

244

the patrolman says they've set up a mini communication tower.

Thomas hobbles over to the easels and begins to pore over the maps, making annotations in a journal. He says that as long as there's nothing to assemble in the way of my ship, he's going to familiarize himself as best he can with the bowl. This finally gives me an opportunity to do something I've been wanting to for a while: Study the piece of debris that Nikolaos recovered from his Village. One of Mr. Pujol's men brings it to me upon request, and I use the food table as an observation platform.

The metallic rubble is charred, mostly likely from when it pierced this planet's atmosphere. As a whole, it's not very heavy, but it's not light either. I can tell, even past the damage, that the alloy used in my vehicle's construction is powerful and unique.

And then there are these weird, faded inscriptions. The rune-like letters are very angular – with no curves – and they're cut off. Like the rest of the word is inscribed on the missing half of this debris.

Does it read, Prison? Banishment? I certainly felt like I was imprisoned or enduring banishment when I was with the stars. Coasting through galaxies as my weak conscience slowly slipped into nonexistence. I sense a shiver coming on. I don't want to return to that choking, smothering cycle. Facing uncertainty in a foreign planet is, without a doubt, preferable to that...

Will I lie? Tell Farah and this excavation team that the lettering spells something it doesn't, just to protect myself? I may not have to be faced with a decision like that because, in the end, I may not remember how to translate the inscriptions.

Think, Rubik. What word or words do these letters form? I recall my dreams for assistance. So far, I've had a conversation with a female, where I proved my inability to carry on a simple conversation. But I also revealed to her that I'm running, though I couldn't specify from whom. She suggested my past, my family. I told her I hadn't spoken to them in a while. Years.

There were other conversations. With someone who has apparently sworn allegiance to me. Why? I'm someone worth swearing allegiance to? We argued, this person and I, because I wanted to hide – split up. They suggested we stick together. I then mentioned closure. From what? Next I said, Ready the Leaper. What's a Leaper?

The clues are all over the place, spinning around my head so fast that I don't have a good chance at reaching out and grabbing one. I want to flip this table over I'm so overwhelmed! Why can't I remember anything? I pick up the piece of my ship, seconds away from throwing it off to the side, when a small moment of clarity begins to transpire.

This writing...I believe I know it. I've been looking at it wrong. My insides start to pulse with exhilaration. It's been there, right in front of me all this time, and I've just been overcomplicating it.

"Thomas," I say, pronouncing his name better than anything I've managed to say yet. "Look at this."

He turns from the maps, an expression of surprise on his face. He's noticed the change in my voice. The poise and self-confidence. He limps toward the table, but before he makes it all the way, Mr. Pujol rushes inside the tent.

"Third alarm," he says intensely. "We've got to brace our encampment at once. Storm's on the approach."

Chapter 46 | Farah

Storm clouds billow over distant dunes like smoke from a wildfire that can't be tamed. I watch them slosh through the sky slowly, monstrous mouths bent on consuming everything.

Patrolmen work around me quickly, hammering and clamping down our gear. Mr. Pujol shouts orders into the air, and his crew obeys. I wipe grit from my face and rush toward Dad, who's being helped out of the main tent by Rubik.

"The vans," Dad says, putting a hand on my shoulder. "Mr. Pujol wants us to ride this out in the vans." The vehicles are parked only a short distance away from our camp, and I can already see Lois and Digs waiting in the middle seat of the van we rode in earlier.

"C'mon!" my best friend yells, opening the side doors. We make it to her a few seconds later, and between the three of us, we've helped Dad into the middle seat in no time. Beyond the vans, I see torrents of rain and sand plowing through the desert destructively. Nikolaos and Father Cash race over from the crater, rolled-up sheets of paper sandwiched between their arms.

"Everyone okay?" the Father asks, and he has to

raise his voice slightly over the increasing winds.

"So far," I reply. Rubik opens the passenger door, motioning for me to take cover. Before I do, one of the patrolmen runs up, pointing a weather apparatus at the far off skies.

"It's heading east," he says over the wind, studying the readings on the screen. "With any luck, we'll only catch blips of it."

I look around us. Our hair and clothes are blowing. Tent flaps flutter crazily. Sand clouds are appearing outside our camp. If this is just a ripple effect of the storm, can we outlast a blip of it? Or worse, the heart of it? I stomach my fears and step into the van. Rubik shuts the door behind me, waits as Father Cash and Nikolaos climb inside, and then hops in last – slamming the side doors emphatically.

I peer through the window, watching Mr. Pujol and his patrolmen finish up their tasks and seek refuge in the other two vans.

"Mr. Miles," a voice cackles through the walkie on the dashboard. I peel it from the Velcro and pass it to Dad, who sits between Lois and Digs.

"Yes," Dad says.

"This should move on soon. However, if it worsens, I'm coming over there. We'll have to race out of the storm and abandon camp."

"Understood." Dad hands me the walkie, and I put it back. Abandon camp. That would be a cumbersome, counter productive task. It means we'd have to return to our Village and stock up on more supplies – losing an entire day in the process.

Who knows, though? This storm might be enough of an excuse for Dad and me to stay behind. Could end up being a blessing in disguise. If nothing else, Lois and Digs would be forced back home.

The whole atmosphere around the crater has grown dark. Nikolaos clicks on a flashlight just as our van begins to sway and careen subtly in the wind. Droplets of rain smack against the side and roof every so often.

"Haven't seen a storm this bad in years," Father Cash says in his deep tone. A flash of lightning blossoms in the sky quickly about a mile away. Thunder cracks.

I need a distraction. "Were you guys able to figure anything out at the crater?" I ask Nikolaos.

"Took some semi-complicated math," he replies, pointing his flashlight out the back window, "but Father and I were able to estimate some crash sites based on the speed of Rubik's ship and the fall patterns of the debris. If we didn't have the footage, it'd be like looking for marbles in a pitch black warehouse."

"Wait, so you know where we have to go next?" Digs asks, turning to face Nikolaos, who sits between Rubik and the Father.

"We have a general idea," Father Cash answers. "Which is better than nothing. Turns out a large piece of Rubik's ship fell pretty close to where we are now."

Outside, the winds are now screeching and howling. Pushing against our vehicle like they're testing our weight. I hold onto the handle bar above my seat.

Please don't let this get out of control, I think. *Please.*

But that's just what it does.

A chunk of minutes later, our van is almost completely teetering. Lois and I let out gasps, and Digs has buried his face in Dad's arm. Dad takes off his goggles, squinting out the window. There's nothing but gusts of sand and darkness. It's like this storm appeared out of nowhere!

The driver's side door opens and Mr. Pujol jumps in. "Seatbelts," he shouts, shutting the door and starting the engine. He stomps on the gas pedal, and we barrel forward. The headlights only do us so good, and Mr. Pujol relies on his compass as he drives south.

I see more lightning in the side mirror. Following us. Chasing us. How are we going to possibly outrun this? We don't stand a chance.

"Hold onto something!" Mr. Pujol shouts over the storm. He doesn't have to offer this command. We all – every single one of us – are either grasping each other, or grasping a part of the van's interior.

We cut left, then right. Our bodies jerk in aggressive synchronization with the vehicle's movement. During one turn, I hit my head against the window, and my vision sputters. I feel blood on my temple, but we're moving so unpredictably I don't have a spare moment to nurse the injury.

The loudest thunder yet seems to resonate through my bones. Digs yelps, and I hear him begin to cry.

"Follow me deeper south!" Mr. Pujol shouts into his walkie. "Follow me!"

We swerve and weave, zigzagging through rainfall and sand clouds. I can't make out anything in front of us, so how can Mr. Pujol? There's no obvious passage to safety. He must be guessing. It's the only thing he *can* do.

Is this how it all ends for us? I figured, if anything, the undergrounders would ambush us. Take Rubik prisoner and kill us off. But this? A desert storm? We never even had a chance to recover what we set out to find...

My bleeding's getting worse. I can feel it dripping onto my forearm now.

"Dad," I whisper, turning to him. No good. He's holding onto Lois and Digs, and the winds are close to deafening. He'll never hear me.

Images are blurry. I pray it's dizziness from the fast driving, and not blood loss. I have a feeling it's a combination of the two.

"Rubik," I say, knowing he doesn't stand a better chance at hearing me anymore than Dad. Yet, I try anyway. Rubik is gripping the back of the seat in front of him. To his left, Nikolaos and Father Cash are doing the same thing. Teeth gritted. Eyes closed.

More lightning. More thunder.

The van nose dips slightly, and then drops back onto all four wheels. Mr. Pujol swears, clenching the steering wheel. I attempt to glance at the speedometer, but I already know we're at full speed. Either that will prove to be enough, or it won't.

I say inward prayers. It's what my mom would do.

It's probably what Father Cash is doing. I can sense my consciousness slipping...ever so gradually...I'm about to black out. I fight it. With what little strength I have left I fight it.

I'm almost successful, but it's pointless. The van suddenly flips forward, crashing and sliding upside down across the sand. Everything goes black.

...

...

...Heavy breathing.

...Panting.

...

...

...Gasping.

...

...

My eyes flutter open. I dangle upside down by my seatbelt. It's dusk outside. The storm has passed, and hours have lapsed. My throat is dry. I want to scream out, but my throat is so agonizingly dry! My view focuses.

I see Father Cash through the rear view mirror, and he's cut and bruised pretty bad. He uses a pocketknife to try and tear through his seatbelt. Rubik is coming to. He coughs into his fists.

Dad is already checking on Lois and Digs, who both begin to whimper as they wake up and assess our predicament. Nikolaos cusses, rubbing his eyes. His nose is bleeding, but because he hangs upside down, it's not a constant drip. If he doesn't right himself soon, he could choke and drown.

"You okay up there, hon'?" Dad asks. I barely hear him. My ears are ringing wildly.

"Y-Yeah," I say weakly, reaching around my waist for the seatbelt buckle.

"Hold on," Rubik tells me from the back of van. He's well spoken and his voice is steady – so much so that I notice it amidst our dismal situation. "I'll come get you." He yanks his seatbelt buckle free in one motion, tumbling down onto the roof of the van a second later.

"W-Where's Mr. Pujol?" I stammer, realizing that the driver's seat is empty. The windshield is intact, albeit badly cracked, but that means the patrolman wasn't thrown from his seat. His door is slightly ajar, and the seatbelt is undone.

He must be fine – checking on his men or something. But...would he do that before making sure we're okay? I want to point this out, but I've said about all I can. I need water. My coarse throat won't take much more talking.

One of the side windows is completely busted out, and Rubik climbs out of the van through the opening. Next, he pulls open my door, and I watch him – upside down – as he holds me secure with one arm, and with his free hand he pulls my seatbelt apart.

He carries me out of the van carefully and sets me on the sand.

"Make sure you haven't broken anything," he says, his speech flawless. "I'm going to free the others." He leaves, crawling back inside the van. How is it that one moment Rubik's struggling with multi-syllable words, and the next, he's speaking like it's been his language all along?

Did our accident revive Rubik's memories? Set something right?

I sit up cautiously, a wave of wooziness almost overcoming me. The bleeding next to my ear has stopped, and I feel around my face for any other injuries. Surprisingly, I find none. Past our van, I see the other two vehicles – one lies on its side, the other is bottom up. There's no visible movement I can make out in the twilight. No sign of Mr. Pujol and his fellow patrolmen.

I push off the dirt and sand, rising to my feet shakily. There's still a high pitched tone vibrating in my head. I concentrate on it, hoping to subdue it, but that only centralizes and increases the ringing.

Don't look up, I tell myself. Don't look down. Just look straight ahead.

I do, and I see Rubik emerging from our van. He holds a shaken up Digs in one arm, and leads a stumbling Lois with his other hand. His instinct for helping others is so natural, it's like he was bred for it.

"You okay?" he asks, setting Digs down gently. I nod, leaning over to check on Digs.

"Help the others," I tell Rubik in a hoarse whisper. He doesn't have to be told twice. A second later and he's jogging back to the upturned vehicle. That's when I note his physical change, subtle though it may be: Rubik's particles and cubes have faded. They're not as

255

bright as they should be, especially close to nighttime. Is his skin losing its see-through quality? Or is my vision just that messed up right now?

"Where do you hurt the most?" Lois asks, tending to her little brother. I see a few cuts on her left arm, but other than that and minor disorientation, she appears fine. Thank God for that.

"All over," Digs replies, moaning. His right eye is swollen shut and blackened. He's also got a busted lip. Lois starts to check his arms and legs for broken or dislocated bones. He doesn't let out any sharp cries, so I exhale in relief. Hopefully, that means he hasn't broken anything.

"Mr. Pujol," I manage to say, trying desperately to form excess saliva in my mouth so I can swallow it. Lois looks up at me and nods.

"I'm fine here," she tells me, smiling. "You go check on the patrolmen." I smile back and make my way toward the immobile vans. The wheels aren't spinning. No smoke rises from the engines. We've been here for a while. So where's the rest of our team?

I check the first van. Nothing.

I check the second van. Nothing.

They're all gone. But to where? There *has* to be an explanation. Maybe they regrouped after we crashed, and they've gone ahead by foot to secure a perimeter? That doesn't make any sense. Mr. Pujol's priority would've been ensuring our wellbeing. He'd have revived us. Checked on us.

"Farah!" Rubik calls out. It's strange enough

hearing him enunciate perfectly, let alone shouting. This is the first time he's risen his voice around me. I turn from the crashed vehicles and walk back to the group.

"Look," Rubik says when I reach them. He's motioning to the ground, where Father Cash is on his knees, pointing a flashlight. Footprints, in the sand. Lots of them, outside the driver's side door and leading away from us.

Dad limps toward me, putting an arm around my shoulder and handing me a canteen. I take it gratefully and pour water over my face and down my throat.

"Thanks," I say feebly, giving him back the canteen.

"This is curious," Father Cash says. He stands up, guiding the flashlight's beam over the sand and down the collection of footprints. "It appears as if Mr. Pujol was dragged away. Look at the wide marks between the boot prints."

"The undergrounders," Nikolaos says, walking up to us. He's bandaged his nose, and he passes Dad the first aid kit. Dad digs through it, procuring a few Band-Aids. I stand still as he applies them to the cuts on my temple.

"I highly doubt it," Father Cash answers. "For starters, they would've covered their tracks. Whoever took our patrolmen left a clear trail in their wake. And, why didn't they kidnap Rubik?"

"Touché." Nikolaos takes the first aid kit from Dad when he's finished.

"Did you notice the same pattern in the ground near the other vehicles?" Father Cash asks me. He flicks off the flashlight.

"No, but I wasn't looking at the ground," I reply. "Plus, the sun's almost all the way down. Could barely see anything anyway."

Father Cash shakes his head slowly. "I'm willing to bet we'll find the same thing." He and Nikolaos leave, striding toward the other vans.

"How are you?" I ask Dad, turning to him.

"Bad news," he utters gravely. "I think I'll have a limp for the rest of my life."

I roll my eyes. "Only you could make light of a situation like this." Rubik and I help him away from the van to where Lois and Digs are sitting. They're both solemn-faced, wearing five Band-Aids between the two of them. Currently, Digs is leaning against his sister, sniffling.

"Right here," Dad says, and we help him to the ground next to Lois. He bites his lip, clearly in pain.

"Dad," I say once we've set him down. "You're hurt." Before I can get anything out of him, Father Cash and Nikolaos jog back over.

"So?" Dad asks, avoiding my gaze. "What'd you find?"

"Same thing," Nikolaos tells us. "Tons of boot prints and drag marks."

"Why?" Rubik says, his insides glowing dimly. I wonder if anyone else will notice Rubik's change in voice and appearance. "Why take *only* the patrolmen?"

258

"If we can figure out who did this," Dad says, shifting his weight on the sand, "maybe we can figure out why. Let's check the rest of the supplies. See if they took anything."

"Don't think they did," Nikolaos replies. "When I grabbed the first aid kit from the back of the van, the trunk was a mess, sure, but it looks like everything's still there. Plus, I had to pry the door back. It hadn't been opened yet."

"And, most of our stuff is back at camp anyway," Lois adds, her tone deflated. "Which majorly sucks, by the way."

"You're telling me." Nikolaos pops his knuckles anxiously. "You have any idea how much camera equipment I have back there?"

"Okay, obvious question," I say, folding my arms. "What do we do next?"

"I propose we find a way to right one of the vans," Father Cash says. "Then, we drive back to camp and salvage our supplies from the storm's aftermath."

"That will only work if the vehicle's are still drivable," Dad says, taking off his goggles and rubbing his eyes. "I suggest we take advantage of the cool evening and follow the footprints before the wind erases them. Those aren't just paid muscles who've been taken from us. They're *people*, from our Village. Some fathers. We have to try and rescue them."

"Too bad our roles aren't reversed," Nikolaos says, "and we're the ones captured, waiting until the patrolmen come to our rescue. Least *they* would know what to do."

"We should still try," I say, coming to Dad's support.

Father Cash sighs through his nose. "I can only respect this decision. So, Rubik, Nikolaos and I will follow the trail then? You four will stay behind?"

"Splitting up is a bad idea," I say. "We'll be more vulnerable."

"She's right," Dad declares in agreement, gesturing for Rubik to help him up.

"Dad, wait – "

"We need to stick together," he continues over me. "It's our best shot at surviving this."

"You should first rest some more," Rubik says, helping Dad up anyway.

"And give the footprints more time to blow off?" Dad chuckles. "Not a chance. Farah, fetch my walking stick, would you?"

"Isn't it back at camp?" I ask. "I don't remember you bringing it from the tent."

It's almost switched from dusk to full darkness, but I can still see Dad pale. He swallows, then puts on his goggles.

"Let's go then," he proclaims, turning on his good foot and limping away from us. Digs and Lois get to their feet, and Nikolaos hands them a water bottle apiece. I reach out to grab Rubik, but he doesn't notice my effort because he's already making his way toward Dad to give assistance.

I was hoping to have a word, see if Rubik can explain these indistinct transformations he's undergone. Although, I shouldn't deem his perfected speech as "indistinct." He's talking like one of us now. I'm shocked no one else has said anything.

I fall in line beside Nikolaos, and the two of us bring up the rear of the procession. Lois and Digs walk right in front of us, then Rubik and Dad. Father Cash is at the lead, flashlight passing over the footprints. He carries a gun in his other hand.

The sky is purple, sprinkled with stars and angled constellations. I look over my shoulder, taking a last glance at the capsized vans.

"I'm sure they're alive," Nikolaos says softly. I face forward. "Mr. Pujol and the other patrolmen are trained for this kind of stuff."

"I'm sure they're alive, too," I say. We're both lying – trying to make the other one feel better. It makes me sick.

Chapter 47 | Rubik

I help Farah's father along, and I hear every grunt and moan he lets out – try though he might to keep them silent. Up ahead, we're approaching a small hill, beyond which I know we'll only find more and more desert.

Thomas's limp notwithstanding, we're actually moving at a decent pace, and our cadence is that of a fast walk. I wonder how long Farah's father will be able to endure this.

"Let me know when you need to rest," I tell him. I hold him under his left arm, gripping lightly.

"I'll rest," he says, panting, "when everyone else needs to." Stubborn man. Can't say I fault him, though: I wouldn't let an injury impede our progress either.

I sigh inwardly. Our current situation – lost in the desert, riddled with injuries – is my doing. If I'd never crashed here, on this planet, Farah and her people would be going about their lives. Safe behind the walls of their Village. They've already lost two patrolmen for my sake. How many more lives will be taken at my expense? Mr. Pujol and his men?

No. I can't let that happen. I won't. All I've done since arriving here is draw the undergrounders' attention, generating panic and fear in the process. I've been a burden, there's no two ways about it, and I have to stop. Even if the only way I can do that is by removing myself from the equation.

I have to turn myself in to the undergrounders.

I know the arguments. Why give in now, when we're so close? Why hand those evil men a potential weapon in the form of my strength and skill? Why put Farah and her Village through so much, only to abandon them when things seemed hopeless?

Yet, the thought of any harm coming to Farah, or her father and friends, is unbearable. I'll deal with those questions when the time's right. For now, I will heed Thomas's advice.

"But we," he told Farah after the assembly proceeding, "have to focus on what we can control."

Here, in this world, where sandstorms run wild and savage men raid Villages, I can't control much. But I *can* control what I do.

So it's time to do something.

"The boot prints lead over this hill," Father Cash says, shining his light across the ground and up the mini dune. He stops, waiting until we catch up to him, and then he grabs Thomas's other arm. Together, Father Cash and I lead Farah's father up the incline. I sniff, suddenly smelling the faint scent of...smoke?

When we reach the top, my mouth drops.

"Wha...?" Farah says, coming up beside us. We're all fixated with the view below us: At the foot of the uneven slope, about a quarter of a mile away, is a large camp. Smoke rises toward the stars from different sources.

"Another Village?" I ask, turning to Thomas, then Father Cash.

"Too small," they both reply, almost at the same time.

"Guys, look." Nikolaos gets to his knees, indicating to the boot prints. The prints all seem to gather in the same area, then disappear, replaced by wider markings with square-patterned tread.

"They had trucks waiting for them," Thomas says, leaning all his weight against me so Father Cash can join Nikolaos. Farah, Lois and Digs huddle around, getting a peek as well.

"So?" Farah eventually says, straightening up. "Do we go on?" I want to tell her no, *we* don't go on – something about all this doesn't seem right. And I mean more than just the patrolmen getting kidnapped. If that's not another Village or an undergrounder base down there, what is it?

But what good will debating do? Farah was right earlier – we can't separate. Too much of a risk.

"C'mon, Rubik," Thomas mutters. "I'm not getting younger." I nod, easing him forward carefully. Because of the subtle drop in elevation, I'm forced to half carry, half guide Thomas. I hear the rest of the group falling in behind us.

"You gonna tell me where you're injured?" Farah asks, coming to Thomas's other side. She grabs his right arm and helps me. We march down the sand in unison, taking extra precaution.

"Probably not," he replies simply, smiling despite his discomfort. Farah sighs, proclaiming her frustration.

"How about you, Rubik?" she says. "You hurt?"

"No," I reply. "I feel fine."

"You certainly sound it," Thomas notes. "Was I not paying attention when you improved your speech and diction?"

I see Farah's face light up. "You noticed, too?" she asks Thomas.

"It happened in the tent," I explain to them, "when I was examining the debris. Something clicked."

"That makes absolutely no sense," Farah's father retorts. "But then, I am talking to an alien. Can't really rule anything out anymore." The ground starts to level, making our trek easier.

"What did you discover," Thomas continues, "back at our camp? Before the storm hit, you were getting ready to show me something."

I open my mouth – the revelation about the strange writing on the tip of my tongue – when gunshots ring out. It's coming from up ahead, in the camp. Instinctively, I lower Thomas to the ground – forcing Farah to do likewise.

I turn around. Father Cash and Nikolaos are already on their stomachs, and so are Lois and her brother.

A minute passes, and the gunshots subside. The camp is too far away to be a threat, yet I ask anyway, "Everyone okay?" Digs is breathing madly, quite shaken up, but he still replies, Yes, along with the rest of the group.

Slowly, we get to our feet. Did we just hear an execution? Were Mr. Pujol and his men shot?

"We have to hurry," Father Cash announces, jogging ahead of us – pistol in hand. Farah and I pick up her father, and the three of us try to sprint walk. Nikolaos passes us, pulling a pistol similar to the Father's out of his back pocket. Lois and Digs remain behind us, their arms around one another.

We hold a constant pace, and, before much longer, we're sneaking in the shadows of a tall, twisted metal fence. Heaps of junk and stacked cars loom above us, and I see a giant crane off to the side. From within the compound, dogs bark and laughter shrills.

"I know what this is," Thomas whispers as we set him down silently. I wave Lois and Digs over, and they each take a place on either side of Thomas.

"Did you grab another weapon?" I ask Nikolaos quietly, and he pulls a second pistol from the waist of his jeans. I take it and hand the gun to Thomas. Father Cash gives Farah the flashlight, and then he creeps right up to the fence – checking for tears or openings.

"Stay here, with your father," I instruct Farah, "and shine this into the sky if you feel the least bit threatened."

"Rubik – "

"It's not safe," I say, putting my hands on her shoulders. I can feel her shaking. Suddenly, I have a strong yearning to carry her away from this place. Hold her against my body until the trembling stops. I stare into her deep green eyes...they're little great nebulas, like the ones in space. Beautiful, terrifying.

"*Rubik!*" Nikolaos whisper shouts from the fence. "Come give us a hand!" I turn from Farah and head toward Father Cash and Nikolaos, but Thomas says, while I'm still within earshot: "Be careful. I know what this is."

I don't have time to stop and ask him to elaborate. Nikolaos and the Father are already peeling back a sliver of the fence. I jog up to them, grabbing the same piece of wire and ripping upward. I manage to create a wide gap – wide enough for us to crawl through one by one.

"Whoa," Nikolaos says as I fold back the fence. "You make that look too easy."

Father Cash drops to his hands and knees and scurries through the opening. Nikolaos goes next, then me. Once on the other side, I reach through the wired fence and bend it back, making it look like it's restored. I catch Farah watching me from several yards off. I show her no emotion before spinning around and following Nikolaos.

The shadows are broad within the compound. We wend around demolished vehicles and canine corpses, and the pungent smell of rust and rot is strangling. Nikolaos and Father Cash hold their pistols in both hands, and they point the weapons out in front of them every turn we take.

The laughter and howling is getting louder.

Finally, after about a quarter of an hour later, we've managed to slink toward the center of the compound unnoticed. The only thing standing between us and the commotion is a towering pile of trucks and junk. Off to the side are two or three steel barrels, and inside them tiny fires flicker in the night.

"Slowly," Father Cash mouths, his back against our makeshift barrier. He inches away from Nikolaos and me, and is the first one to peek around the side. Nikolaos copies him, getting closer to the ground. I inhale softly. I'm not sure I want to see what's on the other side, but I have to look. I step out, careful to remain hidden, and look over the Father's head.

It's our patrolmen. Five of them – gagged and bound to individual poles. They're being held captive in a sort of courtyard vicinity, surrounded by capsized trucks and beams of artificial light. A sixth body lies facedown in the sand, fresh blood pooling around the torso area. He's dead. One of ours has been shot dead.

Nikolaos stifles a gasp and points: There are dozens and dozens of children, ages seven to seventeen, sitting atop the trash and debris that surrounds our patrolmen. They wear primitive clothing made of rags and scrap metal, like it's armor.

"See? See!" a tall child shouts, appearing from the side of the courtyard. He strides with the confidence of a leader, wearing a belt of chains and pointy shoulder guards. I hear a crazed hunger in his voice. "This is what you make us do! You make us do this!"

The patrolmen moan in response, and the courtyard echoes with adolescent laughter. The scene is absolutely disturbing. How can mere children act so barbaric?

"No?" the child leader says, hands on his hips. "Then *tell us where he is!*" That's it. They're looking for me. I can stop this madness.

"Don't," Father Cash whispers, as if he can hear my thoughts. "They're not referring to you. They could've easily taken you from the van." He has a point. Now that he mentions this, how did they not see me? Was I hidden that well in the backseat?

Regardless, I should just reveal myself now, and maybe that will be enough to scare the children off. It's worth the brazen move, especially if it means saving the rest of our patrolmen.

A pack of wild dogs begin to fight over the sixth patrolman's corpse. The child leader charges forward, kicking them away bravely.

"Shoo!" he screams. "You'll spoil your feast!" When the growling and barking dies down, and the dogs finally scatter, the boy turns and walks up to the patrolman in the middle. After he removes the gag, I see that it's Mr. Pujol.

"Now let's try again." The child leader circles Mr. Pujol like a bird of prey. "I ask where he is, you tell me. Simple, right? Simple!" Mr. Pujol's nose is visibly broken. Did the crash do that, or was it these savages?

The child leader stops pacing, standing right in front of Mr. Pujol. "Where is the man named Lark?" he says through gritted teeth.

That's who they're looking for? I glance down at Nikolaos, and we swap looks of bewilderment.

"I-I told you," Mr. Pujol sputters, breathing uneasily. "We d-don't know who t-that is."

"You're lying," the boy replies with bone-chilling steadiness. He holds out his hand, and a girl who wears oversized boots and elbow pads over her dirty garb appears. She hands her leader a spear, and then reverently backs away.

"Your friend got off easy," the child leader continues. "Bullets kill faster than stabbing."

"S-Stop! Please!"

Hearing Mr. Pujol's desperate cries is all it takes for me to act. I push through Father Cash and Nikolaos and sweep into the courtyard. A vast, collective gasp fills the air, and the child leader spins around. He drops his spear in fear, acting like a young boy for the first time.

"Let them go," I say, deepening my voice. I point at the leader, making sure everyone can see my clear skin and sparkling insides. Atop their makeshift seats, the rest of the children begin to whisper. The leader backs into a shadow, overtly wavering.

I move toward Mr. Pujol and remove his bounds. I catch him before he collapses and sit him up against the base of the pole. Father Cash and Nikolaos eventually come to my assistance, helping me free the rest of the patrol.

"Our men require water," I say to no one specifically.

There's a pause, but then I actually hear faint footfalls as someone runs off – hopefully to retrieve canteens. I untie the last patrolman, grabbing his arm and guiding him to the ground.

Then, I turn to the child leader. "You killed one of ours," I tell him, balling my hands into tense fists. I let Nikolaos and Father Cash check on the patrolmen, and I close the gap between me and the quivering boy. He slides to the dirt ground, holding up his hands.

"Wait! Please!" he yelps. "He was dead when we found them! The crash killed him! We just shot him to scare the others! I swear!" I tighten my fists even more, ensuring the taut muscles in my arms overwhelm the boy with intimidation.

"He's telling the truth," says the girl in the elbow pads. She walks into the courtyard with a large pail filled to the brim. Water splashes around as she carries it awkwardly. Father Cash stands up, taking the pail from her and distributing drinks among the patrolmen.

"And what about that spear of yours?" I say, turning back to the leader. "Looked like you were getting ready to do something you'd regret."

"No!" the boy shouts, his face revealing so much dread. That was all an act, I think, when he was parading around the courtyard before his peers. This boy can't be older than thirteen or fourteen. "At worst I was going to hit him a few times with the hilt, but then we'd let them go! We *always* let them go!"

I flip my hand indifferently, and even this small

gesture causes the boy to flinch. I leave him in the shadows and rejoin Father Cash and Nikolaos.

"I told Oliver this was a bad idea," the girl says, standing behind the Father. She looks to be about Digs's age. "But he never misses a chance to grab Village patrolmen and question them." They've done this before? The leader, Oliver, eluded to that when he said they "always let them go," but hearing it come from this child of a girl makes it even more unbelievable.

"You're incredible, by the way," she says matter-of-factly, walking right up to me and prodding my skin. Perhaps she's better suited to be this group's commanding presence than Oliver. She shows no fear whatsoever. Only wonder and curiosity. And, she can apparently read people too – gauge their character – because she knows that I could never hurt her, or any of the other children.

"C'mon, everyone!" she yells to her on-looking peers. "He's safe!"

In a few short moments, a frenzy of excited children flood in around us. Some reach in and touch my arms and back. Others gawk at me from afar – feverishly talking and whispering amongst themselves. I move back a little, but the throngs of children only follow like a shadow. I look over my shoulder. Father Cash is still giving the patrolmen water, but Nikolaos is beaming up at me.

"You're a god to them," he says, getting to his feet. I swallow, turning away from him and watching as my

272

audience doubles. The entire courtyard is packed with teenagers and younglings. Jumping on their toes to get a good look.

I can handle the guardian angel title. But a god? I'm far from that.

"Go get Farah and everyone else," I shout to Nikolaos over the chatter. I can't deal with all this alone.

I need Farah – more than ever.

I can't take this.

I can't stand here, inactive, and do nothing. How long's it been since they went in there? Five, ten minutes? Too long. Did they try and call out to us for help, and we just couldn't hear them? Someone needs to go check on them and –

"I know this place," Dad says again. I stop pacing and look down at him.

"What do you mean?" I ask. "How?" His eyes have a far off look to them. I can tell even though he wears goggles and it's dark.

"The rumors started about a year and a half ago," Dad says, and beside him, Lois and Digs perk up. "Orphans. Sneaking out of Villages at night and disappearing into the bowl."

"I've never heard about that!" Digs says earnestly.

"We don't have an orphanage at our Village," Dad replies. "Not all Villages do. Anyway, the rumor is that they found a place to survive. And, a way to eat and thrive...

"Other Villages sent search parties, and we even contributed to the efforts at one point. But the orphans didn't want to be rescued. When they were eventually found, they resisted with open hostility."

I furrow my brow. "And what, they were found here?"

"Called themselves the junkyarders," Dad says, nodding, and I almost laugh. Digs's eyes have widened though.

"That's so cool," he says. I guess for a ten-year-old, the idea of living without grownups and doing your own thing *does* sound cool.

"Except for the hostile part," Lois says, and then her face changes from somewhat lax to animated. "Look! It's Nikolaos!"

I whirl around, and sure enough see Nikolaos's form materializing in the shadows.

"You guys are not going to believe this," he says, peeling back the damaged portion of the chain-link fence. Lois and I help Dad to his feet.

"Hostile orphans?" Digs exclaims, bolting forward.

"I – how did you know?" Nikolaos scratches his head, and is forced to step aside as Digs crawls through.

"Digs! Stop!" Lois calls out. "It's not safe!" We help Dad slowly, taking little steps because of the lack of light.

"Actually, the situation's almost completely under control," Nikolaos assures. "And it's all thanks to Rubik." Nikolaos catches us up to speed as my best friend and I help Dad onto his knees. He clambers through the opening, then Lois, and I go last. We don't bother restoring the fence once I've reached the other side.

"Which patrolman died?" Dad asks darkly.

"Don't know his name," Nikolaos answers, navigating us around piles of cars and junk. "And Mr. Pujol's kind of in a recovery state right now. You'll have to indentify the body."

Another dead. That's three in over a week. The bowl bestows many hardships upon us, so you'd think I'd be able to swallow pills like this with no sweat. But death...so up close and personal...it's nightmare inducing.

I distract myself by taking in my surroundings while Lois and I help Dad along. If these kids really do refer to themselves as junkyarders, then it's fitting. There are heaps of old appliances and various other things, as well as stacks of crushed vehicles that stretch into the night sky.

It appears as if the kids have repurposed the cars on top of the stacks, turning them into tiny homes. I can tell because little faces poke out and watch us from above as we pass. There are rope ladders that dangle from each "car house," and strings of lights extend from stack to stack.

We're essentially walking through a junkyard village.

"It's just up ahead," Nikolaos says as we approach several steel barrels that flicker and smoke, fires burning within each one.

I can hear enthused babble beyond the last stack of vehicles, and Digs ignores his sister's scolding and runs up ahead. When Lois, Dad, Nikolaos and I finally turn the corner, my breath is stolen from me.

There are children *everywhere*. They wear what appear to be scraps of metal and rags. Some kids even have old hubcaps tied to their backs, like it's protective gear or armor. There are teenagers, too, dressed in similar fashion.

Overturned trucks form a semicircle around us, and I see Father Cash, Mr. Pujol, and the rest of our patrolmen off to the side – drinking from a bucket. Rubik is currently the center of attention. Literally. He's right in the middle of the crowd, arms spread out. Kids leap up and down, trying to get a better look. Others clap jovially, or high-five one another.

"Hi." A little girl walks up to us. She's in baggy clothes and work boots that are too big for her, and she has dual elbow pads on. "I'm June. You guys must be tired."

Nikolaos chuckles. "June, this is Farah, Thomas, Lois and Digs."

"Hi," June says, "again. Tired?"

"Actually we're pretty hungry," Digs answers for us. Lois and I laugh. "Got any food?"

"I think we can handle that," June says, waving for us to follow. I look over, trying to get Rubik's attention, but he's far too distracted at the moment. I shake my head, actually amused by all this, and lead Dad in June's direction.

On the other side of the upside down trucks are two mammoth, rusty turbine propellers. They're leaning against each other so that they form a great triangle with the ground. Inside the propeller structure are three picnic benches, and Lois and I sit Dad down on the one closest to us. June goes to the back, where a stove is rigged up. She turns on a hanging bulb and starts to work.

I raise my eyes. The pointed ceiling is about nine or ten feet up. Each blade in the propellers is about Digs's size. I sit down next to Dad, who rubs his knee under the table, and Lois and her brother take a seat across from us.

"One of your friends is taking Father Cash and the patrolmen to a hangar?" Nikolaos asks June, joining us inside the structure. "Least that's what she said."

"Probably Kit," June replies, her back to us. I smell bread and coffee coming from her direction. Is she really *baking*? "And yeah," she continues, "the hangar is where the spare cots are. It's probably the best place for you guys to sleep tonight."

She sets four mugs on the table before us as Nikolaos leaves again.

"We have lots of water, and lots of coffee," June says, jug in hand. Lois and Digs take some water, and I tell June that I'll wait with Dad for the coffee.

"How do you know how to make all this?" Lois asks, motioning to the stove with her mug. "If Digs was *half* this helpful around our fort." Digs flicks his sister's arm in response.

"The older kids are actually the ones who cook and bake," June clarifies, removing the coffee pot from the stovetop and pouring the dark black drink into our mugs. "But they teach us younger ones how to warm everything up. I like doing it, so I'm hoping it'll be my job next season."

I hold the mug up, and the coffee steam tickles my nose. She's explaining all this to us as if their community operates like a Village. The older ones bear the more difficult tasks than the younger ones. They teach and instruct one another, and have jobs.

There seems to be a surprising, almost fairy tale order to this place.

"Where are you getting power from?" Dad asks, sipping his coffee. June sets the coffee pot back on the stove, and uses two rags to remove the tray of bread from the oven. She tells Dad, while she's doing this, that there are quite a few working generators stationed throughout the junkyard.

Again, just like a Village.

June puts the tray of nut-scented bread on the table, and a shoebox of mismatched forks beside it. We don't have to be told to help ourselves.

"Fhank ew," we all say appreciatively, mouths full. The bread is warm and moist, so much so that it falls apart when it hits my tongue.

"I hope it's enough to hold you over until breakfast," June says. She stands at the end of our table, watching like a proud mother might. Life in the bowl ages you fast, shaving off adolescent years, and June is a walking testament to that.

Confident that we're settled in and our needs are currently met, June dismisses herself to go see if the others need her help in the hangar.

"Living here would be cool all right," Digs says, plowing another forkful of bread into his mouth. We eat in silence for a few minutes – the tension that was previously knotting us up begins to loosen. Even Dad makes a joke while he licks his fork clean.

We did it, I think. Somehow we survived a sandstorm, and we found the patrolmen. Hopefully this means we got the hard part out of the way first, and it'll be downhill from here.

I set my fork down, almost laughing out loud at myself. Who am I kidding? It's only been one full day, and this is the bowl, which means things haven't even begun to get difficult.

"There you are," Rubik says, stepping inside the propeller structure. Outside I see his entourage has followed, but thinned considerably. Only a handful remain, though most of them are teenage girls. They stare, eyes glued to Rubik, and swap whispers.

"Rubik you're okay!" I blurt out, slipping out of the picnic bench and throwing my arms around him.

Out of the corner of my eye, I see the mini crowd disperse – huffy glares directed my way.

"Of course," Rubik says, chuckling. We break away. "Just...overwhelmed."

"Can't imagine why," I joke. "Wanna sit?"

"Here," Digs says as Rubik takes my place next to Dad. Digs slides the now empty bread tray forward. "Have some crumbs." We all laugh, and I grab a fifth mug from the cabinet next to the stove.

"Drink this," I tell Rubik after pouring him some water. He takes the mug thankfully, and downs the drink. It's only a few minutes later that June returns, large tree branch in hand.

"Thought you might want this," she says to Dad, leaning it against the picnic table. Next, she tells us that our cots are prepared, and Father Cash, Nikolaos, and the patrolmen are already settling in for rest.

Dad gets up first, refusing anymore help, and uses the long branch like a crutch instead of a walking stick. We follow June through the junkyard, passing beneath more car houses in the process. Digs points up breathlessly, noticing them for the first time. Some kids climb up their ladders, glowing battery-powered lanterns hanging over their shoulders.

We enter the curve-ceilinged hangar through a side door, and the huge building is reminiscent of the storage units. That makes me gasp involuntarily. Alex. It's been an entire day since I saw him in the backseat of that truck...awaiting his "appointment" with Lark.

"What's wrong?" Rubik asks, grabbing my hand. I'm frozen in place just past the threshold, and everyone else has already gone ahead to the collection of cots at the other end of the hangar. Rubik is the only one who noticed that I stopped.

"Nothing," I reply.

His face changes. "It's Alex, isn't it?" He loosens his grip around my hand, like he's getting ready to let go, but I squeeze his fingers.

"C'mon," he says, looking embarrassed for some reason. "Let's go with the others." I swallow, composing myself, and let Rubik guide me across the pavement. There are about a dozen cots set in the corner, and Mr. Pujol and his men already occupy five of them. Father Cash is lighting candles that sit on upturned crates.

Lois and Digs claim the cots on either side of Nikolaos's. They can't be too close to one another during the night because "Lois snores!" and "Digs talks in his sleep!"

Dad sits down on the edge of his cot slowly and begins to untie his boots. I take the cot next to his, leaving the last few open for Rubik and Father Cash to choose over.

Rubik picks the one next to mine.

"Oliver's gonna want to talk to you guys in the morning, after breakfast," June says, putting her petite hands in her pockets. "He'll want to know why you were traveling through the bowl. Basically he just wants to make sure you're not here to take us away."

"I can assure you right now," Father Cash says, blowing out a match, "that's not why we're heading through the bowl."

I crawl onto my cot, and even though the tight surface is stiff and uninviting, it feels absolutely wonderful to lie down. I don't even fool with removing my boots.

June bids us goodnight after telling us there are blankets and quilts stored beneath each cot. I'm pretty sure I only catch about half of what she says, and that my brain sort of makes up the rest. I am too tired to sort it out. The fatigue is heavy and I let it force me down, into the deepest slumber I've had in months, possibly, in years.

The next morning I'm the last one up. The hangar is already empty. I pull back the quilt that someone must have draped over me last night and swing my feet around. My boots were pulled off, too. I reach under the cot, find them, put them back on, and rise.

I throw my fists up and stretch for so long that the tingly feeling that follows almost pushes me back onto the cot. The cuts on my face throb a little, and I delicately touch around the injury – making sure the bandages didn't fall off during the night.

Outside the hangar, the sun isn't fully up yet. A violet and orange sky stretches overhead, a few swirly clouds here and there. I follow the sound of talking toward the overturned trucks and courtyard area.

There's no one around, but there is a fresh mound of dirt and sand in the middle, and an old shovel is tip-down in the ground. A body has been laid to rest. Our patrolman. I stop at the makeshift gravesite, rubbing my arms even though I'm not cold.

I probably didn't know this man well, but that doesn't mean he had any less of a story than me. I feel a stinging and burning sensation behind my eyes. I ward off the tears with gritted teeth.

"Farah?" a voice says from behind. I bat my eyelids a few times before turning around. Rubik approaches

283

in the morning sunlight. He's changed into cargo pants and a white T-shirt, making him look more human than he has before. His transparent skin still showcases his floating cubes and particles – dim though they might be now.

"Hey." I leave the grave and meet Rubik. Together, we stride toward the propeller structure, where the smell of eggs and more bread is swelling in the air.

"How did you sleep?"

"Fine," he answers, chuckling. "I've grown used to 'cots,' right?"

"Yeah." I smile, nodding. "And I probably could've slept on the pavement I was so tired."

Rubik tells me, as we walk, that the junkyarders lent our patrolmen a few working trucks so they could head back to the crater and gather up the supplies that didn't blow away in the sandstorm. Nikolaos insisted on going with them because his camera equipment was stowed inside one of the tents, and Father Cash accompanied them as well.

We head into the propeller structure, and I see Dad, Lois, and Digs sitting at the same picnic table as last night – all working on a plate of scrambled eggs. The other two tables are occupied with four or five kids apiece. An older girl, who looks about my age, works at the stove with fast hands.

"Rubik! Sit by me!"

"He doesn't want to sit there, you don't bathe."

"That's not true, Mort!"

"He wants to sit next to *me*!"

284

Rubik scratches behind his head, unsure how to deal with all this energy and attention. You'd imagine he would have mastered the perfect response by now, but hearing the frenzied interest coming from all these kids is like a new form of popularity altogether.

"Show them how it looks when you drink water," I say to Rubik, patting his back and leaving to join Dad's table. Rubik scowls after me, and I give him a playful thumbs up.

"Sorry I let you sleep in, honey," Dad says after I've taken a seat next to him. There's already a mug of coffee waiting for me, and after I sip it I find that it's still plenty warm. "You looked pretty peaceful."

"It's fine," I say, giving him a side hug and letting my hand remain on his shoulder. "Felt good to sleep."

"I was wrong about Lois, by the way," Digs says, swallowing his food. *"You're* the one who snores!" Dad and Lois burst into laughter, but don't console me or say that Digs is only kidding.

"Is he serious?" I ask, mortified. I feel my face flushing.

"It started after I put those blankets over you," Dad explains, scooping up some eggs on his plate and taking a bite. That was Dad who covered me in the night? I'm grateful, but I suddenly realize that I was hoping it was Rubik.

The girl who is working over the stove turns from the burners and sets a plate before me. I tell her, Thank you, but she's already returned to the stovetop before I get both words out.

"Should we help her?" I ask before starting on breakfast.

"Already tried," Dad says, taking a sip of his coffee. "She insisted on doing everything herself."

A loud eruption of *oohs* and *ahs* echoes inside the propeller structure. We all turn and see Rubik, standing before his audience and drinking a jar of water. The kids marvel as the liquid works its way down his translucent throat.

When he finishes, there's a round of applause, and he winks at me before sitting back down.

"They may have a hard time letting him leave," Dad notes, finishing his bread. I grab a fork and take a bite. The eggs are actually perfect. Extra fluffy. Not at all what I was expecting.

"Speaking of which," I say, chewing, "when *do* we plan on leaving?"

"Mr. Pujol made it seem like immediately," Lois says, pushing her empty plate forward and drinking some water. "As in, right when they return with our supplies."

"That's if everything didn't blow away," Dad corrects. "Should they be unable to salvage any of our supplies, we'll have to return to our Village."

"Meaning, it's the end of the line for us." Digs folds his arms, sulking.

"You know we did almost get swept away in that storm, Digs," Dad says. "We could've been killed."

"*It was so cool!*" he replies cheerfully. "I don't want to go back to class and chores. Those are equally *un*cool." Lois shakes her head, but instead of calling her brother a moron or a doofus, she reaches over and messes up his hair.

When I'm about halfway through with my breakfast, June shows up for the first time that morning and heads straight for our table.

"Oliver's ready to see you guys now," she informs us in almost a whisper.

"We should wait for the patrolmen to get back," Dad tells her.

"Oliver hates patrolmen," she says. "Now's probably the best time."

"It's fine," I assure Dad, shrugging. "Let's just get it over with, yeah?"

According to Nikolaos, Oliver used our patrolman – the one who was supposedly killed in our crash – as an example. Shot him in the chest to scare Mr. Pujol and the others.

If that's the case, this Oliver kid is a reckless, disrespectful punk. It's probably better for him that our patrolmen aren't back yet. Who knows what they want to do to him...

"Oh, and Oliver has asked that Rubik stay behind," June continues, looking over her shoulder. Rubik is still distracted with the kids around his table. "He didn't like how he embarrassed him in front of the other junkyarders last night."

"Tell Oliver to swallow all that pride of his, that is if it doesn't choke him to death before he's finished." I set my utensil down. "Rubik's coming with us."

June doesn't even argue. "Cool. I told him you'd say something like that, but he didn't believe me. And last thing – "

"Just how many demands does King Oliver have?" I say, narrowing my eyes with incredulity.

June snickers at my insult. Appears as if she doesn't care for this messenger business much, or where the messages are coming from.

"He's going to ask about a man named Lark," June says. "Nobody he asks ever knows who that is, so I don't guess you will either."

Our table goes silent. Lark? Oliver is going to ask about Lark?

"Uh oh." June's tone has changed. "You know him, don't you."

We all nod. June sighs, straightening up. "Well, we'd better head over then. Oliver's going to have a lot of questions for you."

"Why does he want to know about Lark?" I ask as we get to our feet.

June looks down at the ground as she responds: "Lark's the reason Oliver is an orphan."

Chapter 49 | Rubik

Farah and the rest of her table are standing up, so I do as well, but this is met with groans of opposition.

"I have to go with the others," I tell the children, and, before they can really object more, I duck outside after Farah.

"What's going on?" I ask, walking alongside her.

"That Oliver kid wants to talk with us," she replies. "June just told us that he's going to ask about Lark. Oliver believes he's responsible for his parents' death."

Now that Farah mentions this, I remember Oliver screaming at our patrolmen yesterday, demanding to know where Lark was. In the wave of everything else that happened, I forgot to tell Farah last night.

What's Oliver expecting of us though? Does he think we're just going to tell him which Village we're from so that he can sneak into it in the middle of the night and quench his blood thirst?

June guides us south, and we zigzag around the debris heaps that are so prevalent in this compound. A short while later, we approach a tiny shed. The door has been removed, and we see Oliver sitting atop a ripped armchair inside – his face and part of his body draped in shadows.

Two stout teenagers stand on either side of where

the door might have been – one holds a bat, the other a set of chains.

"Is he serious right now?" Farah whispers beside me. We come to a stop, standing in the sunlight and increasing heat while Oliver remains seated in his shed. Thomas is to my left, and Farah to my right. Beside her are Lois and Digs – hands clasped.

June moves to the periphery, but is scolded before she can vanish.

"I said he couldn't come!" Oliver yells, pointing at me angrily.

"We insisted," Farah says, folding her arms. Oliver grips his armrests, but says nothing else on the matter. June excuses herself, stating chores that require her attention.

"Why are you traveling through the bowl?" Oliver says, switching topics. "Were you looking for us?"

"Young man," Thomas intones, "with all due respect, well, you're a *young man*. I'm having a difficult time responding to your demands."

"Oh?" Oliver snorts. "Funny. You're *not* having a difficult time receiving shelter and food from us, are you?"

Thomas pushes up his goggles. "Fair point."

"All I ask is that you answer my questions," Oliver continues, feigning calmness. "Then you can be on your way."

"We're looking for my ship," I say, holding my hands behind my back. "The other two who are traveling with us – Nikolaos and the Father – believe they can map out where the wreckage is."

Oliver rubs his chin. "You're the one, then? That fell from the sky?"

"No, it was me," Farah says, shaking her head. Lois and Digs stifle laughter.

"I don't appreciate your sarcasm!" Oliver shouts.

"And we don't appreciate you disrespecting our dead!" she retorts. She moves forward, but I grab her arm gently. "Did shooting our patrolman last night make you feel big?"

"Farah, get a hold of yourself," Thomas pleads, leaning forward on his branch. She breathes in quickly, but eventually falls back in line. This area of the compound is quiet for a moment, the only sound is distant barking.

"We have a piece of your ship," Oliver finally says, and every single one of us straightens up. "It's a sizeable portion, actually."

"Where?" Thomas steps toward the shed. "You have to take us to it."

"I will." Oliver rises to his feet and steps into the sunlight. "But first you're going to tell me where Lark Persons is."

"Why?" I ask, thinking he won't elaborate. He does.

"I want to kill him," says Oliver simply.

Oliver runs his hand through his bleach blonde hair, looking truly confident for the first time. More so than last night, even, when he was interrogating our men. He must believe he has the ultimate bargaining chip.

Standing in much more light than when I saw him

first, I see that Oliver is pretty fit for his age. He wears a red T-shirt with the sleeves cut off, and fingerless gloves on both hands. His jeans are tattered and ripped, and he has a pair of mismatched boots on his feet. He doesn't have the pointy shoulder guards I saw on him yesterday.

"What makes you think we'll let you kill one of our own?" Thomas says, resting on his branch.

"You know where he is then?" Oliver's icy blue eyes have turned wild, intense. "Lark?"

"I'm speaking hypothetically here," Thomas counters, but it's too late. Oliver can see right through that.

"Tell me where I can find Lark," Oliver says, walking straight up to Thomas. "And I'll tell you where we're keeping the alien's wreckage."

"How do we know you're not lying?" Farah insists. "You could just be telling us you have part of the debris so that – "

Oliver turns, interrupting her: "Charred metal that's made of a foreign alloy? Bits of indecipherable inscriptions on it?"

Farah ingests the rest of her sentence. "That'd be the one," she says, embarrassed.

"So." Oliver reaches out his gloved hand, expecting an acceptance from Thomas. "Do we have a deal?"

No one responds or says anything for a good length of time. Maybe – just *maybe* – they're all considering this. But I can't let them go through with it. No more lives are worth me finding my spacecraft. Not even

Lark's.

"We'll have to respectfully decline," I tell Oliver. Thomas lets out a large sigh, like he'd been holding his breath for a while.

Oliver's face hardens. "Fine. Once the rest of your party returns, I'll have to *respectfully* ask that you leave." Then, he waves for his guard to follow him off.

"Sounded like a solid deal to me!" Digs jokes once Oliver's out of earshot.

"Don't kid like that – Lark is still one of ours," Thomas says, wiping newly acquired perspiration from his face. "Let's get out of this heat, shall we?"

We find our way back to the hangar, and the cool shade and cold cement is ever welcoming. Thomas asks for my help, so I assist him in getting on top of his cot. He suggests that we all rest up, like him, until Mr. Pujol and everyone else returns.

"We're going to have to make up a lot of time," Thomas warns before he turns over. He falls asleep shortly after. Lois and Digs climb on top of their respective cots, and, in no time, they're both napping soundlessly atop the blankets.

Farah lies on top of her cot, too, but her eyes are opened and gazing at the high ceiling. I'm sitting at the edge of my cot, unable to force myself into a lying position.

"Been like that for almost half an hour," Farah says quietly, checking her wristwatch. "Can't be good for your back." She pivots her head, looking at me with soft eyes. This is where I should say something witty and clever. Something that makes her laugh. In a pathetic panic, though, I just bring up the first thing that comes to mind.

"Last night was a first."

"Hm?"

"It was the first time I slipped into unconsciousness since arriving on your planet and I didn't have a dream memory also."

Farah props herself up by her elbow. "Dream memory? Is that what you were referring to last time we talked about this?"

I nod. "And I'm scared that I won't have anymore."

"It's just one night," Farah reassures me. "Could only mean that you were so tired, you haven't remembered it yet."

"That's possible?"

"Sure. I read somewhere once that we *always* dream. We just don't always remember them."

I tilt my head, unable to process how this is possible. "So...there's a way to recall them?"

Farah's face drops. "Not necessarily. I guess it means you weren't meant to remember last night's memory. Or dream. Or, er, memory dream."

"That's unacceptable," I say, getting to my feet. Beyond Farah's cot, her father stirs a little, then resumes his steady breathing. "There's got to be a way."

"If there is, I don't know about it," she replies, looking taken aback. I force myself to sit down again. "It's okay, Rubik." She puts a consoling hand on my knee. "We're gonna figure this out. Together."

I look away, feeling downright foolish for my ill-tempered response. It's just that we're so close to obtaining another portion of my ship, and yet so far away. It could potentially hold some answers, and maybe even confirm my working theory about the writing on the metal, but we'll never know.

Not unless we give up Lark.

It's insulting, in retrospect, that we're willing to protect him when he's put us through so much. He cast out Farah and her father – manipulating the Village assembly into thinking they were absolutely essential to this perilous venture. Then, aside from knocking me out with his weapon and trying to stab me, he promoted an idea of separation. From Farah.

It's the worse thing he's done yet.

"What are you thinking abou – ?"

"Lark," I say, before she's even finished asking. I meet her eyes, and she begins to withdraw her hand, but I catch it – holding her tenderly. "My apologies," I say in a kinder voice. "I was thinking about Lark."

Farah blinks. "Thinking we made the wrong choice?"

"No, it's just..." I trail off for a second, then lightly clear my throat. "Why do you think Lark killed Oliver's parents?"

"No idea. As morbid as this sounds, I was kinda hoping Oliver would explain. Elaborate a little, you know?"

"Guess it makes no difference," I say with a sigh. "I

wouldn't have been more inclined to accept Oliver's offer either way."

"There you go again," Farah whispers, a smile appearing on her face. "Doing good where others would fail. You don't owe Lark anything, and yet you're willing to protect him."

"Actually, I'm protecting the kid," I reply, chuckling. "Knowing Lark, I bet he sleeps with one eye open. Oliver can't be the only one who wants to kill him, and my instinct tells me Lark wouldn't hesitate snapping a teenager's neck."

"Hadn't thought about that," Farah says, her smile vanishing.

"That was an unnecessary detail," I say quickly. "My apologies."

Farah's smile returns unexpectedly, and it deepens. She says, "You can stop with the apologies now."

I look down and notice, with a start, that I'm still holding her hand. She rubs the top of my knuckles, and, as if noticing at the same time, she jerks away.

"Wow, er, my turn to say sorry," she says, tucking hair behind her ears nervously. I want to tell her that it's okay, I like holding her, but calling attention to this moment would only ruin it.

"You gonna tell me about your dreams?" she asks a few minutes later, lying on her back again. I inhale first, then give her every detail I can muster. What is said in my dreams. What sticks out to me. What confuses me.

Which, I suppose, is all of it.

"'Ready the Leaper'?" she repeats, interlacing her fingers and resting them on her stomach. "As in, prepare? Rubik, maybe the Leaper is the name of your ship!" Farah lets her volume get away from her, and Digs grunts irritably in his slumber.

"It might have crossed my mind, sure, but I hadn't considered it fully," I say eagerly. "Except, if it is a ship, I don't remember. I can't confirm that."

"We could file that away in 'possibilities,' " she replies. "What else could 'ready the Leaper' mean?"

I muse for a second. "I suppose a person or persons. Could be an individual title, like lieutenant, or a grouping, like army."

"So you're thinking it has military significance?"

"Maybe...I don't know, honestly. This is all guesswork."

"Sure, but it's another possibility." Farah sits up again. "What else could one theoretically prepare?"

It takes us a handful of moments to think of something else. "An event," Farah says, her whisper threatening to break once more. "The Leaper could be referring to some kind of event, right?"

"I suppose so." For reasons I can't explain quite yet, this explanation makes the most sense to me, even though I hint to the person I'm conversing with in my dreams that the Leaper is something tangible.

"You may not think it's finished," I said. *"But it'll do the trick with the state it's in."* I guess I could've meant unfinished planning, if the Leaper is indeed an event.

"...Because you *designed it,"* I also said. *"And you*

don't fail, so consequently it won't fail." Design. That rules out it being a person, right? One could design an army though. I inch closer to Farah's cot, getting ready to share my thoughts, when faint footsteps ring out.

Farah and I both turn, watching as June's form approaches. She holds an unlit lantern at her side, and when she sees the others sleeping, she stops.

"Came to check on you guys," she says in a low voice, wiping away beads of sweat from her face and tiptoeing the rest of the way to our cots. "I heard about what happened with Oliver. He has no right to deny you that piece of your spaceship."

That's when Farah snaps her fingers, almost waking her father, Lois, and Digs.

"June," she says enthusiastically, "you know where he's keeping it, don't you? The wreckage?"

The little girl's face pales instantly, but it's not surprise. It's a look of expected dread: "Maybe. You want me to take you to it, don't you?"

Farah swings her feet around, careful not to wake Thomas. "Only if you're willing."

"I don't want to put June in jeopardy," I say, shaking my head. "This could get her in serious trouble with that boy Oliver."

June sighs.

"You know something?" she says. "Before you guys showed up last night, I was starting to get really bored and annoyed with my chores. I was even thinking about leaving. Trying to find my way back to the Villages. So, I prayed to God for an adventure.

298

Something to keep me going.

"Guess God answered my prayers."

Chapter 50 | Farah

Rubik and I follow June out of the hangar's side doors, and we sneak toward a section of the junkyard I've not been to yet. Here, there aren't any of the car houses I've gotten used to seeing. There's not really any form of life on this side – not even stray dogs.

It's just like I imagined a junkyard would look. A lonely landscape with metal skeletons and broken appliances everywhere.

"You don't have to do this, June," Rubik says to my left. But I can tell, by the tone of his voice, he's already accepted the outcome. June won't turn back now. I know, because neither would I.

We run over and around piles of damaged inanimate objects, purposefully not exerting too much energy due to the escalating temperature. I don't even want to guess the heat level because I know that will only make me hotter.

"Nobody comes to this part of the junkyard," June tells us over her shoulder. "Oliver's hidden the generators, so no one can hook up fans."

"Meaning, it's the perfect spot to hide something," I say. June nods as she jogs, and she eventually slows to a walk as we approach a refrigerator on the ground. It's an ancient red one, with cursive type on the side.

The appliance is on its back with the door pointing toward the sky. June grabs the handle and tugs, and I half expect the piece of wreckage to just be lying inside.

But it's not. The back of the fridge has been removed, in fact, and beneath it is a hole maybe five feet wide. I can see a rope ladder descending into the depths, but no sign of light or any indication to how deep the descent actually is.

"Hope you guys aren't scared of heights," June says seriously, stepping over the side of the fridge. She clamps the handle of her lantern between her teeth and carefully climbs down.

"This was your idea," Rubik says after I've given him a nervous look. He holds my hand as I circumspectly copy June and lift one leg over first, feeling for the topmost rung on the ladder.

"Thanks for reminding me," I say back. Once I'm confident with my footing, I pull my other leg over and crouch down. "Don't look up or down – just straight ahead." I paraphrase this recital more to myself than to Rubik, and, in response to his confused expression, I say, "Trust me, it'll help."

Then, I step down, grabbing each crosspiece like my life depends on it. I pretend that I'm merely taking a routine descent from my watchtower. Great heights don't typically daunt me. Submerging into a bottomless abyss does.

I'm starting to second-guess this whole venture.

Focus on the cool air, I tell myself silently. At least you're not in the heat anymore. At least you're not –

"*Oof!*" I touch the ground unexpectedly, and my knee bends clumsily. The impact sends a brief prickly sensation up my leg.

"Sorry," June says behind me, clasping her battery-powered lantern in both hands. "I tried to tell you that you were close, but you were talking to yourself."

I feel my face grow warm and redden with embarrassment as I step backward, giving Rubik space to hop down next to us. I redirect my eyes upward. There is no light up above. Rubik must have shut the refrigerator door behind him.

"June," I say, looking down at her. "When you came to the hangar, you already had that lantern. Were you hoping this would happen? That we would ask you to bring us here?"

She shrugs her shoulders and points, indicating toward a passageway. It's plenty tall for her and me, but Rubik has to hunch as we make our way through. I feel like I did when we were being lead to the assembly proceeding...suffocated, claustrophobic.

"Yeah," June finally answers. "I knew you'd ask. And, if for whatever reason you didn't, I was going to suggest it. But, I had a feeling you would."

Wow. I must have become so impulsive that it's predictable now. How's that for irony?

There are a few turns and bends in the tunnel, and after a while I start to get nervous. We left the hangar at least a half an hour ago. Dad, Lois, and Digs will probably be waking up from their nap soon – if they haven't already.

"Is all of this really necessary?" I whisper to June, referring to the underground safe house she's leading us to. June holds her plastic lantern aloft, casting us in a glowing orb as we walk. Past the light there's nothing but darkness.

"You've met Oliver," she replies. "What do you think?"

"Guess you're right." I peek over my shoulder at Rubik, whose particles and cubes – which are ever so noticeably weaker – still burn and pulse as they drift up his arms, neck and face. At least if the batteries run out in June's lantern we'll have some form of light.

"Here," she announces at last, and I hear Rubik sigh in relief with me. June turns around and pushes against a piece of plywood with her back. It swings forward on dual hinges, and, by way of lantern light, a mini cavern is revealed. It's about the size of the hangar, and it looks manmade. There are support beams throughout.

June flips on a loud switch, and rows of exposed, bowl-like bulbs flick on above our heads. We're standing before a junkyard treasure trove. There are rickety, built-in shelves all along the circular wall, packed with engine parts and jars and hundreds of things I can't indentify.

On the dirt floor, there's an equal amount of clutter strewn about. An upside down table missing one leg. A mirror with no glass, only the backing. An assortment of buckets. Kites. Mannequins with missing body parts and arrows sticking from their chests.

"I'm like one of three people that knows about Oliver's stockpile," June says, leading us down a tiny, intentional path through the disorder. "I followed him one night 'cause I was bored."

I chuckle, amazed by this girl's bravery. She takes us to a white, unplugged cooler and puts her lantern on the floor. Then, she opens the boxlike container. Rubik and I walk up beside her, peering inside, and my growing curiosity is instantly sated.

It's a wide piece of wreckage with jagged ends, like a large shard of glass looks. Rubik reaches down and scoops it up in his hands steadily.

"Heavy," he says. "Heavier, in fact, than the piece Nikolaos recovered."

I suck in a quick breath. "Rubik! What if they can't find it, back at the crater?"

"Hopefully these are just fragments to the shell," he says, setting the wreckage on the dirt ground. June sighs rather impatiently – probably realizing we intend to stay a while. So, she leaves us and starts perusing the shelves.

"Which means," Rubik continues, on his knees, "that they're not terribly essential in rebuilding my spacecraft. We can find a substitute metal on your planet to fill in the gaps if we have to."

"I dunno," I say doubtfully, getting down next to him. "There's not really anything like this here."

I run my fingertips over the surface. Even though it's marred and streaked in places, it's still smooth.

There's writing near the top, just like on the other one. Straight and slanted lines that are cut off. I move my index finger over the inscription, feeling the machine-perfect grooves.

"Dad said you were about to show him something," I say as Rubik picks up the wreckage and turns it over, examining the other side before ultimately putting it back down. "Back at the crater. Did you remember what this says?"

Rubik doesn't verbally respond, but only nods. Then, he inclines forward and writes something in the dirt with his thumb. My jaw drops. He's purposefully written on the ground right above the inscription on the debris – *finishing* the letters where they're cut off.

INTAKE.

"It's...it's English," I mutter, staring at the half dirt, half engraved word. It, like the other piece, had been sliced across the middle so that we were only looking at the lower portion of the letters. That's what made it look so foreign. So alien.

"Our language." I shake my head. "How's that possible, Rubik? You're not from here."

"No, I'm not," he says, proffering his arm forward – basically confirming this fact with his inner flow of lambent cubes. "But I'm apparently connected to your planet in more ways than we can fathom."

I put my hands on my legs before standing back up. "But wait, so, how come with both pieces we've examined so far, the word was perfectly sliced off? Seems like a pretty convenient...well, inconvenience, don't you think?"

Rubik grabs the wreckage and stands it on its side. We both lean in. There's a straight, barely noticeable lip that runs across the edge. It's so small and thin it's no wonder we didn't see it at a quick glance.

"It's supposed to break off here," I say, poking the brink.

"It seems so..." Rubik agrees, delicately setting it back down and then rubbing his wrists idly. He stares at the debris. If I'm baffled and slightly frustrated with the new set of questions this poses, I can't imagine what he must be thinking. Every time it seems that some progress is on the horizon, more obstacles get put in our way.

"Guys, come check this out!" June says from the other end of the cavern. Rubik rises, placing the wreckage back inside the cooler. Together, we join June near a portion of the shelf. There's a large pile of stuff around her feet because she has removed armfuls of items and cleared nearly three shelves.

"June," I say in a scolding tone. "What are you – ?" I don't even finish because I see what has her excited. Hiding behind this shelf is another, smaller tunnel.

"I only noticed it because of the draft," she tells us, proud of her discovery. "I got chills when I walked by. Where do you think it leads?"

Her guess is as good as ours, I think. I lean down, looking into the tunnel, and goose bumps span across my flesh. It's so dark and eerie down there. Who in their right mind would take a passage like this?

Well, considering whose sanctuary this is, it's not difficult to accept that Oliver would be willing to crawl down that damp hole.

"Uh oh." June drops the tin teapot she's holding and spins around. I hear it, too. Voices. Coming from behind the plywood door.

"We have to hide!" Rubik whispers, grabbing my hand and sweeping June up into his other arm. He takes us to the opposite side of the cavern and deposits me behind a large trunk, where I immediately crouch to my hands and knees.

I make sure he and June find an adequate hiding spot – one that's behind a pile of rolled-up carpets – and then I cover my head below my arms and close my eyes. Like this will help me disappear or something. A few beats later, Oliver and another person enter.

I've never heard two people cuss this much.

"Make sure it's still there!" he bellows, and hurried feet patter in my direction. Please don't come near this trunk! But I hear something else opening instead, and then a sigh of relief.

"They didn't take it," a girl's voice says, but to this Oliver only curses some more.

"No! No!" he screams, kicking an assortment of objects. One even smacks into the trunk I'm hiding behind, and I almost betray myself with a startled gasp. I stifle the urge, scrunching my eyes as shut as they'll go.

"Whoever found this place is in the tunnel!" Oliver has changed from furious to panicked in a matter of

307

two heartbeats.

"Hell," the girl says, rushing over to join him. "But that leads to – "

"Quick! Help me board this up!"

"We can't just leave whoever's down there locked on the other side!"

"You and I are the only ones who know about this storage space, Harlow." Oliver sounds like he's losing his mind. "Therefore, we're the only ones who know about that tunnel! Whoever's down there *is not* authorized, got it? It's their own damn fault!" He kicks something else, and then I hear heavy dragging. I want to get a look, but I don't dare the possibility of being seen.

Because of the crazy urgency in which Oliver and this Harlow girl work, I suddenly find that I'm scared along with them. I know, unlike them, that no one's in the tunnel and at risk of being trapped.

Yet it's important to Oliver – so much so that the mere fact that it was discovered unhinges him. Where could it possibly lead?

After a few minutes, my back is starting to cramp and ache. I wish they'd hurry up and leave so Rubik, June and I can sneak out and never go near this place again. Oliver and Harlow finally collapse onto the ground and pant – their task apparently complete.

"We need to round everyone up," Oliver says, short of breath. "Find out who's taken the tunnel."

"What good will that do?" Harlow says, her voice grave. "Whoever's down there is bound to get caught.

You know this. Our home...our refuge here...is now in jeopardy."

Oliver spits on the ground, sighing in resignation. "When was the last time we were in here?"

"It's been at least half a day."

"Meaning that's potentially ten to twelve hours ago our trespasser could have found the entrance."

"Oliver, let's think about this." Harlow's voice is strangely soft now. "No one would crawl for that long. Not unless they knew where it was leading."

"What are you saying?"

"Maybe they're heading back now? Didn't get far before they realized they were in over their head?"

"Dammit!" Oliver gets to his feet. "We can't just board this up. We have to be sure. Give me your kneepads."

The sound of Velcro ripping tells me that Harlow is obeying without argument. Oliver's a loose cannon. One second he's cursing and blocking the passage, the next he's changing his mind altogether.

"We're not abandoning our home unless we absolutely have to," Oliver says, sliding whatever he and Harlow barricaded the tunnel with out of the way. "If I don't return within the usual timeslot, assume the undergrounders have caught me, and that our channel into their food stores has been discovered."

It takes me a minute to put together what Oliver has just said. Assume the undergrounders have caught me. Our channel...discovered. That's it. That's where the tunnel leads. Oliver found a way to sneak into the undergrounders' lair...their food storage, more specifically...and he's been stealing from their reserves.

This means, I realize with a flurry of shivers, Mr. Toff and his undergrounders are only hours away from the exact spot I'm currently kneeling in.

We have to leave as soon as humanly possible.

Chapter 51 | Rubik

Once Oliver's companion – the girl named Harlow – watches her leader crawl into the tunnel, she spins around and bolts for the exit. I peek further around June's and my hiding spot, ensuring that Harlow and Oliver really are gone for good, and then I step out into the light.

"When Oliver reaches the end of his passage," Farah says quickly, standing up and jogging toward us, "and finds no one there, he's going to be livid. Hopefully Mr. Pujol and everyone else have returned. We need to get far away from here. Now."

Farah takes June's hand and leads her off, and I run up behind them – frequently checking over my shoulder in anticipation of Oliver. I keep thinking he's going to change his mind again and back out of the tunnel.

June snatches up her lantern in passing and then throws open the door for us. She clicks on the light, reigniting the radiant sphere amid the darkened trail. We fumble our way around the bends, and twice I bump into Farah and have to apologize.

When we reach the ladder, Farah sends June up first and scrambles after her. I go last, and when I make it to the top, Farah's there with her hand outstretched. I let her guide me back into the sunlight, where the ferocious desert heat is waiting.

"Did you have any idea the undergrounders were based so close to you?" Farah asks June as we sprint back to the hangar.

"No," she replies, and it's the first time I've heard true fear in her voice. "They used to come through here a lot though. We have watchers that would spot them in the distance, and then we'd have to work quickly to hide our valuables and ourselves.

"Lately, they've left our junkyard alone. Probably they figured if they didn't find anything in the past, they're not going to find anything now. We do a good job of making this place look abandoned when we have to."

Farah wipes the sweat from her brow with the back of her arm. I can tell what she's thinking. The undergrounders are far too close for comfort. Any slip on Oliver's part and he might be discovered, which would lead them here. To us.

We need to be thinking about this new information as an advantage. We now know where the undergrounders' hideout is. Farah's Village can add the coordinates to their maps to ensure avoiding that particular surface of the desert, below which the undergrounders lie. In many ways, happening upon Oliver's stockpile, and, subsequently, the hidden tunnel, should be viewed as a positive find...

...Especially if I still intend to surrender to the undergrounders.

As we jog up to the hangar, I see that two of our

three vans have been recovered. The vehicles are banged up pretty badly – dents and long scratches cover most of the exteriors. They're parked off to the side, where Mr. Pujol and the other patrolmen are cleaning sand out of containers and crates. Nikolaos is among them, going through his camera bags, and he waves at us before we enter the hangar.

We have to instantly compose ourselves because Harlow is there, talking with Thomas anxiously.

"Ah, here they are now," Farah's father says, leaning against his tree branch. When Harlow turns to face us, Thomas replaces his happy expression with an indignant one. You'd better have a good explanation, he is demanding with his eyes.

"Where on earth have you been?" Harlow yells.

"Not many places," Farah says coolly, walking right past Thomas and Harlow and grabbing the water bottle next to her cot. She passes it to June first, letting the small girl drink her fill. "Especially not Rubik. He's from another planet, you know."

Harlow folds her arms and sticks out her hip. Her shaggy hair is up beneath a hat, and below the brim her sharp eyes dart from me, to Farah, to June. She looks absolutely disgusted with Farah's literal response.

"I-I gave them a tour," June says, wiping her mouth.

Harlow snorts. "A *tour*?"

"Oh," Farah says, acting appalled. "Should we have cleared that up with Oliver first?" She's overdoing it, I think as June hands me the bottle. I offer it to Farah, but she gestures for me to drink first. So I do.

"Don't think that just because there aren't adults here our rules aren't important," Harlow says testily, turning on June. "*You* have chores to be seeing to."

"I'm already finished!"

"With the whole day's worth?"

June's face drops. "No..." she trails off, looking up at Farah and me apologetically. I catch a glint in Farah's eyes as she watches the tiny girl stalk off with her head bowed. Farah has gotten attached. She's going to want to find a way to get June out of here. Mr. Pujol won't stand for it – not with Lois and Digs already present, and certainly not with us short a vehicle now and who knows how many supplies.

"Make sure you don't wander off," Harlow scorns Farah.

She spins on her heel and stomps out of the hangar. Thomas turns on his tree branch, facing his daughter and me, but he doesn't get a chance to reprimand us. Farah marches up to him, puts her hands on his shoulders, and tells him everything we witnessed in Oliver's secret storage cavern.

When Farah's finished, Thomas strains and sits down on the edge of his cot. "We can't leave. Not yet, at least."

Farah glances at me, making sure I heard what she heard. "What do you mean we can't leave?" she demands.

"These are children," he says, setting his tree branch on the pavement next to his feet. "We can't abandon them for slaughter. It's what we'd be doing if we left right now. This instant."

Farah whips back her blonde hair, then starts tapping her foot. She's trying to keep calm. Trying not to lose her wits.

"Farah," I say, hand on her back. "I have to agree with your father on this – "

She cuts me off, saying, "I know." Then, after a few breaths, she adds, "I know because I agree, too." She walks away from us, pacing back and forth.

"Okay." Farah sighs heavily. "Okay, so what do we do?"

"We wait." Thomas takes off his goggles and wipes the lenses with the corner of his blanket. "Ensure that Oliver returns safely and unnoticed by the undergrounders. Only then can we resume our mission."

"And if Oliver gets caught?" Farah asks, a noticeable amount of color-loss in her cheeks. "Awakens the sleeping giant?"

"June mentioned their protocols earlier," I offer, folding my arms. "She said they could easily stage this compound to appear deserted. We could help the junkyarders, then wait it out – "

"I'm afraid that won't be an option," Thomas says, putting his goggles back on. "The undergrounders will have tortured the boy at that point, getting him to reveal this junkyard and its residents. If they come here and find it 'empty,' they'll just burn it to the ground. Smoke us out."

I know it won't come to that. If the undergrounders do catch Oliver, the boy will do anything to save himself. He'll barter for his life. Offer something up in exchange for his impending torture and ultimate death.

Me.

It's just as well. I'd convinced myself yesterday that the only way to prevent more suffering for Farah and her Village was to turn myself in. If Oliver is captured, and he brings the undergrounders here, I'll have the opportune moment. It won't seem like I'm forsaking Farah or her people, either, because this way I'll be protecting more lives. My submission will actually be the best scenario.

It dawns on me with a chill that I'm *hoping* the undergrounders apprehend Oliver. It's the best chance I have at preventing more deaths in my name. Oliver's the key to me relieving Farah of my encumbrance.

"We found you!" Digs's voice calls out. He speed walks over to us, Lois and Father Cash shadowing behind.

"Everything okay?" the Father asks, clearly sensing the morose atmosphere.

"I think you and I better have a word with Mr. Pujol," Thomas says, and Farah comes to his side and helps him to his feet. Father Cash nods, and together they stride across the pavement and out the side doors.

"Uh oh," Lois says, walking up to Farah. "What now?" She fills her and Digs in on the developing situation. They both, brother and sister, look depleted. I feel like I should say something. Again, they wouldn't be here, in this current predicament, if it weren't for me. No expedition out into the bowl to search for scattered spacecraft wreckage, no vans for Lois and Digs to hide in.

"I'll make sure you're safe," I say to all three of them. Farah meets my eyes and smiles. Digs takes a deep breath, and Lois puts her arm around him.

"I believe you," Digs says, looking up at me through his curly bangs.

Lois sniffs, then agrees: "So do I."

"What should we do?" Digs asks Farah with determined eyes. "How can we help?"

"Right now I don't know there's a whole lot we can do except wait," she replies, reaching into her pocket and retrieving a band. She puts her hair up and, when she's finished, she chews on her thumb with a thoughtful look on her face. "I guess we can tell Harlow that we intend to wait a little longer until our departure."

"Do we say *why* we're waiting?" Lois asks.

"Don't think that's a good idea," Farah answers. "If we do that, we're exposing June. She'd make the perfect target for Oliver to direct his anger toward after he gets back."

Farah's point here is a good one. Sure, we could have immediately revealed ourselves to Harlow and Oliver in their supply cavern, preventing him from going any further down the hidden tunnel, but at what cost? Oliver is like a wild animal that burst free from its cage, and there's no telling how he would've reacted toward little June once he had the chance to get alone with her.

"Okay, well, we can handle that," Digs says, nudging his sister. "Right?" Lois appears as if she doesn't want anything to do with this. Like she just wants to find an unlit crevice in the junkyard and hide.

"Yeah," she says anyway. "Let's find Harlow. We can say the patrolmen need to redo our inventory of supplies or something. You're good at lying" – she tells her brother as they head toward the exit – "so this should be a *breeze*."

"I don't lie!" Digs cries, pushing her as they walk. "You're the one that lies!"

Once they're gone, and only Farah and I remain in the gigantic hangar, Farah takes my hand in hers. "What is it?" she whispers. "What's bothering you?"

I almost flinch. "What?"

"Don't, Rubik. I know there's a lot going on right now," she says, motioning for me to sit on the edge of my cot. I do, and she sits across from me on hers. "But you look more than just troubled. You look consumed."

Only a week and some odd days on this planet and she can read me that well? "Farah, it is nothing but fatigue and – "

"I said don't," she says firmly, squeezing my hand, "as in, don't lie. You can tell me what's going on, and I *know* there's something going on. It's written on your face...in your eyes."

My biggest quandary is that I don't remember my past. Who I am, what my origins are. Yet even though this is the case, I feel – with unshakeable certainty – that Farah is the most unique and extraordinary individual I've ever known.

With a razor-sharp pang, the realization that these could be my last hours with Farah washes over me.

"Your life is something special, Farah," I say, taking her other hand. "Hold it, like it's tangible. Like it's something sweet, something you never want to let go of."

She angles her head, looking baffled. "Rubik – "

The large, wide hangar doors slide open, and then Mr. Pujol steps inside – directing the vans as they back in. Farah and I rise, holding our arms up to shield our eyes from the blasting sunlight. Nikolaos appears via the side doors, and he walks up to where we're standing with his recording equipment bags hanging from his shoulders.

"Guys," he says with a broad grin, "all my cameras are accounted for!" Beside me, Farah tries to look excited for him, but her expression is rather unconvincing. Nikolaos glances back and forth at us awkwardly.

"Oh," he mutters, "er, did I interrupt some – ?"

"Interrupt *what?*" Farah scoffs. She's upset – I can tell by her tone. But there's no way I could have possibly explained to her what my plan is. How I intend to set things right.

"We were just getting ready to help the patrolmen." She steps past me wordlessly and marches toward the vans.

Nikolaos chuckles, scratching his head. "In my experience," he says to me, "I would start now."

We both watch as Farah reaches Mr. Pujol and they exchange words. "Start what?" I ask Nikolaos.

"Start figuring out how you're gonna get her to forgive you," he says, absentmindedly adjusting one of his bag straps. "They say time heals all wounds. Not with women. No sir, not with women. It's up to us to 'bandage' those wounds, you know why?"

"..."

"Because," he explains, sounding like he's had this conversation before. "Most times, *we're* the reason they have those wounds."

I raise the part of my forehead where eyebrows would be. "You speak on this with authority."

Nikolaos chuckles again. "Well, I like to think of myself as an expert on the subject."

"..."

"What!" he says, sounding insulted. "I do!"

Whether that's true or not, there's merit in what Nikolaos is saying. If there is a way to mend Farah's feelings before I follow through with my intentions, then I should seize the opportunity. I just don't know how that will be possible, because that will mean telling her everything.

Nikolaos and I eventually join everyone else at the hangar entrance. Two patrolmen slide the doors shut as Mr. Pujol explains to Farah what arrangements have been made. Thomas and Father Cash walk over, listening from behind the row of patrolmen, who now stand at attention with their hands behind their backs and their feet shoulder width apart.

Mr. Pujol has agreed to wait until nightfall. If Oliver still hasn't returned by then, he's leaving with his men – with or without Farah, her father, and everyone else – but he's taking Nikolaos with him. They will press onward into the bowl to try and accomplish what we started.

I can see by Farah's and Thomas's facial expressions they don't like this decision, but Mr. Pujol's rank is obviously unchallengeable.

Nikolaos leaves, saying he's going to find a generator to charge his batteries. Father Cash offers to help the patrolmen, who have opened the vans' engine coverlets and are starting routine maintenance on the hardware. Thomas and Farah take pales of frothy water and rags and begin scrubbing the interior and exterior of the vehicles.

I take my leave, stepping out through the side doors. The sun and heat greet me, grabbing hold of every single inch of my body. I raise my hands up in the shadow of the hangar and study every finger and knuckle and detail. Since my conversation with Farah by the crater, my skin has maintained the sand-like tint. My translucent body must have absorbed this coloring in the desert and sunlight, and now my internal elements and cubes are morphing to match the new shade.

"But I'm apparently connected to your planet in more ways than we can fathom." It's what I told

Farah, in Oliver's storage cavern. When I finally submit to the undergrounders and give her a chance to get on with her life, I'll be burying all of my unanswered questions in the ground. I'll never know how I'm connected to Farah's planet, or why my body possesses the ability to adapt to this atmosphere.

I feel myself wandering aimlessly through the junkyard, unsure to where my feet are taking me. This is an appropriate ending to my journey, I think to myself. I was trapped in a prison, sailing through space without a compass. Everything I've gotten to experience in these past few days has been on borrowed time. I didn't deserve any of it. I was in prison. Apparently *that* is what I deserved.

So, surrendering myself to the undergrounders is the fitting outcome.

I turn a corner of stacked vehicles. A small boy climbs up his rope ladder, a bucket of water sloshing at his hip where it's clipped to his belt. I used to think children his age – maybe five or six years old – could look up to me. That I was a shooting star. But I'm not. I carry no magic or wonder. All I am is lost and –

Wait. I'd forgotten. Oh how so easily I'd forgotten. I stop walking, standing in the shade of a junk pile – my thoughts racing in loops as I remember something. When I was in space, there was someone watching me. Someone who drew me to this planet. Someone who saved me, set me free. I didn't just happen here of my own accord. How could I have?

This person, who I could sense and feel...are they

from my planet, or this one?

Lois and Digs appear, walking from the direction I was headed. They have two jars of water between them, and, when they get closer, I smell that their drinks are herb-scented.

"Rubik?" Digs says, drawing my attention in. Even as they approached I was still swimming in my thoughts. "You all right?"

"Thinking," I reply, smiling down at them.

"Want something to drink?" Digs says, sipping his flavored water. "There's more in the coolers back at their mess hall."

I let them lead me to the propeller structure, and Lois heads to the back. There's a large cooler beside the stove and cabinet, and she pulls a clean jar out for me as I sit at a bench across from Digs.

"How did your conversation with Harlow go?" I ask as Lois brings me the chilled drink. I thank her and sip the water.

"Not good," Lois answers, topping her little brother's drink off before putting the water jug back inside the cooler. "She reminded us that Oliver wanted us gone as soon as the patrolmen returned."

"But," Digs says, "because Oliver's *not* here, she said she couldn't tell us what to do one way or another."

"Their loyalty to that kid is kind of unreal," Lois says thoughtfully, sitting on the bench next to Digs. "Especially given the circumstances here, you know?"

I nod in agreement, taking a second sip.

"Did you guys find that piece of debris when you

were down in Oliver's cave thing?" Digs asks between gulps. Farah left that part out when she told them about our experience in the cavern. She probably figured the discovery of the undergrounders' base trumped everything else.

"Actually, yes, we did," I say, and then I explain where it was hidden, and how it mostly resembled the other piece that Nikolaos found in his Village. I leave out the detail about the cut-off word. It doesn't seem like the right time to reveal this. Or, perhaps, I just don't want to get into that again. I'll have enough time in solitary confinement when the undergrounders take me to ponder my queue of questions.

For now, all I want to do is drink the cold water.

I stay with Lois and Digs for the rest of that afternoon. We talk in the shade about unimportant things, and it manages to be an enjoyable distraction from everything else. They tell me about their parents' boot shop. School. Their least enjoyable classes. Friends they've made and friends they've lost.

Lois talks of Farah at one point, too. She's like the sister I never had, Lois tells me. She confides that once Farah and Alex started dating, Lois started to see less of her. Meaning that, consequently, Farah and Alex were seeing *more* of each other.

Before we spend too much time on the topic, I steer the conversation in a different direction. Digs appears grateful for this.

Once the sun nears its setting, Oliver still hasn't returned to the surface. The three of us walk under the lavender, semi-cloudy sky toward the hangar. Inside, the patrolmen are playing a game of cards on the pavement. Mr. Pujol is cleaning his rifle, using a cot as a table. Father Cash is reading, and Nikolaos is napping in one of the vans.

Farah and Thomas are both lying on their cots and watching the card game. She perks up as Lois, Digs, and I stride over, but quickly glances away a split second later.

"Perfect timing," Mr. Pujol announces in his deep accent. He clips on the last piece of his weapon and gets up from his knees. He checks his wristwatch, and then takes the rifle and hangs it over his shoulder. "We're leaving. The choice of whether or not to join us is yours." He says this to the entire group, addressing each and every one of us.

The patrolmen gather up their cards and stand, making their way to the vans and prepping for departure.

Thomas sighs from his cot, reaching down and grabbing his tree branch. "Well," he mutters, "do what you have to do." Mr. Pujol nods knowingly before walking over to assist his men.

"Lois, Digs," Thomas says as Farah helps him up. "You two will be safer with Mr. Pujol."

At my side, I hear Lois and her brother open their mouths – getting ready to object – but a loud, booming horn resonates from outside. The pitch is hollow, sounding like a nautical creature might.

Mr. Pujol and his men curse, instinctually drawing

weapons.

Farah gasps. Father Cash shuts his book and hops off his cot. Nikolaos jumps out of the van, his hair standing up in the back. Lois and Digs begin to tremble as Thomas says, his words almost drowned out beneath the horn's second blast: "Oliver's been caught."

And the undergrounders are here, he doesn't say but doesn't have to.

Chapter 52 | Farah

The large hangar doors grind open, and four teenagers rush inside. They wear more quantities of the scrap metal armor than I've typically seen on them since we arrived at the junkyard, and my gut tells me why. There's no time to hide. Our only option is to fight.

The junkyarders have suited up for battle.

"They're on the east side of the junkyard!" one girl shouts, running right up to Mr. Pujol. I help Dad along in their direction so we can hear better. Rubik immediately swoops in and helps me. "And they're in the sand ship, cannons drawn on our fence!" The sand ship. She must be referring to the same vessel Mr. Toff brought to our Village as part of his diversion.

"They're waiting for us," Mr. Pujol says with realization. "It's why they haven't opened fire."

The girl nods beneath the hockey mask she wears. A shimmer of reflected light catches my eye, and I see that she has a pistol tucked in the side of her pants.

"Come with us," the girl says to Mr. Pujol, running out of the hangar. She and the other teenagers mount four dirt bikes, and before Mr. Pujol can object, Dad breaks from Rubik's and my grip and fumbles into the passenger seat of the van. He has to recline the chair forward because Nikolaos was previously sleeping in it.

Rubik says to me, "Stay here with Lois and Digs – "

"I'm not letting you leave me again," I interrupt him defiantly. I bolt forward and slide into the seat behind Dad. Rubik grinds his teeth, but he doesn't argue.

"Farah! Stay back!" Dad yells as Rubik jumps in and takes the backseat. Mr. Pujol starts the engine and drives the van outside, racing after the four dirt bikes. Rubik and I reach over and yank the side doors shut.

Dad mumbles something angrily as I look out the back window. I watch Father Cash and Nikolaos slide the hangar doors shut after the second van zooms out. Lois and Digs will be safe with them. That counts as one thing I won't have to worry about. I face forward, feeling my chest rattle as my heart punches with every beat.

The undergrounders have found us. There's no doubt Oliver told them we're here. They will demand we hand over Rubik, or they will flatten this junkyard with their warship.

I was wrong about the desert storm, I think as Mr. Pujol takes sharp turn after sharp turn – speeding after the dirt bikes through the junkyard. I was wrong to fear that the sandstorm would take our lives. It didn't, but only because our destiny would lead us to this. A showdown with the undergrounders.

We have five banged up patrolmen who barely survived a car crash. We have a small army of teenagers with pistols. We're trapped in a cage-like enclosure. How are we ever going to come out of this in one piece?

I glance over my shoulder. We do also have Rubik. He currently stares out at the soon-to-be night sky, that distant look in his eyes. There's something he's not telling me. Why? Is it about the discovery we made in Oliver's storage cavern? The English writing on his debris? I shouldn't be this upset over it. Rubik doesn't owe me an explanation for anything, so why am I acting entitled?

Because Alex does the same thing, I realize, and look where it got him. If only he had talked things through with me, I *might* have been able to help him. Get him out of whatever mess he's landed himself in. But it's too late for that. Now, instead of being frustrated with all the stuff Alex withholds from me, I'm losing sleep over whether or not he's even alive...

"What's the plan, Mr. Pujol?" Dad asks from the front seat. Mr. Pujol responds, telling him what I pretty much assumed to be his answer: We have to take this one step at a time. Assess the situation. See what Mr. Toff's demands are, even though everyone in this van can assume what they are.

"You know what has to be done," Rubik says mysteriously. "You have to hand me over. It's the only way to ensure everyone's safety."

"Not a chance," Mr. Pujol says as the automatic headlights finally turn on. "My men are already radioing in to our Village. Help is on the way. All we have to do is stall – "

"And what's the fastest time reinforcement can get here?"

Mr. Pujol hesitates, then sighs. "We're about eight hours away." Dad curses and shakes his head. That's far too long. This place will be a pile of ashes by then.

"Can we radio in to another Village?" I ask. "See if someone will help us?"

"Ours is the closest Village," Dad says. "The next one over is about a two-day drive." We're truly on our own then. This whole mess is the most frightening horror that could possibly come to fruition.

I hear Rubik inhale and exhale softly behind me. I want to tell him not to blame himself for any of this, because I know that's exactly what he's doing, but the van is slowing to a stop.

The junkyard doesn't have a tall and protective fence, like the one back at our Village. No, the only partition standing between our vans and the mammoth undergrounder ship, is a puny chain-link fence with partial barbed wire intact.

Mr. Toff's ship towers above us in the sunset, ripped sails flapping in the wind. The eighteen-wheeler, upon which the old ship is built, revs its diesel engine in response to our approach. Retractable square slats have been pulled up all along the expanse of the ship, where ancient cannons and gun turrets poke out.

"Ahoy there!" Mr. Toff's whimsical voice exclaims through some loud speakers. Because of our angle, we can't see if he – or anyone else, for that matter – is on deck. There are a few lit torches clamped to the masts, and the flames flicker against the starry, twilight sky.

"Let's not bore one another by dancing around the issue," Mr. Toff continues. Mr. Pujol turns off the engine after parking. He gets out, and then I reluctantly open the side doors. Surprisingly, neither Dad nor Rubik stops me.

I step out first, feeling even more dwarfed by the sand ship now that I'm outside the van. Rubik is next, and the two of us help Dad out of the passenger seat. We walk up behind Mr. Pujol, who is slowly drawing his pistol from his holster. He stares up at the faded, angelic figurehead at the bow of Mr. Toff's ship.

"We have a child," Mr. Toff's voice echoes through the speakers. The four teenagers we were following jog up to us by the fence. "A boy by the name of Oliver."

The junkyarders gasp. "How!"

"He's as good as dead!"

"What are we gonna do?"

"I'll make this simple for you." Mr. Toff clears his throat. "Give us the being who is with you, and we'll return the young man to you...*mostly* unharmed. Deny us this exchange, and I'll still return the young man.

"But only so he can burn alongside you."

A knot starts to form in my throat – one so bulky I can hardly swallow. The rest of the patrolmen have parked, and they're filing out of the van with rifles at the ready. Mr. Pujol tells us to get behind the van as he strides over to confer with the other patrolmen.

"You have ten minutes to comply," Mr. Toff says, adding with a giggle: "But my pocket watch is fast, so

331

don't expect a full six hundred seconds!"

The junkyarders start exchanging frenzied whispers, and it sounds like they're drawing up verbal strategies as they disappear into the shadows. I call out to Rubik, who is standing as still as a statue...gazing up at the colossal sand ship. If I didn't need his help to guide Dad behind the vans, he'd probably already be climbing over the fence to turn himself in.

This is the one time I'm thankful for Dad's limp.

"Honey," Dad says to me though grunts as Rubik and I lead him away from the fence. "There's nothing we can do here. We should have never left the hangar. I've put you in danger, and we need to leave."

"There will be no danger," Rubik says after Dad sits down on the dirt ground, "because tonight, I will make sure this ends."

"By turning yourself in!" I blurt out, laughing wildly. "Rubik, that's not how we solve this!"

"You're right," he says calmly. "It's how *I* solve this."

"What makes you think Mr. Toff still won't obliterate us?" Mr. Pujol says as he and his men walk over. "Even after you make yourself their prisoner?"

Rubik doesn't reply.

"These are the undergrounders we're talking about." Mr. Pujol reaches over and opens the back of the van, pulling out an assault rifle. The junkyarder with the hockey mask returns, lantern in hand.

"Oliver hates all adults," she says, raising the flickering light and casting ghostlike shadows across her mask. "Not just patrolmen. He wouldn't want us giving into the undergrounders, so we won't. We fight instead."

"We've got about three or four minutes," Mr. Pujol tells her. "My men and I will move the vans, then position ourselves at various vantage points – concentrating our firepower on the gun turrets and cannons."

"I've already got ten to fifteen boys and girls hiding up in the trash towers," the masked girl says, a thrill flashing in her black eyes. "On my signal, we'll open fire." She holds up her other hand, showing us a label-less beer bottle that's half-filled with what smells like gasoline. There's a rag stuffed in the bottle's opening, serving the purpose of a wick.

"Molotov cocktails," Mr. Pujol says, then he points over his shoulder for two of the patrolmen to move the vans. "Undergrounder's are usually the only ones who use those things. Guess they'll be getting a taste of their own medicine."

"We like to fight fire with fire," the girl says before turning and vanishing again.

"You three," Mr. Pujol says as Dad holds up his hands. Rubik and I help him up carefully but quickly. "Get back to the hangar. If things get out of control, take the truck these kids lent us earlier today and leave."

He tells us this like it'll be a last resort. Like he intends to not only keep the undergrounders at bay, but to finish them off once and for all. Doesn't he know that, for the undergrounders, reinforcement and backup is a signal away?

"Please, wait – !" Rubik tries, but Mr. Pujol is already dashing off to find cover. I can't help but feel slightly relieved as we assist Dad away from the fence and behind the trash heaps. At least now too many things are in motion for Rubik to turn himself over. It's selfish relief, I admit, but I don't feel guilty for it.

At least not yet.

"Ah," Mr. Toff's voice bellows behind us. "So this is how it plays out, hm?" We hear the large vessel begin to back up in the sand, and Mr. Pujol and his men start firing at will.

Dad trips over something on the ground, falling forward. It's so sudden that neither Rubik nor I have a chance to compensate for the yank. I even lose my balance and tumble over Dad, nicking something against my hand during our collapse.

I cry out in pain, but the sound is lost below the deafening *cracks!* of bullets that explode into Mr. Toff's sand ship. I feel warm blood trickling down my palm as I roll over, giving Rubik a chance to help Dad.

"Are...okay, Farah!" Dad shouts, parts of his sentence muffled by the firepower.

"Yeah!" I shout. "I ju...cut...hand!" Rubik slides my dad across the ground as if he was light as a doll, propping him up against something sturdy. Next, Rubik tears off a strip of his white T-shirt. Using dim starlight to see, he wraps the fabric around my cut.

I sit up when he's done, crawling toward Dad. A second later, the shooting stops. Rubik hunches next to me, equally shielded behind our barrier, but he stands slowly to chance a look at the damage. I copy him, instantly forgetting about the pain in my hand.

Mr. Toff's sand ship never returned fire, it only moved aside – paving the way for a second, larger ship. The vessel is so enormous, in fact, that it requires *two* eighteen-wheelers beneath it's weight – driving in flawless synchronization. The new ship charges forward, crashing through the chain-link fence like it's constructed of paper.

Now the battle really begins:

A wave of the junkyarders' homemade grenades slowly glides through the air.

An act of perfect timing, not haphazard.

It is preconceived chaos, not random chaos.

"*Run!*" Rubik shouts after the Molotov cocktails collide into the side of the big ship, fire and glass splattering against the wood viciously. The undergrounders return fire, blasting their cannons and gun turrets every which way. Bullets pierce into the junk heaps and towers, raining shards and bits of metal all around us.

Rubik grabs my hand and pulls me next to Dad, who's covering his head with his arms. Rubik finds a random car door on the ground and slides it over, holding it above our heads for protection. My panting and breathing is intensifying so much that I'm on the verge of hyperventilating.

"We need to run!" Rubik shouts over the battle. "Find better cover!"

Dad nods, and I mean to as well, but I have no feeling in my neck. I can't think about moving or responding – or doing anything, really, except breathing. I need to concentrate on that, or I'll pass out.

"Farah!" Rubik's there...calling out to me. Focus on his voice. Dad. He grabs hold of my arm, clasping me tight. I look up, squinting in the powerful light of expanding blues and reds. The junkyarders have resorted to launching fireworks at Mr. Toff's ships, and the sails on both vessels have gone ablaze.

The larger of the two vessels veers right, weaving between three trash pillars, where groupings of junkyarders are pelting more Molotov cocktails down at the deck of the vast ship.

Two gun turrets redirect their muzzles, spinning without ceasing fire, and focus on the base of the nearest tower. The centralized force of bullets works fast, thinning out chunks of the column and blowing debris as far as fifty yards away. The tower made of crushed cars starts to sway, and then it eventually topples over – crashing into a second tower with a deafening boom.

Tiny bodies fall from the sky...arms flailing about. Some even crash onto the deck of the ship, disappearing beyond the vessel's broad railing. The smaller ship rears into a third tower, using its figurehead like a battering ram.

Rubik tosses the car door aside and guides me to my feet. I'm not exactly sure how the muscles in my legs are functioning right now. Seconds. Mere seconds is all it takes for the undergrounders to generate destruction on a scale this big, and it makes me numb.

I grab Dad's left elbow, and Rubik grabs his right. Showers of ember and flakes of debris hit our backs as we pull, helping Dad up. One of Mr. Toff's sand ships sounds its horn, and the second ship responds. They're communicating, I think as we hobble away from the massacre. Sending messages back and forth.

We cut a corner, rounding an upturned tractor. I can still see the battle out of my peripheral...horrifying images imprinted in my mind forever. The large ship fires its cannons into every trash heap and tower it can set its sights on. The explosions are ear-splittingly loud. Dirt and metal spray into the night sky, and so do limbs.

"...Need...fight!" I shout, jerking back against Rubik's pull. He and Dad stop walking and look at me. "We need to fight! To help!" I have to scream until I'm hoarse to ensure they'll hear me. Neither of them says anything right away. They just gaze past me, watching the carnage as it unfolds some hundred yards off.

I don't know what we can do...how we can help...but if there's one thing I've learned in the past week, it's to react with your instinct. It's how I formed my relationship with Rubik. It's how we were able to discover Father Cash and Nikolaos's true intentions when they showed up at our Village.

But if you hadn't acted on that same urge, you would have never followed June into Oliver's storage cavern, and you would have never started this war. The voice in the back of my head nags at me with a truth so knife-like, I can almost physically feel it as it thrusts into my heart.

All the more reason to act. Attempt to right what I wronged.

I glance around our feet, trying to find something we can use, but it's Dad who points. "There!" he yells, and I look to where his finger is indicating. Three junkyarders are running toward the battle. They're wearing rucksacks stuffed with fireworks. Two of the teenagers carry a large crate between them, and it's packed with more of those Molotov cocktails.

"Wait!" I scream. Somehow, they hear us and stop. Rubik and I lead Dad in their direction, and I realize that I recognize one of the girls as we get closer. She was the one who cooked us breakfast. Now, she wears a feathered Mohawk headpiece and shoulder pads.

"How can we help?" I ask her. She looks at her comrades, then back at us. I can tell she's sizing up Dad and his condition, but I can also tell that – given the circumstances – she's not about to deny help.

"C'mon!" she says, waving for us to follow. A series of three consecutive explosions sets off up ahead, and spirals of debris jut out of the ground as a result. My shoulder muscles are rapidly growing weak. Dad must be really hurt because it's the most he's had to lean on us since needing our assistance.

We slow our jog the closer we get to the battle. We cut south and stalk through the shadows once the smaller ship is throwing distance away, its back to us. The girl with the headpiece guides us behind a fallen telephone booth. Fireworks torpedo into the ships from unseen starting points and blossom into colorful displays as they puncture the undergrounders' vessels.

The junkyarders may be thinning out, but they're holding their own.

"Here, here!" Dad orders, and Rubik and I dip down and set him on the ground. The two junkyarders carrying the crate move quickly and set up shop beside the rectangular booth.

"Mae," one of them says, pointing. The girl with the headpiece looks on, and I see by the light of fireworks and battle explosions, she has subtle war paint on her face.

"They're maneuvering west," she says, taking off her rucksack.

"Meaning?" Rubik asks beside me. He takes off his blood-drenched T-shirt and balls it up. I check my hand. I've not bled through Rubik's makeshift bandage, so I'm not the source of all that damp redness. It must be —

"Meaning," Mae answers, pulling out rocket-shaped fireworks, "they're turning deeper into our junkyard."

"Let's concentrate all our ammo on the tires!" one of the boys cries out, procuring a lighter from his pocket. Mae nods, handing Rubik her rucksack and me a box of matches.

"Don't worry too much about aiming," she tells us, taking two beer bottle grenades out of the crate.

"Those are big targets. If you hit any part of it, you're good." Then she holds out her hands as one of her teenage comrades lights the Molotov cocktails. The wicks catch fire, and Mae's on her feet – charging forward like a madwoman. She hurtles the bottles forward with two overhand pitches, and they fly through the air at impressive speeds. They eventually hit their marks, colliding into the rear tires of Mr. Toff's largest ship and cracking into the rubber and metal.

The eighteen-wheeler wavers and sputters slightly, but it's enough to throw off the alignment it has with the other diesel vehicle. The great trucks brake, trying to compensate for one another, and the effect is that the wooden ship splits and cracks in places. If there's a support beam holding the two vehicles in place beneath the large ship, it's been damaged now and compromised.

Mae throws up her fists, shouting to the stars. The two junkyarders beside us light their fireworks after propping them up on the telephone booth. Mae bolts back toward us and slides down. The rocket-shaped fireworks sizzle at the wick, then wail as they launch. On the ground between Dad and Rubik, I cover my ears, and the very next instant wood shatters and splinters when contact is made.

Rubik stands in a crouch, copying the junkyarders and setting up a slew of fireworks at an angle along the surface of the booth. ' Dad grunts and grinds his teeth, but he presses on through the pain and finds a way to help. I see glints of blood leaking from his side, and I immediately stifle a yelp – dropping the matchbox with a flinch.

Mae crawls around our improvised barricade and snatches up the matches, completely disregarding my alarm. She and Rubik work fast, helping the other two junkyarders as I kneel beside Dad.

"You're bleeding a lot!" I shout over the diesel horns. The smaller ship with the figurehead is rearing back around, probably to finish us off. Dad pulls a handkerchief out of his pocket and applies pressure to his wound.

"I'm fine!" he lies, motioning with his head. He wants me to assist Rubik and Mae, but I can't leave him. Not like this. Not even for a fraction of a second.

"Here," I say, pushing down with my palms. The cut in my hand starts and stings, but I swallow the discomfort with a lot of effort.

Nearly a week ago I stood, frozen in shock, as Alex tried to save Morgan's life. I was on the cusp of nausea, wondering how Alex could keep himself composed amid those elements and bloodshed.

Now I'm utilizing that same type of control.

Dad forces a wan smile, and I want to tell him to stop. He needs to save his energy. The smallest exertion could drain him. Yet before the words form on my tongue, a series of crackling noises hiss beside us. Weakly, Dad reaches up and covers my ears with his soaking hands as the dozens of wicks sparkle.

The fireworks shoot off the side of the booth and fire

into both ships. Sparks cascade into the air. Existing flames expand. Mae hoorahs, and I hear Rubik mimic her. The two junkyarders on the end don't skip a beat and are already lighting Molotov cocktails.

If nothing else, Rubik has helped Mae stall the undergrounders, and the brief window of time appears to have been enough: As I press against Dad's injury, I peer over his head and the telephone booth and see Mr. Pujol's form sprinting out from behind debris piles. He and his men flank around the vessels, shooting their assault rifles and shotguns relentlessly.

Rubik and Mae shout again, and I find myself joining them. Flurries of more Molotov cocktails wash down over the ships from the four or five still-standing trash towers. Undergrounders begin leaping from the ships for their lives, where they are met on the ground by our patrolmen. Mr. Pujol takes them out using both hand-to-hand combat and firepower: he shoots a round here, jabs with his elbow and knee there. The undergrounders never stand a chance. Some are even dead before their feet hit the sandy ground.

Then, in the nick of time, Mr. Pujol and our patrolmen scatter. The great big sand ship lights up in an explosion that transcends all previous explosions. I hunch over Dad, feeling jets of air gliding over me from soaring wreckage. I clamp my eyes shut, praying that a massive piece of rubble doesn't roll our way and bury us alive.

After a while, everything finally settles, and my ears ring so loudly I can't even hear my thoughts. I feel

Dad's hands move on top of mine as he takes over, pushing down with what little strength he has left. I open my eyes and he blinks a few times, then mouths, I'm okay.

With reluctance, I rise – just to get a fast look at where we stand. I cough in the thick smoke and sand dust, squinting through the vapors. There are soft, flashing glows in the distance. Fire. Everywhere, but not spreading. To my left, Rubik grabs his wadded-up T-shirt and unfurls it. He crawls around me and starts to work on Dad's wound, when –

A deep horn sounds beyond the settling smoke. An angel appears, her face mournful. She's coming for me, hands clasped against her exposed breasts. A second later, the rest of Mr. Toff's ship materializes in the raining ember. It charges right for us...its deck and sails alight with pockets of fire.

This is how it ends, I tell myself as the vessel gets bigger and bigger – its marble figurehead leading the charge with a saddened expression. Beside me, Rubik stops what he's doing, straightens up, and holds out his right arm. He flattens his hand, using the "stop" gesture.

There's no time to move. No time to scream. In the one second that I have to think, I wonder what possessed Rubik to stand up against the blitzing vessel...like holding out his hand will be enough...

And yet, it *is* enough. With a strident bang, the giant ship is swept from the ground mid-charge. It was a few breaths away from barreling over us, perhaps ten feet off...   Now it's practically airborne, eventually crashing onto its side beyond a row of trash heaps and wreckage. The tires spin. Fire swells. The tattered, singed sails flap to the ground pitifully.

Rubik just moved Mr. Toff's warship.

Chapter 53 | Rubik

That's when the last of the dust and debris settles, revealing a gigantic yellow crane. Father Cash sits behind a pane of glass in the cockpit a few yards off, and he pulls back on two levers. The crane rises, then swings overhead slowly.

Father Cash saved us, and not a moment too soon.

Farah starts to laugh. It's a tired, delusional laugh, but Mae joins in. I reach down and secure the knot around Thomas's torso, using the light from my hand and arm to make sure the bandage is stable. Thomas nods appreciatively, grabbing my forearm and squeezing it. He doesn't have much time. He needs to be stitched up quickly.

I get to my feet as Father Cash hops down from the crane's belted tires. Coming seemingly from nowhere, crowds of junkyarders rush toward the Father – chanting and applauding.

"For a second," Farah says beside me, holding my hand in her wrapped-up one. "I thought you moved that ship out of the way. Why did you do that, with your hand?"

"I have no idea," I confess, gazing down at her. She's acquired more cuts and scratches on her soot-covered face, but those green eyes and that hopeful smile of hers cuts through it all. I want to say more...perhaps even *do* more...but the moment has passed when she breaks away to check on her father.

Mae and her comrades leap over our barricade and join Father Cash. Exuberant cheers and clapping fills the dust-coated air. A victory – albeit a small one – has been attained. Now we must get everyone out of here before –

"Didn't see that one coming," a projected voice declares. I spin around, feeling every muscle in my body clench. Behind a haze of more fading sand and dust, four figures appear, striding toward us. Nikolaos. Lois and Digs. *Mr. Toff.* And behind them are six more sand ships – rolling so gradually their engines are nearly soundless. They're huge...equal to that of the big vessel we defeated first.

"But then," Mr. Toff continues, "I'm full of surprises, too, aren't I?" He speaks through a cornucopia-shaped device that amplifies his speech, and with his other hand he grasps a weapon with a long nozzle. There are tubes that snake out of it and connect to a cylindrical container on his back, where gasoline swishes inside. Mr. Toff is wielding a fire-torching weapon of some sort.

He jabs Nikolaos in the back with the nozzle, indicating for him and Lois and Digs to get on their knees. My fingers furl into tight fists – all three of them are gagged and bound at the hands, and they each have a bruise or two on their faces. Most of all Nikolaos.

Mr. Toff was never on that ship...the one Father Cash knocked into oblivion with the crane. It was just his voice projecting through. A diversion, a distraction. We fell for it...*again*. He was making a daring play in the hopes that I stuck behind in hiding, but instead, he found the perfect incentive for me to surrender in the form of Nikolaos, Lois, and Digs.

"Let them go," I command, taking a cautious step forward. I hear Farah's heavy breathing behind me, but neither she nor Thomas object to my actions. They're either stagnant with terror, or they've accepted what has to be done.

"Let them go," I say again, firmer, "and you have my word that I'll come with you."

Mr. Toff redirects his aim to Digs, and droplets of gasoline leak out of the nozzle. I freeze, feeling winded. If he hurts the boy, I think, I'll doom us all because I won't be able to refrain. I won't be able to refrain from darting forward to disassemble Mr. Toff – limb by bloody limb.

"I hope you mean that," Mr. Toff says without using his amplifying device. He holds it out, and one of his cronies appears and takes it. You're a coward, I think with flaring hatred. A coward who can't even show his face. Mr. Toff is draped in rags and dirty linen strips. His head is covered with a baglike mask that has ample tears and frayed stitching. How he can see – or even breathe – is a mystery.

That's irrelevant, I think as I turn to face Farah. What matters is that Nikolaos, Lois, and Digs are in danger, and I'm the way they get saved.

"I have to go now," I tell Farah, who is kneeling beside her father. I see, even in the small light cast from stars and scattered fires, that tears are forming in her green eyes. Behind her, Father Cash and the junkyarders look on with stone-cold faces. They know, just as Farah knows, just as *I* know, that this is the only option.

"Wait," Farah says, straightening up and walking over. Two thin marks streak down her cheeks from where tears have split the grit. I want to wipe her eyes and pull her close. Assure her that I can take care of myself, and that I'll find a way back to her. I stop short because she says,

"What will you do?" Her voice is a whisper. She blinks, and, before I respond, I realize what *she* will do. Once I turn myself over, Farah's going to stop at nothing to try and rescue me. She'll put herself in harm's way. For me. She will risk everything for me. I know because I would too. For her.

"Forget about you," I reply, my throat swelling up. Lying to Farah is causing me actual pain. "I will go with Mr. Toff, and I will forget about you. Whatever he plans to do with me, I'll make sure it doesn't place you or your Village in peril.

"But I will forget about you, Farah Miles. My journey has brought me here, to the undergrounders. All you've done is prolonged the inevitable. They should've been the ones who took me away from the crater, not you.

348

"My advice? Forget about me, too." And then I turn, my last mental picture of Farah taken. Her lip quivering. Eyes watering. The girl who showed me compassion when others showed fear and hate, is now in my past. Nothing but a memory. A memory, perhaps, of a girl I could have loved.

"Go," I say to Nikolaos, looming over him. He swallows, exchanges a glance with Lois, but then stands up anyway. Digs and his sister copy this, and all three of them dart past me to safety.

"You've made the right choice," Mr. Toff utters behind his mask. "And you'll see why soon enough." He steps aside, and I march forward without looking back. How can I? How can I meet the pain in Farah's eyes? She probably feels betrayed, but then, if so, I will have been successful. Farah will never risk her life for me again.

A rope ladder falls from the side of the nearest vessel, and without thought, I grab hold of a rung and pull myself up. I'm ascending into more sand and dust clouds, unable to see where the ladder ends. Two pairs of hands grab hold of my shoulders after a few beats and guide me over the railing.

I plop down onto the wide deck, facing about ten undergrounders with torches in hand. Mr. Toff appears behind me a moment later, and our ship cranks loudly and then turns with a jerk.

This is finally it, I think with choking realization. I'm never getting back home now. I'll never have my answers. I'll never see Farah again.

"This way!" Mr. Toff exclaims, taking off his weapon and handing it to someone. He leads me across the deck, and his undergrounders part so we can walk by. I have to take careful steps because it is tricky striding on the wobbly, moving ship. Mr. Toff's saunter, however, is perfect.

We pass the helm of the vessel, where an overweight man in a duster jacket is steering. I see black, taut cables at the base of the helm that disappear through the floor and probably lead into the vehicle's cab, where they're undoubtedly rigged up to the power steering. The driver spits on the deck as I move by.

"Right in here," Mr. Toff says over his shoulder while opening a wooden door. I follow him into the cabin, where three lanterns are lit and swing from the low ceiling. Old, crinkled maps cover the window-less walls. A small desk is set in the middle, and Mr. Toff sits behind it and motions for me to close the door.

"We have so very much to be thankful for, you and I." Mr. Toff pulls out an old bottle of wine and two jars after I've shut the door and taken the chair opposite him. "And now, a drink."

He's treating me like a guest, not a prisoner. Doesn't he know I killed ten of his men? Doesn't he know what I'm capable of?

"I'm always looking to toast something," he says, prying the cork off. He carefully divvies out two portions of wine. "Once I even toasted the stars, for the hell of it." He puts the bottle away in a desk drawer, moves the sheets of parchment on his desktop, and slides me my jar.

Mr. Toff holds up his drink and eyes me through the slits in his mask. "Well?"

I stare at the liquid as it sloshes in the glass.

"It's not poison, if that's what you're thinking." Mr. Toff pulls back his mask – just enough to show his mouth. He takes a delicate slurp, swallowing slowly to savor his drink. "See?"

I take the jar and sniff it. The scent is sweet, unlike anything I've smelled in the bowl since crash-landing here.

"To our futures," Mr. Toff says, raising the jar. "Though uncertain they may be." I hold my jar up, mimicking Mr. Toff, and he clinks the drinks together before swallowing a huge gulp. I take a drink, but one much smaller than his. The bitter liquid burns slightly as it trickles over my tongue and down my throat.

"Now," he says, crossing his legs under the desk. "How's that for a toast?"

I put the jar back on the desktop wordlessly. What's with this act? Why is he using civility when he talks to me? Like a conversation between two casual acquaintances? He's scheming. Trying to best me.

But why this way? Is this how he gets amusement?

"It's quite remarkable," he murmurs, leaning forward and studying my bare chest and arms. "Your internal patterns of cubes. Oh what you must think of yourself!"

"What do you mean?" I ask, folding my arms and flexing my muscles. If Mr. Toff is scared or feels threatened, I can't see it in his body language or tiny eyes.

"Once we get to the grotto, your questions will be answered." Mr. Toff stands and actually *bows*. "Until then," he says, looking up, "have some more wine!"

He whisks past me and slams the door shut in his wake. The grotto. As in, the undergrounders' lair. The den of killers and bandits. And what then? Will Mr. Toff finish what Farah's Leader started? Will they engage in more tests? Subject me to examinations and never-ending analytical rounds?

I can take it, I tell myself. If Farah and her Village never have to endure what they've been through this past week, I'll force myself to suffer through whatever the undergrounders have waiting for me.

I was trapped in space for who knows how long. This is merely an extension of that punishment. My destiny, as it were, is coming full circle. Best to just accept that now before I start having worries or doubts.

The hours tick by with a slowness I can almost taste. It's foul, like the sour drink Mr. Toff poured me. I get up from the chair and walk around the desk, examining the maps. They're similar to the ones the patrolmen had propped up on easels back in their tent. Markings indicate where Villages, canyons, and dunes are located.

But there's another score on one of the pages that draws my attention. A small 'x' at the top of the illustrated region. I look for a legend, and find it at the bottom right of the largest map.

Why is that significant? I turn from the wall and start to rummage through Mr. Toff's desk. There are journals and papers and all sorts of files, but nothing appears to hint at why the archives are so special.

I do find something, however, that causes me to gasp. A picture. Buried and hidden in the corner of one of the drawers. It's a headshot of Alex. Farah's Alex. Why would Mr. Toff have this? I flip over the photograph and read the small, cursive writing:

Sworn allegiance indicated by the scar.

No, it can't be. Alex is working with the undergrounders? Is he the mole that sold out my location? Put Farah and her entire Village in jeopardy? I feel a chill work up my spine... Alex isn't the only one that has that branding scar. Father Cash does, too. Why did he save us from the undergrounders then? Is he having a change of heart? Or is that scar on his neck simply a coincidence? Farah didn't think so, and neither do I, I realize.

Before I can search around for more clues, the sand ship tugs suddenly, then dips down at an incline. It's all I can do to stay on both feet. I fumble out of the cabin and into the moonlight. Stretches of infinite desert surround Mr. Toff's fleet.

I make my way around the helm and to the railing,

holding on as our incline intensifies. We're heading down a spacious ramp, leaving the surface behind. All around the deck the undergrounders work via torchlight to collapse equipment and stow away crates of supplies.

We've reached their home.

After nearly half an hour, the ship levels. We've entered a great tunnel that shames the junkyarders' tall hangar. This passage is enormous and seemingly eternal. It may very well lead to the planet's core for all I can speculate.

"Are you ready?" Mr. Toff asks, walking up to me with a flickering torch. "Are you ready for your answers?"

Don't respond, I order myself. He's still playing you. It's all part of some elaborate plot Mr. Toff has designed to get me behind him. Believe whatever he plans on feeding me. This way, it'll be easier for him to accomplish what he has set out to.

But, there is one thing I can do to make things difficult. I can be less predictable. Keep him guessing.

"I've been waiting for too long," I say. I can tell by the way he cocks his head he wasn't expecting a response. "I have memories. Fragmented images of a follower who spoke of allegiance.

"Maybe our paths have crossed so you can carry on that person's mantle."

I have no idea where I'm going with this, but Mr. Toff doesn't appear disoriented and thrown off. "That," he says breathlessly, "would be an honor."

He bows again, then spins around and barks out orders. The sand ship's speed quickens a little, and the cool cavernous air is brief relief amid the aches and bruises I've come to acquire. It seems that everything that's been transpiring has flown by so fast that I've not really had a chance to evaluate my injuries.

I bend my arms and legs, then I swivel my head. I hear a little popping, but nothing in my body seems worse than mere soreness. That, in and of itself, is a miracle. I feel the truck's tires turn, and the broad wooden vessel sways in accordance with this maneuver. I see pale light up ahead. We're almost there.

Mr. Toff returns to where I'm standing around a quarter of an hour later, flanked between two armed undergrounders.

"You will not be bound when we enter the grotto," he says, "but my only ask is that you allow yourself to be escorted by me and my men."

"I would expect nothing less," I lie, clasping my hands in front of me. I turn and look out over the railing as we emerge from the tunnel and enter the undergrounders' bustling city.

This is no lair or hideout, I realize as my jaw drops. This is like a *metropolis*. Streets. Forts built into the craggy walls. The hum of chatter and activity, and all the other noises produced from the goings-on of a city.

Mr. Toff's sand ships dock between scaffoldings, where men and women wait to assist with the unloading. They connect a retractable plank to the side of the vessel, and Mr. Toff and his men guide me across the walkway.

The whispering starts immediately.

"It's him!"

"I knew he was alive!"

"Everything's about to change."

"He's our *future*."

I've been called that before. By the undergrounders, when they first happened upon me at the crater. I didn't know what that meant then, and I certainly don't know now.

"Come," Mr. Toff says as we pass through the workers. We take a side staircase with four switchbacks, and, once we're on the ground, we move under the shadows of the sand ships and turn onto a long, cobblestone road.

Backlit waterfalls drape the sides of the city like curtains – colors of purple, green, and red bleed through on timers. Three-story buildings and brick homes extend before us, intersected with other cobblestone streets. Skimpily clad women loiter under lampposts and call out to us. Intoxicated men stumble out of taverns. The pungent smell of smoke trickles from nearly every other window.

This place is right where it should be. Underground.

"Here we are," Mr. Toff says, turning a corner.

We walk down an alley-like pathway, and for a flash of a moment I'm panicked. Like they're taking me back here to execute me. Logic seeps in and rids me of that fear. The undergrounders wouldn't bring me back to their city just to kill me. So then where are they leading me?

Mr. Toff hands me his torch once we reach the end of the path. I take the light hesitantly. Then, he leaves his men and me and crouches down before the cavernous wall we've dead-ended at. He tugs on a tiny lever that was hidden in the shadows. There's a subtle grinding noise. An instant later and the wall is raising. The rock outcroppings must be artificial, concealing this passage.

"After you," Mr. Toff says, straightening up and taking a step back.

"My quarters then?" I ask, staying put. I'm not about to enter that darkened cave without an explanation. "Is this where you mean to keep me?"

"Not at all," Mr. Toff says. "Look." He reaches inside and pulls a switch on the interior wall. Strips of hanging lights click on, revealing a tall ceilinged room. And it's in this very room where my spacecraft awaits, blackened and damaged, but very much in one piece.

Chapter 54 | Farah

The ground is soft against my touch. It's not sand and dirt. It's ash.

I look up. I'm on the ground. I've fallen to my knees. There's vomit between my hands, too, not just ash. Father Cash helps me up. Together, we watch the large sand ships turn through the junkyard and disappear into raining dust and debris...like wispy, ghostly figures.

Rubik is gone.

"Farah," the Father's low voice says. I don't think he has anything to say. I think he just wants to say my name, make sure I'm all here. But I'm not. I'm on that ship with Rubik, ensuring that he's safe while he ensures I'm safe. Together we'll weather whatever the undergrounders have in store. Rubik and I will keep each other going, because we –

"Farah?" I turn and meet Father Cash's eyes. He looks concerned for me. Don't give me your empathy, I think. There's no point. Why? Because this is *not* how it ends.

"C'mon," I tell him apathetically, wiping my mouth with my shirtsleeve.

I walk past him toward Dad, who is slowly rising to his feet. I grab him under his arm and help him sit atop the fallen telephone booth.

"Does anyone know how to stitch up a wound?" I ask Mae, who is done untying Digs and Lois and has set to work on Nikolaos's bound wrists.

"Yeah," Mae answers, "I've done it several times. We'll have to use the alcohol Oliver keeps in his fort."

"Good." I walk up to Lois and Digs. "Are you guys hurt?" They both shake their heads, avoiding my eyes. "This isn't your fault, guys. You didn't purposefully get taken. Okay?" Lois looks up, eyes watering. I pull her in for a tight hug, then, after breaking away, I kneel down and hug her brother.

"I'm fine," Nikolaos says reassuringly when Mae's done cutting through his binds. "Don't worry about me."

Father Cash chuckles, putting his hand on Nikolaos's shoulder. "That mean you don't want a hug?" I look over just as he's rolling his eyes in response to the Father.

"We don't have much time," I tell everyone, turning around. The junkyarders have congregated around us, forming a loose circle. They look exactly as I imagined – beaten down, dirty, and sore from battle.

But they also look eager. Hungry for something, anything.

Dad sighs, adjusting his sitting position. "Farah, honey – "

"Don't," I interrupt him. "Don't you *dare* say it's over, because it's not. It's nowhere close to over. Rubik has just made it possible for us to pursue him, rescue

359

him."

"What are you talking about?"

"He was lying," I say. "It was so blatant I can't believe the undergrounders bought it. Rubik wants them to think he's done with us. That he wants us to move on…'accept' what has come to pass."

Nikolaos clears his throat behind me. "Farah, don't you think you might be stretching here?"

I close my eyes. "No. You heard him, I heard him. He was saying what he wanted the undergrounders to hear." I open my eyes and walk up to Nikolaos and Father Cash. "All Rubik has done since arriving on our planet is get us out of pinches. It's time we return the favor."

I hear a few of the junkyarders begin to whisper excitedly. Then, the chatter grows and grows, spreading like the Molotov cocktail fires.

"Twice," I say, holding up two fingers. "Twice Mr. Toff has outsmarted us and caught us off guard using the element of surprise. Don't you think we should use this opportunity to beat him at his own game?"

Digs takes a fist and punches his other hand. "Yeah!" Lois glances down at him, surprise in her face. Digs flushes, glaring at his sneakers, but Lois startles us all by saying to me, "What exactly did you have in mind?"

"Well," I say, a little thrown off but committing to my response, "I think it's safe to assume the undergrounders have closed off Oliver's food channel" – to this the junkyarders whisper confusedly – "we'll explain later. Anyway, we could start there?"

"But you just said the undergrounders would have closed it off," Father Cash says, walking forward and pocketing his hands.

"Yes, but if they haven't blown up and collapsed the entire tunnel, we could still theoretically get down there," I say, the plan just rolling off my tongue before I can fully formulate it. "See, what if *we* plant explosives down there? Blow their entire food cache to bits? We'd be using that as a diversion to then do what Mr. Toff would never expect."

"Enter his lair through the front door." Nikolaos rubs his chin, then nods.

"You're assuming Mr. Toff doesn't have methods of clearing his tracks in the desert!" Dad says, shaking his head. "You have any idea how long our Villages have been searching for their hideout? Lark spent most of his young adult life doing that very thing!"

"We've seen where the ships go," Mae says, removing her feathered Mohawk. "Oliver took a few of us into the bowl one afternoon after they scoured our junkyard for salvageable goods. You're right – they have fans and blowers that cover their tire tracks, but we made a map. Oliver figured it would be valuable one day."

Dad nurses his side, wincing in pain.

"Need to get your cut cleaned up," I say, walking over to him. He nods once, putting a hand on my shoulder.

Mae calls out and orders for a kit to be brought over, as well as some lanterns and a bucket of water. Three

361

junkyarders disband from the circle and hurry off.

"You're going to have to stay here," I tell Dad, kneeling down and getting eye level with him. "You have to heal."

He knows I'm not referring to just this instance, but in the grand scheme of things. I can tell he knows because he doesn't reply. He just looks at me.

"This was never our problem, Farah." He prods his stomach, checking for fresh blood. "Never your problem."

"But Dad," I say, reaching out and holding his hand. "I'm not thinking about it – any of this – as a problem. It's a responsibility. *My* responsibility to Rubik." He wants to argue further, and even goes as far as opening his mouth, but then he ultimately refrains.

"And if I lose you?" he eventually says, visibly fighting back tears. "I will have failed in my responsibility. Don't you see that?"

Mae comes to Dad's side once her peers return with the supplies she had them fetch. I pull up Dad's shirt as Mae begins to clean off the dry blood around the wound. I'm thankful for this distraction because I didn't know what to tell Dad next.

"You're on the Path, aren't you?" a little voice says behind me. I turn, seeing June's form walking over from the crowds of junkyarders. "Back at your Village?" I chuckle, holding out my arm to hug her. She squeezes back, looking up at me after we break away.

The Path. It's the hard, conditioning years of a

362

Leader in training. Few petition their names for the chance because few want to bear the types of duties that come with a Leader's job.

"I could tell," June says before I answer, "when I first met you. You seem like you're built for that job."

"I'm not a Leader in training, June."

"Oh. You're not?"

"No." I shake my head. "Truth is, I don't have a job I want yet. I couldn't ever decide what to choose."

"That's dumb," she says matter-of-factly, and even Dad chuckles at her bluntness.

"It is?"

"Yeah," she says. "You're supposed to be a Leader. Anyone can see that."

I tuck some strands of hair behind my right ear. "Well, uh, thanks, I guess. Maybe I'll consider it." June heaves a dramatic sigh, unconvinced, and then starts helping Mae sew Dad's crooked cut.

Mae says he'll be fine, but he can't walk for a while. He needs to spend days in bed, preferably weeks, to guarantee no infection and complete healing. Father Cash, Nikolaos, and a few other teenage junkyarders carry Dad back to the hangar on a cot, using it like a gurney.

Lois, Digs, and I take direction from Mae and start cleaning up the battlefield. We put out fires and pull injured kids from beneath collapsed debris. I eventually find where the patrolmen have been this whole time. Near the far east side of the junkyard, where the fighting began, Mr. Pujol and his men tend to dozens of kids sprawled out on the ground.

There's crying. There's moaning. Almost half of the bodies don't move. Lois sends Digs back to the hangar to help out there, and then she and I both assist Mr. Pujol as best we can.

"He's gone then?" Mr. Pujol asks, wrapping a boy's leg in bandages. "Rubik?"

"Yes," I say, pouring water from a canteen into the boy's mouth. "He's gone."

I tell Mr. Pujol about my intentions of rescuing him, and the patrolman doesn't argue. He just exhales through his nose and moves onto the next wounded junkyarder.

About two hours later, well into the night, and we have buried around twenty-five orphans. I can't figure out how I'm able to work through something like that...seeing the innocent, lifeless eyes gazing up at the stars...chests frozen...no air in their lungs... But it needs to be done.

The least I can do for the kids that are still alive is make sure they don't have to see their siblings and friends as mangled, broken remains.

I swallow a round of tears, patting the last mound of dirt with the flat side of a shovel. What was once a space of dirt between car houses is now the gravesite of many brave children.

"I hate the undergrounders," I say out loud. "I hate them and everything they stand for." Lois and Mr. Pujol come up beside me, each placing a hand on my shoulders.

Mr. Pujol says, "Me too."

Lois says, "Me too."

We walk back to the hangar with the rest of the patrolmen. No one says a word. Father Cash is waiting by the side doors, and he opens them for us as we approach.

Inside, Digs is helping June and another boy pour hot soup into wooden bowls. Earlier, two of the patrolmen used our vans to transport the wounded junkyarders here, to the hangar, where they now lay in rows of cots.

"How many?" I ask Father Cash as we make our way to the opposite end of the hangar, where our cots and supplies are stationed.

"Between thirty and forty," he says gravely. "Most have broken bones, few will never walk again." I bite my tongue until I'm sure I taste blood. When we reach our collection of cots, I see that Dad is already lying on top of his covers – his goggles pulled down and hanging around his neck. He snores softly, fast asleep.

Lois receives a bowl of soup from her brother, and she offers it to me first.

"I'll wait," I say, sitting on the edge of my cot. "Not really that hungry anyway." She sits beside me and starts sipping what smells like chicken broth. I watch Mr. Pujol and his men gather around the ammunition trunks and begin to tally up numbers – estimating the remaining inventory.

"Didn't realize this is what I was getting myself into," Lois says between slurps. "Guess I just thought we'd get lost in the bowl. Maybe find a few pieces of Rubik's ship. Then turn around and come back after a few days. I'm not really built for this kind of stuff, you know?"

"Me either," I say, slouching. Working that shovel for so long earned me quite a few aches. I turn my hands upward, examining them under lantern light. I earned a few blisters, too. I see fresh blood on my bandaged palm. I'll have to clean that out soon.

"Sure you are," Lois says after swallowing a mouthful. "Didn't you hear June? You've turned into some kind of a leader."

Great, I think. Not my best friend too. What exactly makes them think I can lead? Is it because I'm the only one who proposed going after Rubik? There's nothing special about that. I just know it's what he'd do for us. I can't possibly be the only one in this group who thought of that. And, aren't they forgetting that I *threw up* when Rubik was taken away?

What kind of a Leader does that?

"If Alex were here, he'd be really proud of you," Lois says, giving up on her spoon and tilting the bowl back to her lips. Alex. It's only been a couple of days since I saw him, or heard his name spoken out loud, yet my heart lies and says it's been longer. Months. Years. A lifetime.

I don't want Leader's accusations about him to be true. I don't want to find out that he was tortured to death as a result of his involvement in starting a war. This giant separation between us, however, is worrisome, because I haven't thought about him as much as I figured I would.

Especially since he said he loved me.

I'm not being fair to Alex. At the end of the day, I need to decide if I love him, too. He deserves that – regardless of whether or not I can tell him yet. So...do I? Should it be this hard, like choosing a job? Shouldn't I just know?

"Alex is a great guy," I tell Lois. "He may not show it a lot, but he cares about me. I can tell."

"Er, okay?" Lois chuckles. "Why are you telling me thi – ?"

"I hope he's okay," I blurt out, staring at the cement ground.

"I hope so too." She puts a comforting hand on my arched back. "Alex *and* Rubik."

Without warning, I get to my feet – brushing Lois's hand off my back. I turn, and almost bump into Mr. Pujol in the process. He has a steamy bowl of soup in his hands, and he holds it forward.

"You need to eat and then rest," he says. "We've got a big day tomorrow."

I can feel my face lighting up. "Y-You mean you're going to help? You're okay with us trying to rescue Rubik?"

"It's not going to be easy."

"It's the bowl," I say, taking the soup from him. "Nothing's ever easy."

"Verdad," he says in Spanish. "Eat, then rest. In the morning, the hard part will begin." He walks off to fetch himself some dinner, and I sit back down and tear through the soup with renewed energy. Having Mr. Pujol and the patrolmen on board is going to bolster our chances of succeeding.

"I'm sorry," Lois says next to me, setting her empty bowl down. "Whatever I said to upset you, I didn't mean it, and I'm sorry."

"I'm not upset," I say, and it's true, because, "I'm just confused."

Lois nods without having to ask me to elaborate. She knows, for probably longer than *I've* known, that there have been growing feelings for Rubik inside of me. A longing. A need. He's protected me and kept me safe and I need him. Why did it take me until he was gone – possibly forever – to admit that?

"Wanna talk about it?" Lois asks, but I shake my head. Now isn't the time. Really, I don't know when a better opportunity could potentially present itself, but I just can't talk about it. Definitely not now.

After I finish my soup, I help June and Digs with the cleanup. Then, I walk up and down the rows of cots with Lois and give water to those who request it, and drape extra blankets over those whose tremors are greatest.

This is all we can do for them. Earlier, when we were racing through the junkyard in Mr. Pujol's van, he mentioned radioing in to our Village. With any luck, backup will be here soon. They'll have better medical equipment and the wherewithal to mend the bloodiest injuries.

368

I just pray these kids can make it through the night.

Lois breaks away about an hour later, bidding me goodnight, and the lights in the hangar begin to shut off. Only a few lanterns remain on, so I step outside for a breath of fresh air before retiring.

Father Cash sits on the ground beneath the stars a few yards away, holding a necklace in the air before him. It dangles in suspension, catching a glint of moonlight every once in a while.

"I gave this to Rubik," he says when he notices me. "The day before we left your Village."

"You did?"

The Father lowers his hand, running his thumb over the nail necklace. I join him on the dirt, sitting cross-legged – like I used to in my watchtower for hours on end.

"I found it on your kitchen table though," Father Cash continues. He doesn't sound hurt, or even sad – he merely tells me this. Conversationally. "Guess he wasn't too fond of it."

"Not necessarily," I offer. "He probably just forgot he set it there. There was a lot going on, you know?"

Father Cash smiles, handing me the keepsake. "It's yours then. For now."

"Um..." Reluctantly, I take the necklace from him. I'm surprised with how heavy it actually is. "Sure, but only till Rubik can have it back."

Father Cash sighs, gazing up at the sparkling firmament. His eyes reflect some of the stars. "I haven't been entirely forthcoming with you, Farah."

"What do you mean?" I store the necklace in my pocket.

"You asked about my scar the other night," he says, looking down at me. I see a lot of remorse in his face. Heavy, weighty remorse. "A few years ago, before I was ordained, I was a patrolman. A high-ranking one, at that. There are codes we follow. Rules and guidelines upheld by leads, who then report up to the Leader. It's how it's always worked.

"Although, there are some who viewed this as a flawed system. Radical patrolmen who, in hungry desperation, formed alliances outside the confines of their respective Villages."

I shut my eyes, not wanting him to finish this explanation. I know it will mean that Alex is connected to all of this, too.

"Those alliances weren't just with other radical patrolmen, Farah," the Father says in a low voice, "but with undergrounders as well." My eyelids are forced open by tears. Burning, scorching tears.

"I'm so sorry, but you have to know, Farah." Father Cash holds out his hand, but I scoot back – getting to my feet and yanking his necklace out. I throw it on the ground in front of him.

"So, w-what?" I yell between sobs. "The scars are m-marks of loyalty?"

He nods, Yes, but I already knew the answer. "Some cut their arm below their shoulders, others down their calves, but few had the mark on their neck. It was a bold, foolish thing, and not a day goes by that I don't regret the things we – "

"What things!" I shout, almost panting. I can't believe my ears. I can't believe – no, *accept* – that Alex really is a part of some movement that has ties to the undergrounders. The evil, ruthless men who are responsible for the death of twenty-five orphans.

"Farah," Father Cash says, holding a finger to his lips in the hopes that I'll quiet down. "I knew you'd be upset, but I didn't expect you to react like this. Those days are behind me! I've repented – !"

"Sure, that's you, but what about Alex!" I fall to my knees, feeling lightheaded. Father Cash's expression gradually begins to change as he puts everything together.

"Alex...your boyfriend." He breathes in and out steadily. "You've seen the scar on him. It's how you recognized mine. I'm so sorry – "

I don't wait for his apology to come all the way out before stumbling away and heading back inside the hangar. I get a hold of my crying long enough to reach my cot, and then, after pulling the blankets over my head, I resume. My sobs are quiet, starting at the pit of my stomach and clawing their way up my throat.

I was right to ask Alex about his scar. I was right to wonder why he kept it so secret. In this moment, bawling under this quilt, I *loathe* being right.

By some act of God, I end up falling asleep. Hours later and I'm the first one up. I drop the blanket from my face and look around. It must still be early because Mr. Pujol and the patrolmen are still asleep in the parked vans. Tiny hints of morning sunlight appear outside the rectangular hangar windows, and I gently slip out of the cot.

I just need to make it outside, where I can think about what Father Cash told me last night and attempt to sort it all out in my mind. I roll my feet as I walk, and the only sound is the tips of my bootlaces hitting the paved ground.

I reach the exit without my name being called, so I know I'm in the clear, but when I turn the handle and pull open the door, an involuntary scream escapes my lips.

It's Alex, standing over the threshold and staring back at me.

Chapter 55 | Rubik

The spacecraft is stout and long, like a torpedo. There are chunks and bits missing along the bottom, but, for the most part, it is astoundingly intact. The long, faded letters that spell *LEAPER* curve up, partially disappearing on top of the vehicle's bandied shell.

So the Leaper was referring to the name of my ship after all. Farah was right to guess that first.

I hand Mr. Toff the torch and walk into the mini hangar. I run my hand across the metal, touching and feeling every groove and chink and dent. They found it. The undergrounders actually found my ticket home.

The retractable door slams shut behind me. I turn, watching as Mr. Toff punches a code into a keypad, probably locking us inside. His guards move and stand on either side of a desk I hadn't noticed before.

"What do you think?" Mr. Toff asks, walking over to my ship and me. "Exterior is in pretty good condition, considering. Of course, that's trivial if we can't get the damn thing to work.

"And yet, I think you'll find that getting your ship's engine repaired is quite meaningless."

That's it. I'm tired of his fuddling and confusing words. I have him and only two undergrounders alone,

373

and it's time I get answers – by force if necessary.

As if sensing my frustration, Mr. Toff pivots on his heel and heads toward his desk. He collapses into a high back armchair, behind which are floor-to-ceiling stacks of speakers. Long ones. Cracked ones. Some with grates, others without.

"You said that when we arrived here, my questions would be answered." I stride over to where he's sitting, broadening my shoulders and trying to look as menacing as possible. "We're here, and I'm ready for those answers."

"Yes," Mr. Toff says, putting his booted feet on the desktop. "Where to begin then?"

Is this part of his game? Only one way to find out.

"My ship," I say, choosing to start there. "How did you find it?"

"We summoned it," he replies simply. "Rerouted your coordinates and brought you home earlier than initially planned."

Home? He doesn't mean *my* home. He must be referring to his.

"You did this?" I point back at the spacecraft. "You're the reason I crash-landed here? On this planet?"

Mr. Toff nods.

"Then how come your men seemed so surprised when they showed up at my crater? You'd think if they'd been expecting me, they would've acted with more confidence and intent."

"You'd think." Mr. Toff chuckles. "Except that my

men didn't know *what* to expect that night, if anything at all. See, my discovering your ship in the stars set a secret plan into motion I didn't dare share with anyone who lacked importance, like hired muscle."

"You're not making sense, Mr. Toff." I lean both fists against his desk and incline forward. The two guards cock their rifles nervously. "Why not see to my capture personally? Why send a few thugs out into the bowl?"

"Because I was expecting you in the ship!" he declares, swinging his feet down and standing. "Those men who discovered you at your ejecting point were on a routine scavenge. They had no idea what to think when they found you because they were not informed!"

I push off the desk and begin to pace. I almost buy this explanation, but there's far too many holes in it to be true. What's he not telling me?

"And *how* did you discover me in the stars?" I ask, walking back to the desk and folding my arms across my chest.

"It started with legends," Mr. Toff says quietly, slowly sitting back down. "Legends that turned into rumors. Rumors that turned into *possibilities*. Could it be, that the once fabled young leader, who was known by all yet known by none, who started political-altering waves of change, who lit the wick of an exploding turning point in our nation, was still alive? That he'd somehow found a way, through medical science, to prolong his days and wait out the wars...wait in hiding, among the stars, for that day when his followers would call upon him again?"

He's not referring to me. No. He can't be. He's lying. HE'S A LIAR!

"WHAT ARE YOU TALKING ABOUT?" I reach down and grab him by his collar, hoisting him into the air. Two rifle muzzles poke into my back, but I continue to throttle Mr. Toff over his desk. I shake him violently, but he only holds out his hands and commands his men to stand down.

"This w-was your plan, Mr. Macklin!" he shouts through gasps. I toss him against his wall of speakers, sending plastic shards and wires into the air. "We found the journals! The instructions! It was hidden...in the archives! *But we found it! We found you!"*

I tip over his desk and flip it aside, and the furniture crashes into one of the undergrounders. Mr. Toff holds up his hands like a frightened child. "Please! This was your will: Prolonged days...enhanced strength capable of superhuman things...*it's how you planned on leading the new world, Mr. Macklin!"*

"THAT'S NOT MY NAME!" I thunder, reeling back my fist and dropping punch after punch after bone splitting punch. Blood sprays on my chest and fist, contrasting against the particles and cubes inside of me.

"B-But it *is* your name," Mr. Toff manages to say. I fall to my knees, still clutching his raggedy shirt. "Randall A. Macklin. O-Or, as you liked to b-be called...

"...RAM."

To Be Continued And Concluded In...
TOWARD UNCERTAIN FUTURES

Acknowledgements

First and foremost, thank you to my Savior, for making it possible for me to pursue my dreams. Your provisions are unending. This is for You.

Thank you to my wife, for her patience. For reading the first draft and giving great guidance. A writer's wife is the most resilient and tolerant human being. Trust me.

Thank you to my editor, Pam, for laboring over the early, error-laden manuscript. I don't envy your job, and your polishing was ~~invaluible~~ invaluable.

Special thanks to Chris, for being the first one to add *RFL* to his shelf, and to Justin, for accepting an ARC and reading through it and giving feedback. And thank you to Wesley G., because I didn't have an acknowledgements section in *Capernaum* and she worked her you-know-what off for me.

Lastly, to my family. Thanks for your love and support and encouragement. Without my parents and sisters, I may not have ever found my niche in this world. To my friends who I consider family, too – a big thanks for your prayers, and for nudging me along.

To you, reader, I acknowledge the utmost thanks for sticking it out to the acknowledgements section. I appreciate the dedication. You're why I keep writing.

Soundtrack

Perhaps this is something that should've been mentioned at the start of the novel, but hey, now is as good a time as any. I have many artists to thank for the completion of this novel, because they provided a great deal of ambience and atmosphere while I was writing. They are, in no particular order: Ellie Goulding, M83, Strange Talk, First Aid Kit, Empire of the Sun, and Godspeed You! Black Emperor.

Thank you for your sounds.

About The Author

Julian R. Vaca was born in Long Beach, California. He moved to Tennessee in the early 2000s, where he later graduated high school from Nashville School of the Arts. Julian holds a BFA from Watkins College of Art, Design & Film, and he currently lives with his wife in Green Hills.

Running From Lions is his sophomore novel.

Visit him online at: www.JulianRVaca.com.

CPSIA information can be obtained at www.ICGtesting.com
Printed in the USA
LVOW07s0959200315

431325LV00020B/363/P